Fred & Leah: A True Life Second World War Drama of Love, Loss and Captivity.

M J Dees

Published by M J Dees, 2019.

Get M J Dees' first novel FOR FREE

Sign up for the no-spam newsletter and get LIVING WITH SACI for free.

Details can be found at the end of FRED & LEAH

Fred & Leah: A true-life Second World War drama of love, loss and captivity.

At a time of war, soldiers are not always the only casualties.

On September 3rd, 1939, Fred knew he would have no choice but to go to France and fight. However, when he found himself among the thousands of men stranded after the Dunkirk evacuation, he had no idea when he would see his wife Leah and his two children again.

Leah is left trying to raise her two children by herself but even she can't stop the bombs from falling on her street.

M J Dees' fourth novel and his first historical novel, Fred and Leah, is based on a real life love story of two people whose lives were irrevocably altered by war.

Sunday, 3rd September 1939 - Dover, England

Fred wasn't a big fan of Brontë novels, even film versions like this, although Merle Oberon was nice enough as the leading lady. He looked around at the faces inside the Granada cinema, everyone else seemed to be enjoying the film. Leah liked these types of stories and with Fred leaving for France soon, the two of them had to make the most of whatever time they had together. Fred wasn't sure whether he was relieved or disappointed when the film was interrupted and the words: "All officers and soldiers return to your barracks" flashed up on the screen.

They were stationed in Dover because Fred's Battalion, the 2nd Royal Northumberland Fusiliers, was meant to be preparing for a war which, until now, had been uncertain, but which most had always felt was inevitable. Fred was tired with this perpetual preparation, and his men seemed fed up too. He was spending more and more time trying to keep his fusiliers from getting into fights, annoying the locals and, in one case, stealing a car. Sports was always the best method of occupying them. The Battalion had a strong football team with a history stretching back to the last century, and the team relished beating local teams or rival Army units. Boxing was also popular, and they even managed to organise the odd horse race.

Fred liked sports. He had been a sprinter when he was younger. He didn't know anyone in the army who could run faster than him. If it hadn't been for this falling out with Hitler and Fred being in the military, he reckoned he would have given anyone in the Olympics a run for their money. You wouldn't know to look at him. He didn't look muscular. He still had his puppy fat, but that was deceiving. He was as strong as the best of them.

Leah was strong too, though not a big woman, eight stone and below average. However, her true strength lay in her personality. Woe betide anyone who crossed that woman. She had her sensitive side too. She had cried that morning when Neville Chamberlain had announced on the wireless that the country had declared war, his voice so slow and solemn. The air raid sirens had gone off not long after, and everyone had rushed to the shelter fearing the worst, until the wardens announced that it had been a false alarm.

Fred was glad he lived in married quarters, where he could spend his evenings with Leah and support her until his battalion was mobilised. Until then, his days were spent at Connaught Barracks with his platoon of regular soldiers whom he had trained how to use the Vickers Machine Gun. He was glad he didn't have to try to teach a ramshackle platoon of 'terriers', 'reservists', and 'conscripts', like some of his contemporaries he knew from his days back in India and Shanghai.

As they left the cinema, Fred looked at his wife. She was disappointed that the authorities had interrupted the film and, as he led her out of the cinema, he could see that, after three months, she was beginning to show.

"You all right, love?" Fred asked when they got outside, knowing she wasn't. She had a quietness about her, and that worried him. She wasn't often quiet, and when she was, it spelt trouble. He stopped to light one of his Woodbine cigarettes.

It was a warm afternoon, and Fred hung their coats over one arm as they ambled along the street together.

"It's just that I'm worried, Fred," she confessed.

She hadn't complained about his smoking. This was serious.

"About what?" he asked, trying to be nonchalant.

"What do you think, you daft apeth? About what's going to happen. You'll be off to war any time now, and then what's going to happen to me and Jim and ..."

She touched the lump in her tummy, which to Fred now seemed much larger.

"Don't worry, luv," he said. "It'll be over by Christmas. You'll see. This Hitler's just a playground bully. He only needs someone to stand up to him and give him a bloody nose."

"I wish that someone wasn't you," she said, straightening her hat.

"Come on," he said. "Let's get Jim from that babysitter of yours before she ruins him."

Leah allowed a laugh to escape and slapped Fred on the arm for spoiling her bad mood.

"It seems a shame to declare war on such a lovely day," she mused as they strolled along.

"It's a shame to declare war on any day," said Fred.

"If they didn't have wars you'd be out of a job," she said.

"Very funny."

"I'm serious though, Fred," she said. "Never mind Christmas. I'm due in March. Am I going to be by myself, with Jim to look after as well? It's his birthday soon."

"We've talked about this, luv. Why don't you go back to Sunderland? Your sister and your father are there, they'll help with Jim."

"I want you, Fred."

"I know, dear."

"I wish mum was here," she said.

Fred didn't say anything, he just squeezed her arm.

Leah was still feeling sensitive, and as she looked up at her husband, she began to sing.

"Kiss me goodnight, Sergeant-Major. Tuck me in my little wooden bed. We all love you, Sergeant-Major."

"Stop it, you daft sod," Fred laughed. "It's Platoon Sergeant Major. I won't have been gone five minutes, and you'll be working and in pants."

"Why do you men have such a problem with women in pants?" she asked. "If I have to, for work, then I'll wear them."

"Told you," he laughed then launched into song himself. "Ain't she sweet? See her walking down that street. Yes, I ask you very confidentially, ain't she sweet?"

Leah batted Fred on his arm.

"You're very violent you know," he said. "Has anyone told you that before?"

"Yes, but I hit 'em." she laughed.

"Look at that," said Fred, pointing to a lamppost on which someone had attached a poster. "Wanted: Adolf Hitler."

A group, chatting away, passed them.

"Yesterday, someone told me that Hitler had committed suicide," said one.

"Well that's not true, is it?" said another. "If he'd killed himself, Chamberlain wouldn't have declared war, and he wouldn't be dropping poisoned balloons on Polish babies."

"Who? Chamberlain?" asked the first.

"No, Hitler," said the second.

"I heard it was poisoned chocolate they were dropping on the babies," said a third.

"I heard the bombs hadn't gone off and just contained goodwill messages from Slovak arms workers," said the first.

"And someone told me today that some Germans had landed in Folkestone," a fourth said.

"Rubbish," laughed the second.

"I don't believe it either," said the fourth. "But I do believe what he said about them transporting Turkish troops through Britain."

"Worse things happen at sea," said Fred to Leah as they passed the group.

Leah could see them staring at Fred's uniform.

It hadn't been easy being a professional soldier after the Great War with so much anti-war sentiment about. But his father had been a sergeant in the Royal Northumberland Fusiliers, and Fred had seen that as his destiny, too. He'd enjoyed the time he served in India and Shanghai and met Leah when he returned to England. She had worked in the NAAFI in Leeds where he had had a temporary posting.

"I just thought they would come up with a solution," Leah mused.

"I think we all did," said Fred. "But there's no magic wand for this one."

"Pity," said Leah.

Monday, 4th September 1939 – Connaught Barracks, Dover, England

There was a mixture of feelings at the Barracks as Fred inspected his platoon.

"What are the feelings amongst the men?" Fred asked Corporal Jack Cooper, his right-hand man, and friend from as far back as India. Jack was a Scot by birth, but had somehow ended up in the Fusiliers. He was thin, freckled, with a smile and a shock of fair, curly hair, with which he managed to woo all the girls.

"Well, they all heard Chamberlain's 'bitter blow to me' speech yesterday which wasn't very helpful," said Jack. "It might be a bitter blow, but with everyone depressed at the prospect of war, in many ways, it's a relief. At least the suspense was over and there's only one course to pursue. Most of the men are relieved to have some certainty at last. They're a long way from home and want someone to put a bit of heart in them, some kind of instruction and encouragement."

"They certainly will. Soon we'll be leaving for France with the 4th Infantry to join BEF." Fred's battalion was attached to the 4th Infantry as a machine gun unit.

"The BEF?"

"The British Expeditionary Force, that's what they're going to call the Army in Western Europe."

"You've heard something?"

"Only what they're going to call us," Fred laughed. "The Major is in with the Brigadier now. It's only weeks, maybe days."

Monday, 4th September 1939 - Dover, England

Leah sang *As Time Goes By* as she did the washing.

Even when the darkest clouds are in the sky
You mustn't sigh, and you mustn't cry
Spread a little happiness as time goes by.

She sang it to herself with the optimism of someone trying to convince herself that everything would be fine, but she felt herself struggling, and her head throbbed. She decided to turn the wireless on and listen to the gramophone records they played on the BBC home service in between the monotonous news and announcements. Once the wireless had warmed up, she heard the baritone of one of her favourites, Nelson Eddy, singing *The Mounties* from *Rose Marie*. She was trying to ignore her tiredness. She had woken up at 3 am with a nosebleed and struggled to get back to sleep. The street outside her window had seemed busy with passing fire engines and a strange man walking up and down, whom she assumed must be an air raid warden.

Jim was hanging around her wanting to help with the laundry. The dolly stick she used to agitate the clothes in the tub fascinated him. She let him try to turn the handle of the mangle, but the handle would escape from his grasp at the zenith of its turn, and it was too heavy when there were clothes in it. Leah had her hands full trying to work the dolly stick while keeping Jim away from the hot water and the copper.

She thought that there would be no point making a Sunday roast any more once Fred went away to France. She thought about his suggestion of going back to Sunderland to be close to her family and wondered whether she could spend Sunday afternoons at her dad's house. He could do with the company now that Mum was gone and all the children were married off. Even young Beattie had married Isaac and moved to Billingham. The house must seem empty now all twelve of them had gone or moved out.

*

When she got Jim to sleep, Leah sat in the living room next to Fred and opened the old shoebox she had brought down from the bedroom.

"What are you doing?" Fred asked.

"I thought it might be a good idea to sort through the photographs and pick out a few to take with me in case the house is destroyed by fire."

Fred sighed.

"Cheer up, luv," he said. "Worse things happen at sea."

Leah couldn't shake her melancholy. Her headache hadn't gone away. She'd had it all day, despite taking aspirin.

"Look at this," she said, showing Fred a photo.

"Nice," said Fred without paying proper attention.

"It's Humph," Leah said in a tone, which let Fred know she wasn't happy about his lack of interest. Humph had died in an accident at the pit when Leah was 18.

"Sorry, luv."

"I remember it well. My dad bought his shop with the compensation."

"I know."

"Have I told you before?"

"Once or twice," Fred smiled.

Leah rolled her eyes, set the photo aside and moved on to the next one.

"Oh look, Catherine is in this one." She waved the photo at Fred, who feigned interest.

"She was 14 when the flu took her," Leah mused as she studied the image.

The photos of Catherine and Humph also reminded Leah of the brother she had never known because he had died before she was born. He had been two years old. Leah supposed she should think herself lucky. Maybe Fred was right. Maybe worse things did happen at sea.

There was a picture of her mother. Four years had passed already since her death. Leah missed her. In the photo, her mother was standing next to her father.

"I worry about Dad, you know," she said as she showed Fred the photo.

"Why?"

"The way he wheezes. I worry that he might not be long for this world."

"That's what you get for working down the pits," said Fred. "All that coal dust."

The next photo was of Leah's sister, Bessie, with her husband and their four children.

"This must have been taken around the time mum died. Look, Lydia is just a baby. There are Audrey, Ray, and Joe. And here's one of Becca and her husband and their two, Reeby and Bill, taken at young Bill's christening."

"Aye, I remember that. We'd not been married long, eh luv?"

"Ah, here's Beattie, look. Do you know where this was taken?"

Fred shook his head.

"When she came to Leeds to visit."

"Ah, Leeds," Fred smiled. "The NAAFI."

"You came in because the Woodbines were cheap."

"And you used to always tell me I should give them up."

"Those things smell terrible."

"They're cheap."

"Typical Yorkshireman."

"What do you mean?" Fred pretended to be offended. "I used to take you out."

"To Harry Ramsden's."

"What's wrong with Harry Ramsden's?"

"Nothing," she relented. "It was very nice."

"The train fare to Guiseley cost a fair bob, I can tell you."

"Last of the big spenders."

"But it was worth it."

"Yes, delicious," Leah pulled a postcard from the box. "Look, it's the NAAFI."

She showed it to Fred.

"Ah, the Tudor style tavern. There's a couple of blokes in the photo. Don't think I know them," Fred laughed as he squinted at the photo. "Look at those comfy seats in the lounge and the 'theatre/ballroom'," Fred read the caption.

"I remember those upholstered chairs under the stairs," Leah pointed, as she took the postcard back. "They were happy days. Beattie came down to stay for a weekend, and I showed her the sights of Leeds."

"You know how to live," Fred joked.

Leah sighed.

"What is it, luv?"

"We were happy in those days."

"Aren`t you happy now?" Fred sounded offended.

Leah placed an apologetic hand on his arm.

"It's just that, since Jim arrived, I've responsibility now and I'm running a household. I didn't need to worry about bills and cleaning and meals in those days. I hadn't appreciated how much mum did when she was alive until it was my own turn to don my pinny and scrub the steps, do the washing, cook the meals, wash the dishes, make the beds, make the fire, take out the dust and ashes."

"Worse things ..."

"... happen at sea, I know," Leah interrupted. "I'd always dreamt of a cottage in the country with a beautiful garden full of flowers, but right now I'm glad we have this small backyard. I don't know how I would manage with all the weeding on top of what I'm doing now. And there's another one on the way."

"Look, that's our wedding photo," Fred said, pointing to the box.

She took it out and looked at it.

"You'd better behave yourself when you're in France. You'll forget all about us with all those French girls around."

"Don't be silly. You know I'm not like that. And even if I was, I've got Jack there to keep an eye on me."

Wednesday, 2nd October 1939 - The Maginot Line, France

Jack was leading the men in a sing-song.

Now imagine me on the Maginot Line, sitting on a mine in the Maginot line. Now it's turned out nice again, the army life is fine.

Fred was glad the men were in good spirits, but he missed Leah and Jim and wondered what they might be doing at that moment. He was sure now he would miss Jim's birthday, and he wished he hadn't promised Leah he would be back by Christmas.

"Hello." An old Frenchman approached the platoon. Fred thought he might be a veteran of the last war.

"Bon joor," it was the only word Jack knew in French, and the villager chuckled at his mispronunciation.

"What do you think of our defences?" the old man asked.

"Very impressive," Fred said. "But we'll have to see whether they'll be sufficient to contain the Germans."

"Do not worry. I have absolute confidence in the defences of the Maginot line," the old man smiled.

Fred wished he could be as optimistic as the Frenchman.

"You know that this war has been organised by the international bankers," Jack told the Frenchman, who appeared confused by the accusation.

"Come on," said Fred to his corporal. "We need to get the men back in the trucks."

"International bankers," Jack shouted back towards the old man. "They're the ones who will profit from it."

"I wish you would keep your politics to yourself," Fred chuckled as they climbed back into the truck.

The transport left the village for the muddy landscape punctuated by a few lines of thin trees.

"Bit sparse, isn't it?" said Jack.

"Still recovering from the last war. Soon it might be facing a new one." Fred lamented.

"I don't want to wish the war to arrive," said Jack. "But all this waiting around is very frustrating. Half the time we're getting the men to dig trenches and then getting them to fill them in again."

"We've been laying telephone lines and camouflaging positions," Fred reminded his corporal.

"But we've spent days digging ground for it to become waterlogged. And all the time with the enemy watching us a few hundred yards away."

"We're watching each other."

"Why? So that we can work out whether they were building up their forces ready for an attack?"

"Come off it, Jack," Fred laughed. "You've spent most of your time sunbathing and playing cards."

"Cheeky bugger. It's getting too cold and damp for sunbathing now."

"Don't forget I'm your superior."

"Why can't we fire at them, sarge?" Jack offered a mock salute. "We've been training the men all summer to fire the Vickers, the Germans are over there, and we're not allowed to shoot at the buggers."

"It's not so much fun when they start firing back at you," Fred reminded him.

"It can't be any worse than working in the co-op," a fusilier next to Jack chipped in. "This is an adventure."

Fred and Jack had had their fair share of conflict in India and China, and Fred wondered whether that was the kind of adventure that the Fusilier was looking for and whether he would still want it once he had found it.

"It's almost noon." Fred showed Jack his watch.

"Ah yes, time for the daily raid," said Jack, looking to the sky.

Sure enough, soon as the sound of the German planes was heard and, under Jack's direction, the platoon began singing:

Run rabbit run rabbit run run run
Don't give the Farmer his fun fun fun
He'll get by by without his rabbit pie
So run rabbit run rabbit run run run

The men in his platoon were imagining the Germans running away as they sang the song, that they were the farmers and the Germans the rabbits.

It wasn't just the young fusilier who was chomping at the bit for some action.

FRED & LEAH: A TRUE LIFE SECOND WORLD WAR DRAMA OF LOVE, LOSS AND CAPTIVITY.

15

Monday, December 25th 1939 - Dame Dorothy Street, Monkwearmouth, England

Leah, her sisters Beattie, Bessie and Rebecca, and Bessie's daughter, Audrey, were tripping over each other in the tiny kitchen.

"Look at you, well on your way to starting your own family," Bessie told Leah as they prepared the dinner together. "Before you know it, Jim and the little one inside you will be having families of their own and spending Christmas with them."

"Give over," said Leah. "Let me give birth to this one first."

"Well, look at Dad," said Bessie. "Four of his boys are married off and spending Christmas with their wives' families."

"Well, they wouldn't all fit in here if they hadn't," said Leah.

"That's not the point," said Bessie. "Look at Audrey here. Before I know it she'll be married off and spending Christmas somewhere else. That's how it starts."

"Stop it, Mum," Audrey complained.

"It would've been nice if Fred and Tom had made it back for Christmas," said Leah, finding herself getting emotional.

"Don't worry, pet," Bessie placed her hand on her arm. "I'm sure you'll be together again soon."

Bessie had become the matriarch of the family since their mum had died, and Leah could rely on her for the advice she used to get from her mother.

"He promised he'd be back by Christmas," she said, as tears welled up in her eyes. "But now they're saying the war is going to last for three years!"

"But it's not up to him, is it, luv?"

"Why did I have to go and marry a military man?"

"Wouldn't have made a difference if you hadn't. Look at Tom. He's still been sent overseas. So it wouldn't have made a difference who you married. They're all getting sent overseas."

Leah grimaced.

"You all right, luv?" her Bessie asked.

"Yes, It's just the heartburn. It's terrible. Do you mind if I sit for a moment?"

Bessie grabbed a small stool from the scullery.

"Here you go, luv. Does sitting help with the acid?"

"Not really," said Leah. "It's my ankles. I just need to take the weight off them for a bit."

"Oh yes, they are swollen, aren't they," said Bessie investigating. "Oh listen to this one. This one's my favourite."

Bessie pointed in the air, in the direction of the wireless, which was playing Christmas carols in the back room.

Silent Night
Holy Night
All is calm
All is bright
Round yon virgin
Mother and child
Holy infant so tender and mild
Sleep in heavenly peace
Sleep in heavenly peace

"Is this what I've got to look forward to in three months," said Beattie looking at Leah perched on the stool.

"It wasn't as bad with Jim," said Leah. "I seem to be getting everything with this one. I had terrible morning sickness for the first couple of months."

"What's he doing in France anyway?" Leah complained. "Nothing has happened since the war was declared."

"Quite a few boats have been sunk," Bessie reminded her. "That one off the coast of Scotland. That was tragic, that was."

"Worse things happen at sea," Leah mumbled.

"What, dear?"

"Oh, nothing, Bessie. Just something Fred was always fond of telling me."

Leah started humming a tune, but not the one on the wireless.

Too many tears,
Each night I go to bed,
I lay awake and shed
Too many tears;
Your memory
Is bringing me
Too many tears.

"What's that, luv?"

"Oh, it's been going around in my head for days. I don't seem to be able to dislodge it. Bert Ambrose and his Orchestra. It was very popular when I met Fred. When I was working in the NAAFI in Leeds."

"Listen, luv," Bessie said. "Even if Fred were here, he'd be down the pub with the rest of the men and you'd still be stuck here making the dinner with us girls, keeping nine children at bay."

Leah laughed.

"Yes, you're right," she said.

"Audrey, get your aunt a cup of tea will you, luv?"

Audrey was already 12 and helped in the kitchen with her aunts. Joe and Rebecca were both 9 and so could be put to work setting the table. At 8, Ray was not interested in helping out and preferred to play with his five-year-old sister, Lydia, who conspired with him in bossing around the toddlers: Bill, who was 3, and Leah's Jim, who was still only two. Ray and Lydia were preparing their own pretend Christmas dinner and making young Bill and Jim do all the work. Leah thought it a blessing that their children hadn't been evacuated. So many from the city had, although there was talk of all the evacuated children coming back in the New Year.

It reminded Leah of something she had read in *Lady* magazine about not letting this be a winter of discontent by keeping Christmas for the children's sake. The Government was already planning to introduce rationing - in fact, petrol was already rationed - so they should enjoy this Christmas while they had the chance. It might be the last decent Christmas they had for a while. This war seemed to be taking its time.

Jim was demanding Leah's attention.

"What is it?" she asked, noticing the irritation creeping into her voice.

She knew she felt stressed. Bessie had bought her a bottle of Sanatogen for Christmas to help 'win her war on nerves.'

It was difficult not to feel stressed, Leah thought, with the blackout and everything. It wasn't safe to cross the road after dark any more. Many people had been knocked down. And if the cars didn't get you, the ice would.

Jim was there asking for attention again. She knew it wasn't his fault, but she couldn't help feeling irritated that he wouldn't let her get on with what she was doing.

*

She sat in a chair feeling bloated. She had eaten too much, but why not? Who knew when they would get a chance to celebrate Christmas like this again? Joe was doing impressions of Lord Haw Haw, which were quite good and made her laugh.

She remembered that last night she had dreamt she was back in Leeds with Fred at the NAAFI. Talk of the war always filled the days, and she was glad that at least she dreamt of other things.

She wished she could be like her new neighbour, Mrs Pearson, who lived next door to the small terrace they had rented near the docks. Mrs Pearson put all her faith in God. Leah could hear her listening to religious services on the wireless at all hours, and she would tell Leah that she was praying for God to strike Hitler dead. Leah wished she could bombard God with all her requests and thought that if God wanted to kill Hitler, he wouldn't wait until Mrs Pearson asked him.

Tuesday, December 26th 1939 - Monkwearmouth, England

Leah was startled at first when the front door opened. She thought that maybe the wind had blown it open and grumbled to herself as she went to close it. But when she entered the hall, she stopped and gasped in amazement at Fred, who was just crossing the threshold.

She cleaned her hands on her pinny while he dropped his kit bag and went to embrace her.

"You're huge," he said looking at the mound where her belly used to be.

"Thanks," she joked. "Nice to see you too."

She smoothed down her pinny over her belly, self-conscious about how large it had become.

"I suppose I can't look very attractive to you at the moment," she said.

"No," he responded with haste. "You look ..."

"Radiant?" she asked with sarcasm.

He smiled and nodded.

"I've missed you," he said.

"How long are you back for?" she asked, unsure of whether she wanted to know the answer.

"I'm not sure yet," he said. "I've been transferred to the 7th at Gosforth Park. They want me to help train reservists and conscripts. I haven't been told if or when we're returning to France."

"I hope you never go back," Leah said, tightening her embrace.

Fred smiled. He had no desire to return to France either, but he thought the chances of him being able to stay in Sunderland were very slim. He hoped his superiors would delay his return to the Maginot Line long enough for him to be around when his child arrived.

Leah slapped him on the arm.

"What was that for?" he demanded.

"You said you'd be back by Christmas," she complained.

He laughed.

"I came as quickly as I could." He said reaching into his pocket for his Woodbines.

"You haven't given up smoking then," she teased him.

"No, but I should. This packet cost me 7d!"

Friday, 8th March 1940 - Monkwearmouth, England

"Come on Jim, put down that stick."

Jim dropped the stick and ran to catch up with his father.

"What were you doing with it?" Fred asked him.

"I was hunting lions," Jim said with pride.

"Come on," his father laughed and led him by the hand into his father-in-law, James', grocery shop.

Fred waited while James finished serving a customer, a short, old woman in a raincoat and a headscarf.

"The co-op didn't have any marmalade either," she was saying. "And do you know what they told me? They said they would sell me 1 pound of lard and if I wanted more, I would have to buy 'compound'. The man behind the counter claimed it looks almost the same. But do you know what? It's a mix of cottonseed oil and animal fat. I mean, how am I expected to cook with cottonseed oil?"

James nodded as the old woman recounted her woes.

"You're very patient," said Fred once the old woman had left.

"I have to be nice," he said. "With all the evacuees, we've lost so much business we have to be nice to the customers we have."

"Any news?" Fred asked.

"Nothing," James shook his head. "I'll let you know as soon as we get a call."

"Alright," said Fred, resigned to having to wait longer to find out whether their new baby would be a boy or a girl.

"Did you hear about Mrs Holmes?" asked James.

"Mrs Holmes?"

"You know. She used to teach at St Benet's."

Fred pretended to remember but couldn't.

"She was found dead on Roker Beach."

Fred raised his eyebrows. He might not have known the woman, but it was still a terrible thing.

"She lived with her invalid sister," said James. "She always seemed very nervy. She had a nervous breakdown last year. I saw her last Thursday. We laughed and joked together. Now she's dead. Her poor brain must have snapped."

"You don't think it was an accident?" asked Fred.

"I don't think so," said James. "And she's left her poor sister penniless. She'll end up in the Institute."

Fred was shocked, but he didn't say so. If anything happened to him, the Army would continue to look after Leah for a while, but if something happened to Leah, he wondered what would happen to the children. James was in no position to take care of a baby and a toddler, and the rest of Leah's family had their own children to look after and plenty of them with more on the way. Even the youngest sister, Beattie, was pregnant and living down in Billingham with her husband, Isaac. He thought of his own mother and sisters in Beverley. Bub was a live-in maid and Minnie was already looking after Bub's daughter. His mother might look after the kids, but she was already looking after his brother Harry's son. The last he heard she was thinking of billeting a soldier and his wife. She might not be able to take on two more. Of course, Fred dare not share these thoughts with Leah and felt guilty for thinking that anything might happen to her.

"You all right?" asked James, noticing his son-in-law daydreaming.

"Yeah, sorry," said Fred. "I was miles away."

*

On the way home, Fred had seen the Army delivering food to soldiers billeted in the area. He was amazed to see loaves on the floor of the van without any covering and the men carrying the food with hands black as soot. No wonder so many men were getting ill. He hoped that they didn't handle the food at Gosforth Park in the same way, but resolved to mention it to Major Potts on his return.

Saturday, 9th March 1940 - Sunderland Maternity Hospital, England

Fred looked at the little bundle of flesh in his wife's arms and then at his wife, who didn't look as pleased as he had expected.

"What is it, luv?" he asked.

"It's nothing," she said, though Fred could see it was something.

She offered him the tiny baby.

"Go on, hold her," she said.

"Are you sure?" Fred asked, looking at his daughter and unsure of what to do with her. His daughter wasn't a Vickers machine gun and was outside his comfort zone.

"Yes, you can give my arms a rest," she said. "I've been carrying the two of them."

"Two of them?" Fred asked.

"Yes, two. I thought I'd had twins at first. They've had me breastfeeding the boy from that woman on the end, she doesn't have milk of her own. It takes it out of me."

Fred held his daughter like a full tray of drinks, scared he might drop her.

"My breasts are so sore," Leah whispered.

Fred nodded in sympathy, not sure what to advise.

"You'll be home in a week," he said.

She just looked at him.

"It's funny," she said, almost to herself. "I could have sworn I had twins. It's the strangest thing. But the doctor insists there was one."

Fred wasn't sure how to take this.

"Are you all right?" he asked.

"I feel so useless," she said. "I thought I would be so happy to see my baby. But I feel so helpless stuck here."

"Are you sleeping all right?"

Leah shrugged.

"Better than I was." She looked at her daughter in Fred's arms. "She'll distract me from all this business about the war."

Fred followed Leah's gaze out of the window where the rain was falling.

"It'll be good for the flowers," she said. "I'm surprised anything survived this winter. I saw snowdrops in the garden this morning, and the crocuses are coming up."

Thursday, 21st March 1940 - Sunderland Registry Office, England

"Where's the other one?" asked Leah as she placed her daughter into the pram.

"What other one?" Fred asked.

Leah shook herself back to reality.

"Sorry," she said. "I was so used to having two in the hospital."

"You all right, luv?"

"I've got a bit of a temperature, that's all."

"Well, let's get you to the doctor."

"No, I'm all right, Fred. No point spending money. It's just a little temperature. I'll be right as rain before long. Just something I picked up in the hospital, I expect." She tucked the blankets around her baby. "And, anyway, if we don't get to the registry office today, we'll have to wait until Tuesday, and the army might have whisked you off again by then."

"They shouldn't have done," he said.

"Well let's not risk it, shall we? You've already booked the vicar for Sunday. What did he say again?"

"He said that Easter Sunday was the perfect day for a christening because it symbolises new birth."

"You see," said Leah. "It's the perfect time. Come on, let's go."

She pushed the pram to the front door. Becca had given it to her now that Bill was too old for it.

"I can smell fish," said Fred.

"It's Beattie," said Leah. "I couldn't get any olive oil, so I have to use cod liver oil."

"Poor sod," said Fred looking at his daughter.

*

"Seems very quiet doesn't it?" Leah commented when they reached the town centre.

Fred nodded.

"Considering it's Easter weekend," she said.

Leah sat down on a bench.

"Are you all right?" Fred asked.

Leah nodded and then shook her head.

"What's wrong?"

Leah sighed.

Fred parked the pushchair next to the bench then sat down and lifted Jim onto his lap.

They sat in silence for a moment. Fred was watching her all the time.

"Is there something you want to tell me?" he said, releasing Jim to chase the pigeons.

"I just can't get it out of my head."

"What's that, luv?"

"The feeling that I had twins."

"But you didn't. You had little Beattie."

"I know. That's what the doctor said."

"And anyway," Fred had adopted a jovial tone to try to lift her mood. "Imagine having to wash two sets of nappies."

"My breasts are still very sore," she said. "The midwife said it was very common. She said it would get better by itself."

Fred looked around to make sure no one could hear them.

"Well, if it's not better by Tuesday, let's get you to the doctor. Did the midwife have any helpful ideas?"

"She suggested I massage my breasts and apply hot and cold compresses to ease the pain."

Fred checked the coast was still clear.

"Have you been doing that?" he asked.

"I've been trying. She also told me to feed Beattie more often. She said that might help."

Fred noticed that Leah had bitten her fingernails to the quick. She was not at all the feisty Wearsider he had met at the NAAFI in Leeds.

"Do you worry?" he asked.

She nodded.

"At times like these we need to be thankful for what we have," he said. "And remember that, though we might be short of a few things, we're still a lot better off than the Poles and Finns and Jews."

"But it makes me feel so little and futile," she said. "And there's always the fear that one day the bombers will come and yet no one wants to talk about it."

"Listen, do you want to hear a joke one of my men told me?" asked Fred, thinking of Fusilier Barnett.

"Alright then," she said. She liked it when Fred was silly.

"A man walks into the records office and asks to change his name. The clerk is not keen on helping but asks the man's name, and the man replies: 'My name is Adolf Stinkfoot.' The clerk is sympathetic and decides to allow the man to change his unfortunate name. 'What do you want to change it to?' asks the clerk. The man replies 'Maurice Stinkfoot.'"

Leah couldn't stop herself from laughing. Fred smiled at seeing his wife in a good mood for a change.

"Oh Fred, that's the first time I've laughed in ages."

Sunday, 24th March 1940 - St Peter's Church, Monkwearmouth, England

"Easter is a time for new things, a time for rebirth," said the vicar.

"Would you hold her please?" Leah whispered to Fred. "She feels so heavy."

He took his daughter. She didn't feel heavy to him at all. He looked at Leah and saw how tired she looked and concluded that maybe ten days of convalescence wasn't enough. Maybe breastfeeding two babies had taken it out of her, or maybe she was getting the flu. He resolved to make sure she went to the doctor tomorrow before he left. He'd left plenty of money in the post office to cover the doctor's fees and enough for her to keep the house and family. She would keep receiving his salary, which she could pay in at the post office.

The vicar's cough brought him back from his own world into the church where the vicar was indicating that it was time to take little Beatrice up to the font. Leah held onto Fred to steady herself as she got up from the pew.

"Are you OK?" Fred asked.

"Just a bit tired," she said. She held onto his arm as they walked over to the font.

"I present," said the vicar looking at Fred.

"Beatrice Leah," said Fred handing his daughter to Leah's sister, Beattie, who had come up from Billingham. They had named their daughter after her and asked her to be a godparent along with her husband, Isaac, and Mrs Pearson, whom Leah had asked out of politeness because she wouldn't stop dropping hints.

"I present ..." the vicar looked at Fred.

"Beatrice Leah," said Fred.

"Beatrice Leah, to receive the Sacrament of Baptism," the vicar continued, addressing the congregation and then turned to Fred and Leah. "Will you be responsible for seeing that the child you present is brought up in the Christian faith and life?"

Fred and Leah read from the Book of Common Prayer.

"I will, with God's help."

"Will you by your prayers and witness help this child to grow into the full stature of Christ?"

"I will, with God's help."

"Do you renounce Satan and all the spiritual forces of wickedness that rebel against God?"

"I renounce them."

"Do you renounce the evil powers of this world which corrupt and destroy the creatures of God?"

"I renounce them."

Fred thought to himself that he was about to go off and fight them, much less renounce them.

"Do you renounce all sinful desires that draw you from the love of God?"

"I renounce them."

"Do you turn to Jesus Christ and accept him as your saviour?"

"I do."

"Do you put your whole trust in his grace and love?"

"I do."

"Do you promise to follow and obey him as your Lord?"

"I do."

Fred felt Leah supporting herself on his arm.

The vicar turned to address the congregation.

"Will you who witness these vows do all in your power to support this person in their life in Christ?"

"We will," the congregation responded.

"Let us join with this child who is committing herself to Christ and renew our own baptismal covenant. Do you believe in God, the Father?"

"I believe in God, the Father almighty, creator of heaven and earth." the congregation responded, reading from their prayer books.

"Do you believe in Jesus Christ, the Son of God?" asked the vicar.

"I believe in Jesus Christ, his only Son, our Lord. He was conceived by the power of the Holy Spirit and born of the Virgin Mary. He suffered under Pontius Pilate, was crucified, died, and was buried. He descended to the dead. On the third day, he rose again. He ascended into heaven and is seated at the right hand of the Father. He will come again to judge the living and the dead," the congregation read in a monotone drawl.

Fred felt Leah's weight on his arm.

"Do you believe in God, the Holy Spirit?"

"I believe in the Holy Spirit, the holy catholic church, the communion of saints, the forgiveness of sins, the resurrection of the body, and the life ever-lasting."

The congregation sounded less than convinced.

Fred felt Leah slip down his side. He dropped his prayer book to grab her before she fell and the curate, seeing what was happening, brought a folding chair for her to sit on.

"Will you continue in the apostles' teaching and fellowship, in the breaking of the bread, and in the prayers?" the vicar asked the congregation without missing a beat.

"I will, with God's help," they replied, some members near the font looking with concern at Leah.

"Will you persevere in resisting evil, and, whenever you fall into sin, repent and return to the Lord?" said the vicar with less certainty, having spotted Leah slumped in the chair.

"I will, with God's help," replied the congregation, some of whom were straining to see what the matter was.

"Will you proclaim by word and example the Good News of God in Christ?"

"I will, with God's help."

"Will you seek and serve Christ in all persons, loving your neighbour as yourself?"

"I will, with God's help."

Fred wondered how many more questions there could be.

"Will you strive for justice and peace among all people, and respect the dignity of every human being?"

"I will, with God's help."

The curate returned with a glass of water for Leah who smiled her thanks.

"Let us now pray for this person who is to receive the Sacrament of new birth," said the vicar looking at little Beatrice in the arms of her aunt.

"Deliver her, O Lord, from the way of sin and death," said the vicar.

"Lord, hear our prayer." the congregation responded.

Fred glanced at Leah, who looked as if she wanted the service to be finished. She was trying to follow the service as best she could, and Fred was mumbling the words while he kept an eye on Leah. He looked to the vicar for a sign that it would all be over soon but the vicar seemed consumed by the ceremony.

"Grant, O Lord, that all who are baptised into the death of Jesus Christ, your Son, may live in the power of his resurrection and look for him to come again in glory; who lives and reigns now and forever. Amen."

The congregation, except Mrs Pearson, mumbled an Amen. Mrs Pearson's 'Amen' echoed around the church and the vicar glanced at her before turning his attention to the water in the font. The organist struck a chord.

"The Lord be with you," the vicar sang.

"And also with you."

"Let us give thanks to the Lord our God."

"It is right to give him thanks and praise."

"We thank you, Almighty God, for the gift of water. Over it, the Holy Spirit moved in the beginning of creation. Through it, you led the children of Israel out of their bondage in Egypt into the land of promise. In it, your Son, Jesus, received the baptism of John and was anointed by the Holy Spirit as the Messiah, the Christ, to lead us, through his death and resurrection, from the bondage of sin into everlasting life."

Fred hadn't remembered baptisms being this complicated. The vicar droned on, dryly reciting the service from memory. Leah looked terrible. Even little Beattie in the arms of her aunt was beginning to get a bit restless, having slept so far.

The vicar dipped his hand into the water.

"Now sanctify this water, we pray you, by the power of your Holy Spirit, that those who hear are cleansed from sin and born again may continue forever in the risen life of Jesus Christ our Saviour. To him, to you, and to the Holy Spirit, be all honour and glory, now and forever. Amen."

Another lacklustre amen from the congregation.

The vicar took baby Beatrice, much to her consternation, and placed some water on her forehead, which encouraged her to cry as loudly as she could manage.

The vicar looked at Fred again.

"Beatrice Leah," said Fred.

"Beatrice Leah," the vicar repeated having to raise his voice over the howls of the child. "I baptise you in the Name of the Father, and of the Son, and of the Holy Spirit. Amen."

This time the congregation's 'amen' in reply was more enthusiastic, perhaps with relief that the service was nearing its end.

"Let us pray," said the vicar waiting for the inevitable shuffling of knees onto prayer cushions to die down before continuing. "Heavenly Father, we thank you that by water and the Holy Spirit you have bestowed upon these, your servants, the forgiveness of sin, and have raised them to the new life of grace. Sustain them, O Lord, in your Holy Spirit. Give them an inquiring and discerning heart, the courage to will and to persevere, a spirit to know and to love you, and the gift of joy and wonder in all your works. Amen."

Little Beattie's wailing was now giving the vicar a run for his money. He marked the sign of the cross on Little Beattie's forehead with the holy water and then offered Fred another quizzical look.

"Beatrice Leah," Fred confirmed.

"Beatrice Leah, you are sealed by the Holy Spirit in Baptism and marked as Christ's own forever. Amen." The vicar then turned to the congregation. "Let us welcome the newly baptised."

"We receive you into the household of God. Confess the faith of Christ crucified, proclaim his resurrection, and share with us in his eternal priesthood," mumbled the congregation in a manner Fred didn't find at all welcoming. The vicar seemed relieved to be able to hand crying little Beattie back to her aunt.

"The peace of the Lord be always with you," said the vicar, who could have been wishing that the tiny baby would stop crying.

"And also with you."

Many members of the congregation shook Fred's hand. Most of them he'd never seen before, but Leah seemed to know everyone who inquired whether she was all right.

Monday, 25th March 1940 - Gosforth Park, Newcastle, England

The scenes at Gosforth Racecourse were chaotic, lorries and men all over the place. Not the neat lines and movement to which Platoon Sergeant Major Frederick Wooll was accustomed.

Fred watched another platoon across the racecourse practising firing at aircraft. He shook his head and turned to his corporal beside him.

"It's all so pointless," he complained. "What use are Enfields going to be against a bloody Stuka. Where is that Jones?"

"Here he comes."

Fred watched young Private Jones run towards them. Bobby Jones was 18 years old, and Fred watched the enthusiastic spring in his step with a mixture of enthusiasm and dread. He knew what Jones was going to say to them as soon as he saw him emerge from the stands and sprint across the racecourse towards them.

"Is it true?" he shouted when he was still twenty yards away. "When do we go to France?"

"You're late, Fusilier," barked Fred. "Shut up and fall in."

Everyone knew what Bobby meant. This had been on their minds for some time. It was the reason they had been billeted on this sodding racecourse. It was the reason Fred was trying to train this odd bunch of reservists and conscripts. The authorities had sent half of his platoon back to work in the mines and had replaced them with short Durhams and cocky Londoners. Bobby belonged to the former.

Bobby and many of the other young men seemed keen to get to France as soon as they could. Fred scanned the members of his platoon in their ill-fitting khaki. Bobby's arrival had distracted them.

Fred had been told this morning that he had a few days to get his platoon ready before they would be shipped out to France to join the rest of the British Expeditionary Forces in helping the French to halt Hitler's march through Europe.

Fred had expected little time to prepare and, although the base appeared chaotic, Fred was surprised at how relaxed he felt. He was bored of the preparations and wanted to get off and get the whole thing over with.

He knew the Vickers inside out, and by the time he finished with them, his platoon would too. He liked working with the men. He'd turned down his commission so that he could continue working with the Fusiliers. Some of the officers thought he was mad, although Fred had felt there were some who had encouraged him to turn it down. Leah wasn't thrilled either, but she said she was happy with whatever made him happy. This made him feel a bit guilty for being so selfish. He was sure Leah would also be thrilled to get out of that pokey terrace they rented by the shipyard. Still, it was a bit late for that. Fred had forty bodies to worry about in addition to Leah, Jim and little Beattie. Forty bodies who had wives, girlfriends, mothers and sisters who would all be worried about them, and Fred had to do his best to make sure he got them all back from France in one piece.

He turned to Jack, Corporal Cooper to the rest of the men. Fred trusted him, with his life, if necessary. It had been needed on more than one occasion when they'd been in India together, though Jack had just been a young fusilier in those days. They could tell a few stories of times they had helped each other out of scrapes. Jack was also Fred's rival in the hundred yard dash. Jack had never beaten him yet, though he had been pretty close a couple of times. When Fred was transferred to 7th, as the Fusiliers expanded their numbers in preparation for war, he insisted that Jack be transferred with him and, to his surprise, his superiors agreed. They both surveyed the platoon, who Fred felt were looking shabby in uniforms dating back to the Great War more than 20 years before. Fred hoped this war would be over by Christmas, for everyone's sake. He looked at young Bobby Jones and wondered what would happen if he came face-to-face with the wrong end of a German gun.

"Right, men," he addressed the platoon with authority. He turned to the gun at his side and pointed to it as he instructed the men. "This, as you know, is the Vickers machine gun, the most reliable machine gun built for the British Army. This, alongside your Enfield, is your best friend. Look after her, and she will look after you. This gun was fired for 24 hours in the Great War and did not jam once. She is water cooled, but she can get very hot."

"Sounds like my wife," came a shout from the back followed by a ripple of laughter. Fred knew it would be Billy Barnett. The cockney could barely keep his mouth shut. Standing next to him, sniggering, was Teddy Taylor, a fellow cockney. He was so close to Billy that Fred thought someone had separated them at birth.

"How did they let those two end up in the same platoon?" Fred asked his corporal.

Jack was invaluable in the barracks as well as the parade ground, helping Fred ensure the platoon had all their kit laid out for inspection. For a while, Billy and Teddy were a bit lazy about getting things right, so Fred made the whole platoon do everything again. He knew this would cause trouble in the barracks room, but after a while, the two cockney lads were laying out their kit, creasing their trousers, polishing their shoes and shining their buttons as well as any of them.

Lance Corporal Tom Johnson was always complaining about Billy and Teddy. Johnson was very religious, and Barnett and Taylor seemed to have endless fun winding him up with their sacrilegious comments and refusal to respect his superiority in rank.

Then there was Fusilier Walter Martin, the signaller and radio operator of the platoon, who was always hearing rumours about the progress of the war of one kind or another.

Sunday, 7th April 1940 - Fresnay-sur-Sarthe, France

Fred looked at his men and remembered how overburdened they had looked with their equipment. They'd barely been able to move as they boarded the lorries to Southampton.

He remembered the looks on their faces back at Gosforth when he told them that all equipment except rifles and webbing was to be turned in. Each man was to keep his field dressing, washing and shaving kits, two pairs of socks, a shirt, a vest, a ground sheet and eating utensils. They had known then that this was it, that they would be going somewhere. The training was over.

Besides his own personal ammunition, each man had to carry ammunition for the Vickers. Fred was concerned about some of the conscripts who had never handled so much live ammunition. He was worried about possible accidents.

The spare kits bags had been filled and placed in order, labelled with the owner's name and the platoon, and assembled with the rest of the battalion on the racecourse, which served for their parade ground before being marched to the lorries which would take them on their way. The journey had a bad start with several drivers managing to get their lorries into ditches. Fred was thankful that someone had seemingly trained his driver.

Close to Southampton, an air raid siren sounded and the battalion scattered. Almost everyone took cover in ditches or under trees, although some took cover beneath some of the lorries, many of which contained ammunition, petrol and, in some cases, explosives.

The convoy got underway again and, by nightfall they were boarding a large passenger ship in Southampton docks.

In the packed hold of the ship, Major Potts approached Fred.

"Sergeant, I would like you to prime and issue hand grenades to your platoon," said the Major.

"May I ask why?" Fred inquired.

"A tanker has been bombed," replied the Major as he walked away.

Fred felt uncomfortable stuck in the bowels of the ship and hoped that the German pilot would not return. Once Fred had distributed the hand grenades to the more experienced members of his platoon, he went to the canteen and bought several bars of chocolate, which he stuffed into his pouches with the grenades.

They made the channel crossing in the early hours of the morning.

"I felt like a sardine, stuffed down there," Jack said as the platoon emerged onto the deck.

"I'm glad to get out in the fresh air," Fred confessed to Jack as they docked in Cherbourg.

They disembarked and marched a short distance to the railway station. Fred had just managed to get his platoon lined up and sat them down on the side of the platform when there was a terrific bang, as if someone had let off a firework.

Fred looked in the direction of the noise and saw that a fusilier from another platoon had blown off his thumb and was screaming and writhing on the ground.

Fred's platoon watched as medics rushed to the scene and bound the fusilier's wound before taking him off to an ambulance train. They recognised him as one of the recent conscripts.

"His career in the armed services lasted a short while," Jack commented.

They boarded a train, which took them from Cherbourg to Fresnay-sur-Sarthe at about 10 mph. The space on the train was as limited as it had been on the boat.

"It's a bit uncomfortable, eh, Sarge?" said Jack, looking at Fred's long face.

"What? Oh, right. No, it's not that," said Fred, shaking himself from his daydream.

Jack observed his friend for a moment

"Aye. I keep thinking about my missus and little 'uns as well, but they'll be fine," said Jack. "They've got family around them."

"That's part of it," said Fred. He had felt guilty about leaving Leah to look after the two little ones, especially with her feeling under the weather, but there wasn't much he could do. There was a bloody war on, after all, and, as a career soldier, it was his job to make something of all these new recruits. "I was thinking about the equipment."

The arrival of Fusilier Jones shook him from his reverie.

"Can I ask you a question, Sarge?" Jones asked.

"You *can* ask me a question Jones," said Fred. "But whether you *may* is something else altogether."

Bobby stared at Fred with confusion.

FRED & LEAH: A TRUE LIFE SECOND WORLD WAR DRAMA OF LOVE, LOSS AND CAPTIVITY.

37

"Sarge?"

"What is your question, Jones?"

"What does DP mean? I saw it stamped on the Vickers, on the top of the trunnion block."

"It means drill purpose," said Fred, glancing at Jack who looked nervous.

"What does that mean?" asked Fusilier Jones.

Fred took a deep breath.

"Jones, the gun you saw has been assembled using the good parts from unserviceable guns or components. They stamped the gun with 'DP' on the worn parts so that no one transfers the parts to other weapons. They used to paint white bands on the water jacket to tell it apart from service weapons. If you look, you will also see that your gun has been marked with 'EY' on the water jacket because it is just suitable for ball ammunition in an emergency."

"It's suitable for instruction," Jack could not contain himself. "Stripping and assembling, that kind of thing. It can't be used for firing ball or blank ammunition."

Bobby was silent, and Fred knew Jack had gone a bit far.

"Don't worry, Jones," Fred said, giving Jack a dirty look. "They've been made in a factory from parts taken from unserviceable guns. They'll do just fine when we need them."

Bobby forced a smile and went back to sit with the rest of the men.

Fred looked at the fusilier and felt angry that this young man was being sent to war, risking his life, with inadequate equipment. So far, they had called the war a phoney war. There had been very little in the way of action apart from the hundreds of mariners who had lost their lives at the hands of the U-boat torpedoes. This tranquillity could not last, thought Fred, and when the Germans did decide to attack, the last thing his men needed was substandard machinery jamming on them.

"I can't believe we still have the drill purpose Vickers," Jack complained. "I thought we were going to use them for training, not bring them to bloody France with us. Do you know why we haven't received full-service weapons yet?"

Fred shrugged.

"Are supplies that short?" Jack was incredulous. "In my opinion, the battalion isn't prepared for war. It's hopeless, we're short of every damn thing.

Taking drill guns to France? It's not a good start. It's not fair that this boy should be asked to risk his life with inadequate equipment," he fumed.

"Let's hope this phoney war stays that way," said Fred.

"True. There's not been much in the way of action," said Jack.

"The Navy might disagree with you." Fred reminded him. "They've been right in the thick of it. This quiet can't last."

"Yes," agreed Jack. "And when the Germans decide to attack, the last thing we need is substandard machinery jamming on us. All our attempts to train this set of .... well, it might not be enough to prepare them for the battlefield."

"Not if the newsreel images are to be believed," said Fred.

"Did you see the Germans with their modern aircraft, tanks, artillery, troop carriers? It made me realise that we're not prepared for war."

"At least we have men," said Fred. "They've recruited so many and seem to have sent them all here. We have a good chance against the Germans, even if it is a case of sheer numbers."

"Some said the German tanks on the newsreels were made of cardboard," said Jack.

"I hope so," said Fred.

Jack decided to try to cheer the men up by starting a singsong.

We're going to hang out the washing on the Siegfried Line.
Have you any dirty washing, mother dear?
We're gonna hang out the washing on the Siegfried Line.
'Cause the washing day is here.

Fred smiled at Jack's ability to lift the spirits of the platoon even though he was in a bad mood himself. However, even this induced jollity couldn't distract Fred from the nervous feeling that, despite their numbers, they were not prepared. He'd done some calculations and estimated no more than about 50 rounds of ammunition per man. He hoped that CSM McLevy had more ammunition on its way. They had fired just ten rounds during training at Gosforth, though Fred had done his best to get them to understand the art of marksmanship. Even some of the transport he'd seen looked like they might have been repainted butcher's vans.

Monday, 21st April 1940 – Gruchet-le-Valise, France

Fred took the platoon in regular marches to improve the fitness of the men, and these weekly events had reached 18 miles.

"They're starting to shape up," Jack commented.

"You're right," said Fred. "When I first saw them, I thought they had bandy legs and wouldn't be able to stop a runaway pig."

"I tell you what," said Billy Barnett to his best mate, Teddy Taylor. "If I get my hands on one of those Krauts he's going to know about it."

"Yeah," said Teddy. "I'd make him think twice about going around invading half of Europe."

"Oh yeah?" Lance Corporal Johnson chipped in. "I'd like to see it. You wouldn't know what to do if you got your hands on a real Jerry."

"More than you," said Billy.

"If you came face to face with a German soldier," laughed Johnson. "You'd wet yourself."

Billy got to his feet.

"Oh yeah? And what would you do? Invite him to a bloody prayer meeting?"

"You see this," said Johnson pointing to the stripe on his arm. "This means I know more than you when it comes to the Army, mate."

"You think one little stripe makes you the boss, do you?" asked Billy.

"It makes me your superior, Fusilier."

"In your head," said Teddy.

"In reality, Fusiliers," said Fred walking over to the group. "You will respect Lance Corporal Johnson's stripe, and we will have no more of the argument over who is going to do what to which German whenever or however you get your hands on one. I hope you can match all this bravado with action when things start to get tough."

"Sarge," asked Fusilier Jones. "Would you mind if I just stretch my legs a little?"

"Jones, stay away from that maid," Fred warned. Bobby smiled and left.

Monday, 6th May 1940 - Monkwearmouth, England

Leah thought about the song Fred had sung to her as he was leaving.

We'll meet again, don't know where, don't know when,
But I know we'll meet again some sunny day.

She felt so nervy and jumpy after tea that she couldn't settle. She kept tuning the wireless to see if there was a news bulletin anywhere in English - *not* German. When she found the news, she wished she hadn't. It was dominated by the sinking of the Afridi and the plight of Norway.

Mrs Pearson had collared Leah that afternoon as she was hanging her washing out in the yard. She was going on about the good old days. Victorian life must have been all days of joy and nights of gladness.

Even the Jaffa oranges her dad had given her over the weekend had failed to cheer her up.

Jim wanted to play.

"It's time for bed, luv," she said, much to his disappointment. She had a headache, but little Beattie was already sleeping. If she could get Jim to bed too then, she might be able to enjoy some peace and quiet.

"Get down from there now in case you fall!" she heard Mrs Pearson next door shouting. Leah guessed the boys from up the street must have been playing on the shelter again. Mrs Pearson would get very frustrated with them: "I know your mam," Leah heard her shout. "I'll set Mr. Chamberlain on you!"

Mr. Chamberlain was Mrs Pearson's bulldog. She had bought him a couple of years earlier after her husband died. He had been a veteran of the last war where he had been a victim of mustard gas. Mrs Pearson said he'd never been right again. Leah had no idea why Mrs Pearson had named her dog after the prime minister, but it had done more to get rid of all the unwanted cats and dogs in the street than the rest of the households put together.

*

Leah woke with a start. She had been dreaming of sailors in open boats or rafts in the middle of the sea having abandoned a torpedoed ship. The waves were large and cold and swept the sailors into the brine. She felt their struggle to keep afloat, the hopelessness, succumbing to the waves, and the numbing coldness of death.

Nights seemed to be interrupted by nightmares of this sort, or similar. Little children and frantic mothers with no homes.

Perhaps she was so nervous because the shipyard was just at the end of the street, and it would be an important target for German bombers.

Friday, 10th May 1940 - Ebersviller, France

"It stinks around here," said Jack screwing up his nose.

"Not surprised," said Fred. "Did you see all that horse manure piled up outside their houses as we came through the village?"

"They love their shit around here, don't they?" said Jack. "They must have amazing rhubarb."

"Let's hope it doesn't smell like that all the time. This is going to be our home for a while," said Fred, settling into their freshly dug trench. He yawned.

"You OK?" asked Jack.

"Just tired," said Fred. "I couldn't get to sleep after those AA guns woke me up."

"You and me both," said Jack.

Fusilier Martin arrived, tired.

"Sit down, Fusilier. Any news?" asked Fred.

"Germany has invaded Belgium, Holland and Luxembourg."

"You know this for a fact?" Fred asked.

Fusilier Martin shrugged. They all looked up as yet another aircraft flew overhead. Martin yawned.

"Tired?" Fred asked.

"I think I must have done eight miles today," said the fusilier. "It must be two miles between each platoon. And it's up dyke backs."

"We'll have to get you fitter then," said Fred.

"The village is deserted," said Martin. "It's like a ghost town."

"I'm not surprised," said Fred. "The French know the Germans are on their way."

"I wish they'd taken their shit with them," said Jack.

"The wood is anything but deserted," said Fred. The variety of sounds that came from its depths amazed him.

The French troops had been preparing their defences for a long time. Fred felt they had underprepared the log cabins they had built in the woods, which were not bulletproof, and overprepared the digging of trenches. Fred's platoon had to fill in some of the trenches again, either because they had become waterlogged or because there were too many and they needed to be flattened to prevent the Germans from occupying them. At least they had sandbagged and revetted the trenches. The platoon's task over the next few days would be to replace the log cabins with more serviceable positions.

Saturday, 11th May 1940 - Mowbray Park, Sunderland, England

Leah was in Mowbray Park when her father joined her after closing up the shop. He had brought a flask of strong tea, which Leah welcomed.

Leah still hadn't recovered from the announcement yesterday that Germany had invaded Belgium and Holland. Where Fred might be and what was going to happen to him had filled almost all of her thoughts. Jim didn't seem to know what was going on and had enjoyed the trip on the bus to the park. The people on the bus had seemed as stunned as they had last September when Chamberlain had declared war.

Leah sat and looked at the lake while her father wheezed and coughed beside her. He had brought some buttered brazils, which Leah loved, but today she chewed them but couldn't seem to swallow.

"Would you like some ice cream?" her father asked.

"No thanks," said Leah. "You'd just be throwing your money away."

"Do you mind if I get one for Jim?"

"Of course not."

"Jim." her father shouted, launching into another coughing spasm, as he approached the toddler who was playing by the side of the pond. "Would you like ice cream?"

While her father took Jim to get ice cream, Leah wondered whether the postman had been while she was out and whether there would be any news from Fred.

"Did you hear about Churchill and the new cabinet?" her father asked when he returned. "I heard it on the news. I'm surprised Hore-Belisha isn't in the new cabinet. I have to say I'm not very impressed by the new coalition, but I did laugh when Lloyd George was not mentioned."

"Poor man, what would he do?" said Leah.

"I don't know," her father said. "But his vitriolic sense of duty might goad someone into anger that might have good results."

"If I had to spend my whole life with a man," said Leah. "I'd choose Chamberlain, but I think I'd sooner have Mr. Churchill if there was a storm and I was shipwrecked."

Her father laughed.

"You can be funny sometimes, you know?" her father said.

"Churchill has a funny face, like a bulldog," said Leah.

"He came to the shipyard once to see a ship launched," said her father. "The men in the shipyard were very impressed by 'something' he had."

Leah thought about Mrs Pearson's bulldog next door and thought about how ironic it was that she had named him Mr. Chamberlain and not Mr. Churchill.

"Would you like to come back to ours for tea?" Leah asked her father. "We can listen to Saturday Night Music Hall together."

"That sounds nice," said her father. "Listen, someone told me this in the shop. It'll cheer you up. Hitler visits the front and talks to a soldier. Hitler asks: 'Friend, when you are in the front line under artillery fire, what do you wish for?' The soldier replies: 'That you, my Fuhrer, stand next to me!'"

James waited for his daughter to laugh but Leah just sat there with longing in her eyes.

"Come on," said her father. "Let's go."

Sunday, 12th May 1940 - Ebersviller, France

Fred had just returned with his men from another training march.

"I can't take much more of this," Barnett complained. "Even my beard-splitter's getting sore."

"That's because you're a rantallion, mate," laughed Taylor.

"If you two weren't so lazy you wouldn't mind a little exercise," said Lance Corporal Johnson.

Fred felt for Barnett and Taylor. He hadn't slept well. The anti-aircraft guns firing at enemy aircraft had woken him again. The battalion's guns must have fired about 40 rounds that night.

"Sarge," Fusilier Jones, who was staring west through a pair of binoculars, called him over.

"What is it, Jones?" asked Fred, taking the binoculars.

"Enemy parachutists observed dropping into the woods to the west."

"Martin?" called Fred. The fusilier ran over. "Get a message to HQ that enemy parachutists observed dropping into the woods to the west of Ebersviller and all our sentries are on alert."

Fred handed the binoculars back to Bobby. He wondered whether this might be the start of the real thing. He wondered what was happening in Monkwearmouth and whether Leah might be up feeding little Beattie. The French had meant to relieve them so they could join the rest of the BEF, but he was still waiting for the order to withdraw his platoon.

"Use the Barr and Stroud," said Fred. "See if you can get an idea of their range."

"Is it true, Sarge?" asked Jones. "That the Germans were firing shells and one of the 51st Highlanders has been shot?"

Fred noticed that Barnett and Taylor both looked worried.

"It's true," said Fred. "Maybe this could be a wakeup call for some of you."

There was silence in the platoon. Jack sidled up to Fred.

"Maybe they will take everything a bit more carefully now," he said. "Maybe they will realise it isn't a game anymore. They've been hearing stories of some patrols trying to snatch German prisoners, attacking the enemy positions, and harassing their patrols, but they were frustrated that nothing that exciting has happened to our platoon yet. Maybe now they'll realise that excitement comes with a price."

FRED & LEAH: A TRUE LIFE SECOND WORLD WAR DRAMA OF LOVE, LOSS AND CAPTIVITY.

47

"A passenger train is full, and a German soldier, on leave, shares a compartment with a decrepit lady, a beautiful young French woman, and a young French man," Barnett spoke up, a wry smile already decorating his face.

"Is this going to be a joke?" Jack asked.

"The train enters a tunnel, and no one can see anything," Barnett continues, ignoring the others. "A kiss is heard, then a hollow slap. When the train comes out of the tunnel, the German has a horrible black eye."

"Is this a true story?" asks Fusilier Jones.

Barnett raised his eyebrows and continued.

"'So unlucky' thinks the German soldier. 'The French man gets the kiss, and I get the blame!' 'Well done, my girl!' thinks the old lady. 'You stood up to that brute!' The beautiful woman is puzzled. 'Why would that German kiss that old lady?' The Frenchman, meanwhile, thinks 'How clever I am! I kiss the back of my hand, hit the German and no one suspects me!'"

Barnett burst into fits of laughter along with Taylor. Fred and Jack groan while Johnson shakes his head.

"I don't get it," says Jones.

Wednesday, 15th May 1940 - Monkwearmouth, England

"I never want to hear another radio announcer's voice again," Leah complained to her father as he served customers. Jim was sat under the counter playing with potatoes, little Beattie asleep in her pram.

"Why? Because the butter ration has gone down to 6 ounces?"

"No. Holland."

"It's Holland," he said. "Belgium and France are a different kettle of fish."

"I wonder if I should check the wireless again, in case there's more news."

Her father laughed and then the laugh turned into a cough, betraying his years in the coal mines again.

"I got a letter from Fred today," she said, taking an envelope from her pocket.

"Oh yes?" said her father. "What does he say?"

"Not much. He says they don't get much time." She waited for the customer to leave the shop. "If he's got another woman out there, I'll kill him."

"Don't be daft," said her father. "He won't have time for women. He has a whole platoon to keep an eye on. In any case, Fred's not that type."

She knew it and felt guilty whenever she doubted Fred.

"I worry I'll never see him again," she said just as another customer entered, the opening door ringing the bell that hung above it. "Something about the tone of his letter."

"Don't be silly, luv," her father whispered before raising his voice to greet the customer. "Afternoon, Mrs Sallow. What can I do for you today?"

Mrs Sallow seemed to take an age, but when she had gone, Leah turned to her father.

"I don't know what's wrong with my head, Dad, but, you know, the days of having fun are so far away they feel like they were part of a previous existence. They're so far away I have difficulty reliving them."

"You're old beyond your years, lass. Don't worry, you've plenty of fun left to have. This war won't last forever."

James observed how sad his daughter looked.

"I heard another one today," he said. "How about this one. Hitler goes to a fortune-teller and asks her: 'On what day will I die?' The fortune-teller says: 'You will die on a Jewish holiday.' 'How do you know that?' asks Hitler.

And the fortune teller says: 'Because any day you die will become a Jewish holiday.'"

Leah forced a smile and James sighed.

Thursday, 16th May 1940 - Ebersviller, France

Fred could hear heavy artillery fire to the left of the trench. They had spotted a few enemy planes, but there had been heavy shelling since three that morning. Fred looked at his watch. It was six in the morning.

"Listen," Fred said to Jack.

"What is it?" asked his corporal.

"The shelling has stopped."

Jack checked his watch.

"Three hours," he said.

Fusilier Martin arrived.

"Is there any chance of a motorcycle, Sarge?" he said, out of breath, as he handed Fred a note.

"Ask Major Potts," Fred said as he unfolded the paper.

"What is it?" asked Jack.

"The battalion is being withdrawn from the Ligne de Contact to the Ligne de Recueil," he said, and then sighed.

"And?" asked Jack.

"And we're to cover the withdrawal," said Fred, knowing his phony war would be over all too soon.

"Good. A bit of action," said Taylor.

Johnson sighed.

"Hey, here's one," said Barnett. "Hitler and Goring are standing atop the Berlin radio tower. Hitler says he wants to do something to put a smile on Berliners' faces. So Goring says: 'Why don't you jump?'"

Taylor joined Barnett in raptures of laughter, much to Johnson's annoyance. Jones tittered.

"Yeah, that was quite good," Jones says.

Sunday, 19th May 1940 - Monkwearmouth, England

Leah could have sworn she woke to the sound of a cuckoo, although she couldn't imagine where a cuckoo would nest among these cobbled streets and brick terraces. She heard a blackbird. Its call was unmistakable. It was such a beautiful day that it was almost possible to forget all that was going on. She allowed Jim to play in the churchyard longer than usual after Evensong, and the sky from the scullery window looked beautiful above the silhouetted rooftops.

Tuesday, 21st May 1940 - Ebersviller, France

On the one hand, Fred was relieved that the day's constant artillery shelling had ceased. The noise had been deafening, and his head was aching. Fred had become so used to the whining of the shells that he could estimate where each was going to land just from the sound they made on their approach.

He looked over at Bobby Jones, Billy Barnett, and Teddy Taylor, the youngest members of the platoon. They looked like the novelty of having shells fired at them had worn off.

On the other hand, Fred suspected the shelling had stopped for a reason and instructed his men to be ready with the Vickers.

"Did you hear the one about the general and the fusilier?" Barnett asked.

"No," said Taylor.

"So, the general says to the fusilier: 'Have you come here to die?' and the fusilier says to the general: 'No sir, I came here yester-die!'"

Taylor and Barnett laughed. Jones and Martin joined in, finding the Londoner's outrageous laughter funnier than the joke itself.

"You won't be laughing when the Krauts get here," warned Johnson with his usual grumpiness.

"Alright, Abercrombie," said Barnett to Johnson. "Go polish your bean shooter."

Night had already fallen when the platoon spotted the Germans attempting to sneak through the lines. The Germans had been well-trained, but they were so well-trained they were predictable. Fred was glad he'd had at least some opportunity to train his own men in marksmanship.

"Wait," he told his men, allowing the Germans to draw closer, amazed to see that the leading soldiers were walking without caution as if they expected no opposition. Their helmets were so well polished, it made them easy to spot.

"Fire," Fred ordered. The men opened up the Vickers, and the German patrol scattered and ran back into the woods. Two of them had fallen. They looked dead, but the platoon fired three bullets into them to make sure. Another German, injured from the first burst of fire, staggered out of a shell crater but was shot and fell backwards, back into the hole.

More Germans began to advance. The platoon fired at them, not knowing whether or not they were hitting their targets. Major Potts had told Fred that it was the job of his platoon to hold up the Germans for as long as possible to allow the other companies to withdraw, and some accurate use of the Vickers seemed to be doing do the job for a moment at least.

The Germans used what Fred considered a predictable strategy of running in ones and twos with a gap between each, but the marksmanship of Fred's platoon was proving itself as they picked off the enemy one by one.

Gdoonk, g'doonk, g'doonk

"What the hell is that?" said Jack.

"Not sure. Sounds like a very heavy machine gun," said Fred. "They're preparing for an assault on our position. Martin, get to HQ, if they haven't already gone, ask them to please bring down an uncle target on the spot 100 yards in front of our position."

"What's that?" Fusilier Jones asked his corporal.

"You'll see," Jack replied.

For three minutes, the noise was staggering as shells began to fall where Fred had requested. A couple fell short, but these landed behind Fred's position. After the shelling stopped, there was an incredible silence.

*

When the time came to drop back out of the woods, Fred asked a couple of his best men, Jack and Lance Corporal Johnson, those who he knew he could rely on to cope by themselves, to stay behind for an hour, firing now and again, to convince the Germans they were still in position. They would then sneak out and follow the rest of the platoon.

The platoon had dismantled the Vickers and was lugging them between the trees when they came across a young Highlander who was screaming his head off like a lunatic, his mates trying to subdue him.

Martin and Barnett leapt on the man and helped pin him down. It was then that Fred saw the cause of his distress. Lying on the forest floor a few feet away was another Highlander with the top of his head blown clean off. There was nothing anyone could do for the poor boy. Barnett and Martin tried to calm the hysterical man as much as they could. Before long, an officer from the 51st Highlanders strode over and told the poor wretch to pull himself together and jump in the back of the truck before Jerry came and blew his head off too.

The platoon began the process of dropping back to join the rest of the battalion at the Ligne de Recueil. They were always on the move, firing a few rounds towards the Germans, dismantling the gun into its component parts to drop back a few hundred yards, then reassembling the gun again to fire off another few rounds designed to slow the German advance. Every time Fred heard a shot whistle by he counted his blessings that it wasn't him that time.

"Did you hear the one about the German rifle range?" Barnett asked as they rode in the back of the truck.

The platoon raised their eyebrows in unison.

"So, on the sniping range, the lieutenant says to a fellow soldier: 'That guy over there is pretty good'," Barnett mimicked a German accent. "Yes, indeed, but I have a feeling that we should better check his personal background' says the soldier. 'Why?' asks the lieutenant. 'After every shot, he removes his fingerprints from the rifle'."

Everyone in the back of the truck groaned.

Wednesday, 22nd May - Ebersvillers to Lanheres, France

The buildings in the deserted village of Ebersviller had provided them with some cover, but this became much more difficult to find once they began the retreat into the undulating countryside. They fell into a routine of moving the truck to the next corner, assembling the Vickers, firing as accurately as they could to where they suspected the Germans to be advancing, then dismantling the Vickers, getting into the back of the truck, and moving to the next bend in the road.

Light tanks came into view, with their identifying black-and-white crosses.

"Open fire!" Fred shouted.

The tanks retreated.

"They're not rushing, are they?" Jack commented. "They don't seem that bothered about the Vickers."

Mortar and artillery shells began to fall, and a light aircraft appeared.

"Scouting our position," said Fred. "Better get ready to move."

When the shells began to land too close, Fred ordered the platoon to retreat to the next suitable position. On the way, the trucks passed a few French civilians who looked very sorry for themselves. The next suitable position turned out to be in a hamlet, which had just a few houses.

The men were setting up the Vickers when a Frenchman came running out of his house with glasses of beer, which he tried to offer to Fred's men.

"For goodness sake," said Fred. "Martin! I need you to translate for me. Ask them, please stop giving my soldiers beer! They won't be able to move, let alone fight!"

"Yes, Sarge," said Martin and began to translate. "*Arrête de donner de la bière à nos soldats! Ils ne pourront pas bouger, encore moins se battre.*"

"Aw, Sarge." Barnett complained.

"I'm doing you a favour," said Fred

Thursday, 23rd May 1940 - Lanheres, France

"I won't lie to you, Wooll," Major Potts told Fred when he had managed to reunite his platoon with the battalion and the rest of the 51st Highland Division at Lanheres near Etain. "The general situation is very serious."

The major looked around to check there was no one to overhear.

"You're a career military man, like me. You've been around a bit, you know what it's like. Between you and me, it's now not so much a question of the division re-joining the BEF, as avoiding destruction or surrender."

Fred had imagined the situation was bad, but this had exceeded his worst expectations.

Major Potts checked once more that the coast was clear before lowering his voice to a virtual whisper.

"It's becoming apparent that the French are collapsing. It sounds like they'll try to evacuate the BEF from the coast, so we're going to move somewhere north of Paris, and from there we should be able to make it to Le Havre."

Fred didn't want to show it, but inside he was relieved. News of a boat from Le Havre to England, where Leah and the rest of his family were, was the best news he had received in months.

"I heard the French have been giving up by the thousands, sir. They think they'll be taken prisoner and then sent to their homes."

"Of course, none of this is definite, you understand," warned the Major. "I'm telling you because I know you'll be able to maintain the spirits of the men without going into detail."

"I understand," said Fred.

"Get your men ready to leave tonight. Keep this under your hat, but we're heading to Cornay, near Varennes. It's about fifty miles, but it'll take a couple of nights to get there. The roads are congested with French transport and refugees, and the route may be difficult to find."

Thursday, 28th May 1940 - Monkwearmouth, England

After a morning of tidying the scullery, Leah sat down to listen to the one o'clock news. When it had finished, she sat motionless as a sudden cold seemed to grip her. Belgium had surrendered, and she had no idea where Fred was. She was sure he wasn't in Belgium, but the Low Countries had surrendered so quickly, and now it was France.

It took a large effort to get up and go about her business again, getting Jim and Beatrice ready to go to her father's shop in Dame Dorothy Street so that they would have something for tea.

When she arrived at her father's shop, it was full, and she found her dad rushed off his feet.

"You look tired," he told Leah when she had a moment.

"I know, I feel it," said Leah. "I spent the morning sorting out the scullery."

"Why?" asked her dad. "How could you do such a thing? You need to stay strong. Don't overdo it, Leah."

Leah felt she had 'been told'. She noticed that many of the customers looked sad or withdrawn. She imagined they too must have husbands, sons, or brothers in France. Her father did his best to cheer them up as he served them.

Wednesday, 29th May 1940 - Preuseville, France

Fred looked out of the back of the truck at the road, packed with refugees. There were women pushing prams, old wives, children, babies crying. All able-bodied men and women were pulling carts, all carrying as much of their possessions as they could, using any and every possible means of transport and all wearing expressions of abject misery and dread.

The town, packed with refugees when the German bombers arrived, descended into chaos as the refugees ran for their lives from the heavy bombing.

Fred's platoon had travelled through the night again among terrible traffic congestion, and Fred found himself getting very frustrated. Not just with the clogged roads, but with the constant changes in orders. First, they were going one way, then another. He struggled to contain his emotions every time he received another missive from Major Potts. He knew it wasn't the Major's fault, the indecision was coming from higher up, and Potts must have been as frustrated as he. The major had summoned Fred to report and, as he made his way to the D company HQ, Fred consoled himself with the thought that at least they'd now arrived at Preuseville, near Abbeville on the Somme. Dieppe was about 25 miles away, and even Le Havre was less than a hundred miles. It wouldn't be long now before he was on a boat back home to Leah, Beattie and Jim.

When he entered D company HQ, Fred saw the two other platoon commanders in the company, Lt Jim Stawart and Lt Lovell Garrett, already there.

"Ah, Sergeant, good of you to join us," said the Major on seeing Fred. "I'll cut to the chase if you don't mind."

Fred nodded.

"It is hoped to stabilise a line covering Paris along the rivers Aisne and Somme, from Rheims to Amiens and to the sea north-west of Abbeville. Being attached to the 51st Division, we go wherever they go. The 10th French Army ..." Potts pointed to a map to indicate their location. "Three armoured divisions, three cavalry divisions and eight Infantry divisions. I'm not telling you this for fun. I'm telling you because I think you deserve to know the situation as I see it. In my opinion, from what I have gleaned from above, these troops are in various stages of disorganisation and their ranks depleted. I am being honest with you when I say that, in my opinion, this line is not going to hold without concerted effort. Nevertheless, our orders are to remain here at battalion HQ. A to C companies will be going with infantry brigades of the Highland Division. I understand you might be disappointed to be sitting around here when you could be getting stuck in, but I must ask you to be patient and pray for the success of our colleagues."

Fred nodded. He wasn't disappointed. There was more than enough action for him here with the Germans dropping bombs on their heads. He felt for his colleagues in the rest of the battalion, sent to the front line. Fred hoped they all got back, but he was glad for a respite of sorts.

Monday, 3rd June 1940 - Monkwearmouth, England

After she had put the washing out, Leah had taken Jim and Beattie up Dame Dorothy Street, but before long, she wished she had stayed at home. Everyone she passed stopped to ask her whether or not she knew if Fred was back in England. There were rumours of families having received telegrams, but many more stories of those waiting for news.

Leah let Jim play with the potatoes while she and her father closed the shop.

"Every available boat has gone to help," said her father between coughs.

"Mrs Pearson says that it's the Antichrist appearing because the end of the world is coming," said Leah.

"You don't want to listen to that old woman," said her father. "She'll just put you more on edge."

"Do you have aspirin?" Leah asked her father.

"Of course," said James and disappeared into a back room.

Outside a car was revving its engine, a dog was barking, children were shouting, and an aeroplane flew low overhead.

"Here you go," said her father, returning with an aspirin and a glass of water.

"How can they stand it?" Leah asked.

"How can who stand what?" asked her father, recovering a potato, which had rolled away from Jim.

"All the noise. The soldiers, I mean. How can they stand all the noise? The guns and the bombs?"

She couldn't stop herself thinking about bodies being torn and wounded by shots and bombs, and she shivered trying to get the thoughts out of her head.

"I wonder how many of our soldiers will be left behind," Leah said after she had washed down the pill and handed the glass back to her father with a smile. "They are very brave, aren't they? The rescuers and the rescued."

"I heard someone say today that their son got back and he's in a hospital down south," said James. "His wife wrote to her to say that he has no wounds but is lying flat in bed. He's suffering from shock. Didn't recognise his own wife."

"What if Fred doesn't recognise me?" asked Leah. "What if ..."

"Don't worry, luv," coughed her father. "He'll be back, and he'll recognise you."

Wednesday, 5th June 1940 - Monkwearmouth, England

When Leah had managed to get both Jim and little Beattie asleep, she sat down with the newspaper she'd bought. She read and re-read the accounts of the Dunkirk evacuation. She hoped with all her strength that Fred was among those who had made it onto the boats and out of France.

It had been a very hot day, and Leah felt exhausted. Every task had been an effort, and she was glad now that the children were in bed so that she could relax. She felt optimistic that Fred was already back in England and that they would soon be reunited. She also felt good that they were on the side of right and not on the side of evil.

Tuesday, 4th June 1940 - Preuseville, France

When Fred returned to the billets after his daily briefing from Major Potts, Fusilier Martin ran up to him.

"Sir, I heard that Italy, Turkey and America are in the war against Germany and Dunkirk has been destroyed. Calais has been taken, London evacuated, and the Germans were within three miles of Paris."

Fred wanted to laugh but couldn't. His mind was still full of the information Major Potts had told him.

"I don't know about any of that, Fusilier, but I have just heard from Major Potts that A company have suffered some casualties, six wounded have been evacuated, three seriously, there are eight missing, and the enemy has established bridgeheads over the Somme at Abbeville and St Valery sur Somme."

He didn't tell them how easy the Major thought it had been for the Germans to establish these bridgeheads. Fred had the morale of his platoon to consider.

"I've got a joke about a major," said Barnett.

"I thought you might," said Fred.

"It's about a colonel, but I can tell it about a major."

All eyes were fixed on Barnett with low expectations for the joke he was about to tell.

"So this major goes to the doctor, and the doctor tells him that if he gives up drinking, he is bound to live longer," Barnett begins. "'Are you sure about this?' asks the colonel...er...I mean major. 'I am sure of it,' says the doctor. 'If you stop drinking, it will prolong your days.' 'Come to think of it, I think you are right,' says the Major. 'Six months ago, I gave up drinking for 24 hours, and I never put in such a long day in my life.'"

Taylor joined Barnett in his guffawing. Everyone else present just let out groans and went about their business.

Thursday, 6th June 1940 - Monkwearmouth, England

Leah didn't want to leave the house because of the faces of all the other wives and mothers who had had wires to tell them that their husbands and sons had arrived back in England.

She heard the front door open and went to see who it was. It was her father.

"I didn't see you at the shop today," he said. "Is everything ok?"

"I couldn't face all those people," said Leah.

"What people?"

"All those people who already know their husbands or sons or brothers are all back in England."

"I see. Still no news then?"

Leah shook her head.

"Well, I have some news," said her father with a smile.

"Yes?" Leah's heart began to race.

"Beattie has gone into hospital, she's having her baby."

"Oh." Leah slumped into a chair.

"I thought you would be pleased," said her father.

Leah felt guilty. She knew she should be pleased for her sister, but she couldn't help thinking about her own problems.

"I'm pleased for her," she said. "It's just that I thought you had news about Fred."

"Sorry, luv. I'm sure he'll be all right. They got loads of our lads out at Dunkirk."

"Yes, but not everyone," she said, beginning to cry.

"Eh, lass," her father crouched beside her. "It'll be all right, luv. You'll see."

FRED & LEAH: A TRUE LIFE SECOND WORLD WAR DRAMA OF LOVE, LOSS AND CAPTIVITY.

65

Friday, 7th June 1940 - St Aignan-sur-Ry, France

Fred could see the houses of St Aignan silhouetted by the setting sun as he listened to Major Potts brief him and the rest of the D Company platoon commanders.

"Since we arrived earlier this afternoon, the battalion has managed to put the village in a state of all-round defence," said Potts. "'A' company has still not returned from their engagement with the Germans at Abbeville, which has been disastrous by all accounts. It seems that two German armoured divisions have split the French Tenth Army - the Highland Division, along with their French comrades, are now separated from part of the Tenth. Yes, Wooll?"

Potts acknowledged that Fred was eager to ask a question.

"Sir, there was meant to be a trainload of ammunition to replenish our supplies."

"I spoke to CSM McLevy. He said they're doing their best," said Potts.

"But sir," continued Fred, "without ammunition, the result of this battle will be a foregone conclusion."

"I said, they are doing their best, Sergeant," said Potts.

Fred nodded.

"It's a terrible business," Lt. Jim Stawart whispered to Fred, who nodded in silence.

Saturday, 8th June 1940 - St Aignan-sur-Ry to La Chaussée, France

"The Germans have broken through to the south," Fred told his men. "Prepare for withdrawal."

So started the process of driving the truck to a new position. Setting up, engaging the enemy, and then withdrawing again.

Fred was hungry and tired. His men were physically and mentally exhausted. They kept moving, setting up, and dismantling in a virtual daze, and Fred wondered how long they could keep fighting without relief. The ration was down to two sugar lumps and two tablespoons of mixed carrot and potato per man. Hardly enough to keep them awake, let alone fight.

The platoon drove along the roads passing lines of refugees who were marching in the sun with just the poplar trees, which Napoleon had planted for cover and shade.

"Look," said Fusilier Martin.

He pointed to the distance from where the sound of a German Stuka was already audible.

They pulled off the road and assembled the Vickers, but by the time they set up, the Stuka, already lined up, began to dive bomb the road. As it dived towards the road, the German plane began firing its machine gun, cutting -down women and children as they ran to safety.

The platoon tried firing at the plane with the Vickers, but with no effect. As it approached, they dived for cover.

The bombs howled as they fell, but most of the refugee column looked like they were in some kind of stupor.

When the attack ended, there were old men, women, and children all crying, upturned prams among the scattered dead, while the wounded pleaded for assistance from the platoon.

Lance Corporal Johnson had his legs machine-gunned and his arm blown off. He was a mess.

"My ring, save my ring," Johnson shouted when they tried to pick him up.

At first, Fred wondered why Johnson was so concerned about his ring until Fred realised that Johnson's arm had been blown off.

FRED & LEAH: A TRUE LIFE SECOND WORLD WAR DRAMA OF LOVE, LOSS AND CAPTIVITY.

67

Fred searched the area and found what was left of the arm. The hand was still intact, and Fred saw the ring still on one of the fingers. He slid the ring off and took it over to Johnson, putting it in the breast pocket of his tunic.

"Give us a ciggy?" Johnson asked.

Fred took his packet of Woodbines out. There was one left. Fred had been saving it for the boat journey on the way home. He lit it and handed it to Johnson, holding it up to his lips so he could take a drag.

It was the last thing Johnson managed to do before he died. Fred wondered whether it was because Johnson was a religious man that God had cut his suffering short.

Barnett and Taylor were very quiet for a long time after that. Perhaps it was because they had spent so much of the last few months trying to wind Johnson up that they felt it so much now that he was gone.

Fred sent Fusilier Martin with a message for CSM McLevy, who organised transport for Johnson's body. As they loaded his body into the back of the truck, the refugees were surrounding them, begging for assistance.

Fred had no medical supplies to give them, and even if he had, he wouldn't have been permitted to delay the retreat.

"They're helpless. Can't we do something?" asked Jack.

"I want to help them," said Fred. "But there's nothing I can do."

They watched the desperate faces of the refugees as the truck pulled off, knowing the Germans would be there soon. The platoon, chased all the way, would take up a position whenever retreating infantry found itself under fire from the advancing Germans. Fred's men tried not to panic even when shells were falling close by.

Every so often, they would pass a deserted house, and Bobby Jones would rush inside and come out with a bottle of rum or a loaf of bread. They found a wagon, blown up, and Bobby managed to get some tins of bully beef, which were still intact among the scattered contents.

Fred believed they were on their way to Le Havre, but progress had been frustrating as they seemed to be waiting for the French, who had no transport and progress was too slow. Fred couldn't see how they would make it to Le Havre with the Germans right on their tails.

The platoon would dismount, set up the guns, fire the rounds and then, as soon as they had fired them, pack up again. In the haze of exhaustion, they did their best to keep firing, hoping that the rounds would hold up the Germans long enough for their own forces to make their retreat.

The song, *Run Rabbit Run*, kept swimming around in Fred's head as they withdrew. In the early days of the phoney war, Fred's platoon had sung the song and imagined it was Hitler's soldiers doing the running away, but now the only running the German soldiers were doing was straight towards them.

Sunday, 9th June - La Chaussée, France

"Rouen now belongs to the Germans," Major Potts told Fred. "That's 35 miles to the south. We have been given orders to withdraw to Le Havre, but to make that possible, we need to delay the German advance."

Fred could sense what was coming.

"There is a crossroads, 14 miles south at Totes. We need you to take your platoon there, where the French will give you support. You need to hold up the German advance for as long as possible."

"Yes, sir," said Fred, his heart sinking as he imagined his chances of getting on a boat at Le Havre disappearing.

"Now listen here, Sergeant," Major Potts was solemn. "You must not abandon the French. Do you hear me? I know they slow everything down, but the orders from above are that we must show a united front. For morale."

Fred raised his eyebrows.

"I know," said the Major. "Not our morale. But we must not be seen to abandon our allies. Understood?"

Fred nodded.

*

"King George has been captured, and Chamberlain killed," Fred overheard Fusilier Martin saying when he returned to the platoon. "And someone else said they heard that the Russians had attacked Germany, Turkey has overrun Italy, and the British have retaken Calais."

"Shut up, Fusilier," Fred said.

He called the platoon to attention and explained the orders. They mounted their trucks and headed south with two trucks loaded with ammunition that CSM McLevy had somehow managed to procure in time.

Fred's platoon hadn't got very far when they encountered some French tanks stationary in the road. Fusilier Martin spoke to the French soldiers. His knowledge of French was the best in the platoon, except Bobby, whose ability to communicate with local French girls was excellent, but whose vocabulary was useless when it came to anything related to military matters.

Martin was able to gather that the French were unable to move because their tanks had run out of petrol. There were, however, a couple of light tanks with enough petrol to go with Fred's platoon to the crossroads. French cavalry accompanied these and Fred tried not to imagine what the result of the French cavalry meeting Rommel's Panzer division would be.

"Tell us all a joke, Barnett," Fred asked the fusilier, who had been quiet ever since Johnson had died. Barnett thought for a moment and then decided on one.

"A mother is telling off her son for stealing a penny," he began. "'It is as much of a sin to steal a penny as a pound,' said the mother. 'Now how do you feel?' 'Like an idiot,' said the boy. 'There was a pound note next to the penny.'"

Even Taylor just managed a smile, and Fred wondered what was happening to his platoon and what would become of them.

Monday, 10th June 1940 - Totês, France

Fred ordered the platoon to set up positions on either side of the cross-roads where the road from Rouen entered the town, with the trucks parked where they would be out of sight of the approaching German tanks. He asked Bobby to see if he could get up to the top of the church steeple with Fusilier Martin to see whether they could get a view of the advancing Germans.

As soon as the Germans came into view, Fred ordered the platoon to use short, accurate bursts to prevent the enemy from crossing open areas.

From his observation post in the church tower, Bobby spotted the enemy bringing up mortars on horse-drawn wagons accompanied by more troops arriving by truck. By the time Fusilier Martin had communicated the information to Fred, the mortars had concentrated on the crossroads and the gun positions at the sides of the road.

One of the mortars destroyed an ammunition lorry, which exploded sending high explosives raining down. The wounded were sent into the church cellar and, as there were no medical staff, the stretcher-bearers tried to stop the bleeding and make the wounded comfortable.

The men, issued with chocolate and water, were hungry. Fred took a bite, and stored the rest in his pocket before priming some more grenades to hand out to the men.

They kept up their fire and managed to halt the German advance until the afternoon when a mortar struck the last remaining ammo truck.

Without ammunition, they wouldn't be much use in stopping the Germans, so Fred decided to use the remaining ammunition to get out if they could. If they managed to extract themselves and withdraw, they could rejoin the rest of the battalion and continue the fight.

Fusilier Martin did his best to translate this for the French who seemed more than happy to leave.

Fred ordered the men to leave behind large packs, greatcoats and blankets to make room for more men and ammunition. They dismantled the Vickers and loaded them into the remaining trucks to withdraw to a new position.

The fire from the Germans was intense, and it took its toll on the physical and mental resources of the platoon, also hampered by the speed of their

French counterparts who were on horses. Cohesive activity and coherent thought were impossible as the hungry and tired troops struggled to stay alive.

They had just left the centre of the village when Fred heard a Stuka approaching. He could see from the back of the truck that it was heading straight for them.

"Abandon the truck," Fred shouted, and the men ran to take cover in the adjacent field just in time before the Stuka strafed the truck and French cavalry with machine gun fire. It then circled back, climbing high into the sky.

Fred lay on his back in the open field and watched the Stuka screaming down vertically before dropping its bombs and streaming away. He watched the bombs leave the plane, four of them. The bombs looked as if the pilot had aimed them at him, but he was relieved when they missed both him and the trucks.

"They're not very good shots, are they?" Jack joked.

"We have to fight to the last round," Fred told his men as they climbed back into the truck. "We have to escape."

"What about them?" Fusilier Jones asked, pointing at the wounded French.

"They will have to leave the wounded," said Fred. "They understand. Progress is slow enough as it is and we don't have space in the trucks."

"Can't we just leave them all? We could have managed to get to the coast by now," said Jack.

"No, I have strict orders that they are not to be abandoned. We are to show a united front."

Jack laughed at this. He knew that the front with the French was anything but united.

"They're meant to be our allies," Fred reminded him. "What signal does it give to our allies if we just abandon them?"

They had been on the road back to Dieppe, which was 20 miles to the north, but Fred knew that evacuation by sea was impossible from Dieppe and that his battalion would be trying for Le Havre, which was 50 miles to the west of their current position. He had sent Fusilier Martin out by motorcycle to try and find out what was happening. When Martin returned, he brought news that the German Panzers had already arrived in Yvetot, 15 miles to the west. Fred knew that Le Havre was an impossibility and that their best bet was to cut across country and try to make it to Saint-Valery-en-Caux on the coast, about 25 miles from where they were. Fred sent Fusilier Martin ahead on his motorcycle and hoped that he could get the platoon to a boat before the Germans cut off their means of escape.

As night fell, they continued their withdrawal along the winding country lanes, coming under frequent attack from the advancing Germans and returning their fire long enough to gain an opportunity to retreat further.

Another German plane approached, but this time it was a spotter plane. It released flares, which illuminated the countryside, revealing the position of Fred's platoon and drawing fire from the Germans.

Fred ordered them to move on, and they continued their journey trying to avoid the light of the flares. They had been zig-zagging along small country lanes for most of the evening, but as they were approaching what Fred's map told him was the main road from where they were to where they wanted to get to, St Valery en Caux, Fusilier Martin arrived.

"You're heading in the right direction," he said. "The rest of the battalion is also attempting to reach the coast at St Valery en Caux. However, the road you are about to join is full of Germans. They'll cut off your access to the junction if you don't get a move on."

"Right, let's double our pace," Fred ordered the platoon and then turned to Fusilier Martin. "Tell the French that if they don't keep up, they'll be left behind."

As soon as the platoon reached the junction, they could see the Germans in the distance, advancing from the south.

"Keep feeding the gun," Fred shouted at the men.

They kept firing, but the Germans kept coming. Wave after wave. Fred watched the Germans falling, but more kept coming.

Jack signalled for them all to stop. He pointed through the woods, and when Fred followed his line of sight, he could see three Germans running through the wood a short distance from the road.

The platoon opened fire, and two of the Germans fell. They then came under heavy fire from the flank. The men of Fred's platoon threw themselves on the ground and fired at where they perceived the positions to be, throwing grenades in that direction for good measure. Some of the grenades must have hit their target, judging by the screams coming from the wood.

Fred then spotted around eight to ten Germans running through the trees, but there were others who were still firing at Fred's platoon, which lay flat and was returning the fire as best it could. One of the Germans tried to advance upon them, and they opened fire. The German fell to the ground clutching his stomach, which the platoon had riddled with bullets.

The Germans were now throwing stick grenades, and one landed near Fred's platoon. A piece of shrapnel struck Jack on the forehead, just above the eye, and the blood, which poured from the wound, temporarily blinded him. Fred, concerned for Jack but also concerned for the platoon, which was running low on ammunition, ordered the group to withdraw.

"That was amazing," Billy Barrett said from the safety of their truck. They could still see the German positions in the distance and the occasional shell would whizz overhead. Fred ordered a burst of fire from the Vickers, which seemed to do the trick at persuading the enemy to stay where they were.

They sank as deep as they could in the truck as the mortars flew overhead.

"You need to get your haircut," Fred commented to Jack as he tended to his cut. "You're setting a bad example to the men."

Jack laughed, and Fred told him to stay still.

Tuesday, 11th June 1940 - The road to St Valery-en-Caux, France

When they arrived at St.Valery-en-Caux at 3am, a brigadier was directing traffic, naval guns were firing and the noise was deafening. German artillery was making a mess of the town, destroying the beautiful rows of coloured houses. It was as if each one was being lifted off the ground and then dropped into a pile of rubble. Out to sea, Fred could see nothing because the fog was as thick as pea soup.

There were army lorries everywhere but no tanks.

In one of the houses that was still standing, Bobby found a radio which still had juice in the accumulator. He managed to get the BBC. The men of the platoon heard the announcement that the BEF had been evacuated from Dunkirk.

"Like bollocks they have," said Jack. "We're the bloody BEF, and we haven't bloody well been evacuated. British Expeditionary Force? Boys England Forgot more like."

Fred imagined those thoughts must have been circling Jack's mind for a while.

The platoon found the D company HQ and Fred went to speak with Major Potts while Jack found a medic to look at the wound on his head.

"The Germans have already reached the coast and cut us off from Le Havre," the Major informed Fred. "The Navy is trying to get boats in to evacuate us from here, but the fog and the sea conditions are making it impossible to get anything into the harbour. I need you to take your platoon up to the wood on the outskirts and try to help any groups who are in trouble. We need to hold off the Germans long enough to try and get as many men out by boat as possible."

Fred nodded and turned to leave.

"Fred," Major Potts called, surprising the Sergeant with his familiarity.

Fred turned back to the Major.

"Look, Fred, I appreciate everything you and your men have achieved. You won't be forgotten," he promised.

Fred forced a smile, thanked the Major and left. He knew the odds of getting everyone onto boats was slim. He felt his prospects of seeing Leah, his children and his family slipping away once more.

When he returned to his platoon, they were watching an old Frenchman walking past as if nothing was wrong. Then the shelling started again and, within a few minutes, had more or less destroyed the town.

A small German spotter plane came over, and not long afterwards dive-bombers came over in stukas.

"They're terrifying things," Barnett observed. "Dropping bombs all over the place."

The Germans started machine gunning, and after a few minutes, there was a bit of a lull, which gave Fred's platoon the opportunity to follow the orders Major Potts had given them. They took up a position behind barbed wire fences on the outskirts of the town.

Fred's platoon set up their guns just as three tanks appeared.

"They're big things," Jack observed. "Not the small tanks we have."

Fred could see the German armour moving around in the distance.

"I wonder what they intend to do?" Fred wondered aloud.

"They're heading our way!" explained Jack, nonplussed.

Fred looked at his colleague, whose head the medic had wrapped in fresh bandages in the town while Fred was receiving their orders. He gave him a stare, which suggested he could do without the clever remarks right now.

Fred watched as the Germans drew nearer. He waited until they were within range of the Vickers.

"Open fire!" he shouted, though he thought the chances of the Vickers inflicting much damage on these tanks were small.

The tanks were firing back at them with machine guns. Tracer bullets must have hit a power cable because it was sparking green and white and lashing around like a whip. Barnett was thrown to the ground, but got back to his position and continued firing, covered in blood.

"You bastards!" he shouted.

Fred ordered the platoon to focus their fire on the first tank, and they managed to kill the crew, putting the tank out of action.

The second tank slew around, which meant the platoon was able to shoot at it and put it out of action too. The third one turned around and drove off.

The Germans were soon back with infantry. They began to arrive in trucks and fan out across the field in front of the platoon's position. Fred ordered his men to fire and Germans were falling all over the place until they retreated.

Barnett winced at seeing all the Germans falling.

"It's horrific," he muttered.

"It is a matter of survival, Fusilier," said Fred. "Them or us."

"We've managed to drive them back to the woods," said Jack.

"But for how long?" said Fred, scratching the itchy stubble on his chin.

Fusilier Martin arrived back from delivering Fred's report to D company HQ and handed a note to him. Fred read it and smiled, hope rekindling where it had been abandoned.

"We've been told to be ready to move off at 10 o'clock."

The platoon welcomed Fred's announcement with cheers.

"Go back to HQ and return when they want us to come down to the pier."

*

Martin came at 9.30pm and handed Fred another note, which he read with a mixture of hope and trepidation.

"The embarkation has been postponed until midnight," Fred announced. This time the platoon met his words with silence. "OK, Martin. Go back and try to return with better news next time."

"Yes sir," said Martin and left.

*

Fred's heart sank when he saw the expression on Martin's face when he returned. Fred read the note.

"Postponed until the next day," he announced to a reception of groans.

"Sir, I heard the Americans had landed at Brest with two motorised divisions," said Fusilier Martin.

"Was this from an official source?"

"No, Sir."

Wednesday, 12th June 1940 - St Valery-en-Caux

The German tanks and infantry returned in greater numbers. The fire on the platoon was so intense that Fred saw no option but to abandon the position.

"Every man for himself," he shouted. "Get out any way available."

They made for the town. From their position above, they could see that every building was in flames, there were dead, wounded, and dying people everywhere. It was horrific, and Fred was terrified.

The Germans rained down artillery fire with unprecedented fury while Panzer tanks attempted to penetrate the Allied defences.

Fred realised how low the ammunition was getting and he could see the town in flames. The fog had closed in, and Fred felt pessimistic about their chances of getting boats into the harbour. If that wasn't bad enough, German gunfire was raking the length of the pier, making it impossible to get men anywhere near the boats, even if they did manage to get into the harbour.

The platoon found a new position behind a monument to a French flyer that was safe until some French soldiers wearing white shirts climbed it and brought artillery shelling down on their position.

Barnett looked out to see what was going on. He took a bullet in the centre of his chest and fell back at Fred's feet. Fred crouched beside him to see what he could do, but Barnett was already dead.

"What happened to the RAF?" Fred wondered aloud to Jack.

"I don't know. I haven't seen one of ours all morning."

Fred sent Bobby off to find supplies, and he returned a short time later with a box of grenades without detonators and enough tinned potatoes for everyone.

"Thanks for the potatoes, but what use are these?" Fred asked pointing to the useless grenades.

Bobby looked sheepish.

Fred realised the guns were down to half a belt of ammunition. He gave the order for his men to strip the guns so the Germans couldn't use them and then they sat and waited to be captured.

No sooner had they done this than Fusilier Martin arrived with the order to reclaim the ground above the town.

Following Fred's command, the men began restoring the guns.

FRED & LEAH: A TRUE LIFE SECOND WORLD WAR DRAMA OF LOVE, LOSS AND CAPTIVITY.

79

Once they had finished, they found a suitable position where they had a good view of the enemy and prepared to fire, but Fred was unable to give the order because surrendering French were crossing their path and preventing them from engaging the Germans.

When the path was clear, Fred gave the order to fire, but it seemed that no sooner had the platoon's onslaught begun than it ended, because the ammunition had run out. Once again, Fred gave the order to dismantle the weapons.

They returned to the town, and less than an hour later, the bugle sounded the ceasefire. Fred realised they would be prisoners and have to surrender their weapons, which now meant their Enfield rifles.

Fred was so depressed he felt like shooting himself if he'd had any ammunition. He was kept going by the thought of Leah, Jim and little Beattie waiting for him at home.

They made their way to the town square. As they walked, they watched the British Army dumping their trucks into the sea before the Germans arrived. Fred looked around at the soldiers, many of whom were weeping. He noticed others who were looking in disgust at the weeping men. Fred saw that the officers had changed into their dress uniforms. Fred thought it was nice they were trying to put on a good show, but he was more concerned about where his next hot meal was coming from and how he was going to get himself out of this mess.

There was a torrent of emotions running through Fred's head. Disgust at the fact that the Germans had captured them and that the French had given up. Fear about what might happen next. Would the Germans murder them? Fred felt hunger, exhaustion and relief that he had survived the ordeal he and his men had just endured.

*

They arrived just in time to see the first German tank rumble into the square, and on it was riding General Rommel. An officer from the tank ordered the British to throw all equipment and arms in a pile in a field. The Germans then formed up the prisoners in a column and marched them in an easterly direction.

Fusilier Martin ran up to Fred

"Sarge, they're not going to shoot us, are they?"

"Of course not. They wouldn't dare," said Fred.

Fusilier Martin ran away happier, but Fred wasn't so sure. He thought the Germans might shoot them, but couldn't say that to Martin.

Fred watched the German troops taking control of the town. Some approached what was left of Fred's platoon and shouted orders. The column marched through the town past dead soldiers which lay all around, and the Germans herded them into a hastily erected barbed wire enclosure.

It was raining, but the Germans insisted the prisoners hand over their gas capes and groundsheets, which were keeping them dry. They also searched the prisoners for sharp implements. Fred had his knife, scissors and cigarette lighter taken from him, but was allowed to keep his tin cup and tinned potatoes. He watched as the Germans heaped the confiscated equipment in huge piles.

"We've been sold down the river and left holding the baby," Jack complained. "For a week we've heard stories of the evacuation at Dunkirk and how all the stops were pulled out to make it succeed. Why haven't all the stops been pulled out for us?"

Fred had no reply to this.

They found themselves with a group of French soldiers who offered them some cognac, which Fred thought it polite to accept.

FRED & LEAH: A TRUE LIFE SECOND WORLD WAR DRAMA OF LOVE, LOSS AND CAPTIVITY.

81

5 pm, Wednesday, 12th June 1940 - St Valery-em-Caux to Yvetot, France

Fred marched in the pouring rain with the rest of his platoon, holding an umbrella, which one of the German soldiers had given him. They seemed to be marching back along the route of the German advance, carrying what clothing they had on their backs. Fred looked around at the other British troops, some of which were wearing vests, shorts, and boots. Some were topless. He looked back at the column stretching out behind like a long khaki snake.

At the front of the column, a group of 51st Highlanders were singing *Keep Right on to the End of the Road*.

Fred thought that the German escort looked almost as badly off as themselves. These had been the German soldiers that Fred and his platoon had been shooting at days before. He appreciated what they had been through and felt they shared this silent appreciation.

As they were approaching a village, a van passed, driving alongside the column of prisoners. There was a loudspeaker on its roof and, as they marched through the village, a voice came over the loudspeaker saying: "You are not to accept any food or water from the locals."

Fred's platoon had been picking up any food they saw by the roadside, as they had not eaten for some time. He felt the tin of potatoes in his pocket but knew he needed to save it until times were desperate.

At the far side of the village, Fred and Jack noticed some long grass leading to what looked like a small wooded area. As the column passed, they snuck into the grass. Judging by the rustling, a few others had the same idea. They tried to crawl towards the woods, but heard rustling behind them and turned to see a German pointing his rifle at them.

As they rejoined the column, Fred saw that two Gordon Highlanders had also tried the same trick and been caught and returned to the column.

A German officer told one of them, "For you, British sergeant, the war is over, but there is plenty of work for you to do in Germany".

The Scottish sergeant turned and started walking in the opposite direction to the column.

"I'm not going to Germany. I belong to Glasgow, and Glasgow's that way," he said, pointing in the direction of Scotland.

The butt of a German rifle brought the sergeant to his knees, and this persuaded him to rejoin the column.

"Twelve miles is the maximum we're allowed to march in one day, according to the Geneva Convention. But we've been going for three hours without a halt," said Fred.

"I'd take up your cause," said Jack, "but after what happened to that sergeant's jaw, I don't feel very much like arguing."

"How far?" Fred asked a German.

"Three kilometres," the soldier said without thinking.

A German staff car passed them, and Fred watched as an officer got out and started kicking the British soldiers to hurry them up. As they drew closer, Fred could make out a British captain intervening.

"You should treat the British soldiers as prisoners of war," Fred could hear the captain shout at the German officer.

The officer drew his pistol and fired three shots into the captain. He fell dead, and they left him by the roadside as they ordered the rest of the column to march on. Fred and Jack had to step over the poor man's body as they passed.

*

After what Fred guessed to be a march of about twenty-five miles, they arrived at a makeshift camp. They found prisoners already there who had prepared lentil soup, some of which Fred was able to collect in the tin cup he carried in his pocket. He devoured the soup, but it did little to make up for the energy he had expended that day. Others were not so lucky as to have saved their tin cups, and Fred noticed one soldier drinking his greasy soup from an old sardine can.

The Germans showed them to a stable where they lay down in their clothes.

"Blokes seem to be arriving all the time" Fred commented.

"Forgive me for not being very talkative, but I'm knackered," said Jack, laying his head down.

Fred lay his head down too and must have dropped off straight away, because the next thing he knew was that something had woken him up.

"What was that?" he asked Jack, who seemed to be already awake.

"Gunshots," said Jack. "Maybe someone was trying to escape."

Fred thought about Leah, Jim, and little Beatrice. What would happen to them if the Germans shot him trying to escape? What would happen if the Germans made it to England, which they would, given the speed they'd marched through France? He thought about his mum, dad, brothers, and sisters in Beverley. He'd seen what had happened to the French refugees, the way the German planes had shot and bombed the refugees. Given the speed that Germany had taken France, it wouldn't be long before they were across the channel to Britain, and Fred worried about what would happen to them all.

Thursday, 13th June 1940 - Yvetot to Buchy, France

Fred was in Sunderland. German stormtroopers were in Monkwear-mouth marching down Dame Dorothy Street. He rushed through the back streets to Normanby Street where he could see German troops at the dock end of the street. He ran as fast as he could, seeing the stormtroopers kicking down the door of his terrace. Through the door he could see Leah on the stairs, holding Beatrice, Jim crying as he clutched onto his mother. A stormtrooper raised his rifle to shoot them.

"No!" Fred shouted.

A German officer threw a cup of water in his face.

"You having a bad dream?" asked Jack, standing over him with his tin cup.

"What time is it? Why didn't you wake me?"

"I just did," said Jack. "There was an early morning scramble for water this morning, but I managed to get you a hatful. Should be enough for a shave. You look terrible by the way. You're letting the side down."

"Touché," said Fred, getting up.

"You'd better be quick," said Jack. "There's a rumour that someone is making coffee. Oh and ..."

Jack pulled four hardtack biscuits from his pocket.

"Two for you and two for me."

"What about the men?"

"They've got their own."

"Where are the trucks going?" asked Fred, nodding towards wagons pulling away.

"Taking the officers."

"Lucky bastards."

"Depends where they're taking them," said Jack.

*

The Germans had divided the men into groups of 200 to 300. The first block marched for about an hour and the second block ran to catch up with them - that was how they proceeded. In the heat and with the lack of food, Fred felt exhausted. He watched as other men abandoned the kits they were struggling to carry. He noticed an abandoned infantry kit and gave Jack a nudge. The kit contained a blanket, four mess tins, and a groundsheet.

"This'll come in handy later," said Fred, dividing the kit between them.

Beside the road lay many dead horses and cattle, some blown up like barrage balloons, a terrible stink from their rotting corpses. The surviving cattle were bellowing in pain with full udders waiting for the farmer to milk them, but the farmer was long gone. Fred thought how nice it would be to have a drink of some of that milk.

They hadn't marched much further when they saw soldiers that had been killed in action.

"Those greatcoats will come in handy too," said Jack, pointing towards the fallen men.

"We can't," said Fred

"Why not? They're not going to need them any more. They'll be great as blankets at night. They'd want us to have 'em."

They hurried over to the men and removed the coats, but just as Fred was going to put his on, he dropped it to the floor.

"What's wrong?" asked Jack. On examination, Fred realised it was riddled with bullet holes and soaked in blood. Jack also dropped his to the floor, and the two men joined the column again.

"I'd rather be cold than wrapped up in something this poor sod died in," said Fred.

"Aye, aye, what's happening up there?" asked Jack, pointing to a large gathering of German troops.

As they approached, they saw that the troops were handing over the column to a new group of soldiers.

"It must be the B echelon taking over," said Jack.

No sooner had the new troops taken over than they started pushing the British in the back shouting, "Raus! Raus!"

"What does *raus raus* mean?" asked Jack.

"No idea," said Fred.

"I'll tell you what it means," said a nearby German. "It means that while you are held in captivity, we will soon be in Britain and taking your girls out."

The German let out a loud, unnatural laugh.

Fred and Jack tried to ignore him and just kept moving. After a while, the German appeared to turn his attention to other prisoners up ahead. Jack gave Fred a nudge.

"What?" said Fred, with annoyance.

"Over there," said Jack. He pointed to a field. "Those are potatoes."

Keeping their eyes on the Germans, they climbed the gate and filled their pockets with as many spuds as they could before returning over the fence and back to the column, unnoticed by their German guards. They did not go unnoticed by their compatriots, who followed their lead and pillaged as much from the field as they could before the Germans realised and fired a couple of warning shots towards them, which cleared the field in no time.

*

That night the Germans set up a field kitchen, and Fred and Jack had tattie soup made from the potatoes they'd found in the field. The meal they had that night tasted better than either of them could have imagined, but as they lay on the ground, trying to get to sleep, they both felt cold and miserable.

Friday, 14th June 1940 - Buchy to Forges-les-Eaux, France

The drip-drop of rain on his head woke Fred. The Germans took the early shower as a cue to get the column of POWs moving. Fred, with what was left of his platoon and the thousands of other prisoners, set off into the rain. Before long, it had become torrential, and Fred abandoned the umbrella the German guard had given him. It was useless in the face of this downpour.

As a German staff car passed, an officer leaned out of the window and shouted: "You go to Berlin, we go to London."

"It's rare to see officers these days," Fred commented to Jack. "German NCOs seem to be in charge of the column."

"I don't think they expected to capture so many prisoners," said Jack.

"The troops guarding us now don't seem to have the same modern equipment we saw the Germans using on the front line," said Fred.

There were horse-drawn wagons and guards on bicycles.

"The soldiers seemed much older than those on the front lines," said Jack. "The younger Germans seemed happy to move on to the next frontier once the battle was won, but these older soldiers are miserable."

"I bet they're veterans from the Great War," said Fred. "They don't look very happy to have been recalled to the army."

"Yeah," Jack laughed. "They look like they feel too old to be disturbed by this new conflict. They want to be at home with their families, not guarding vast columns of prisoners."

Fred could empathise with them. He wanted to be at home with his family too.

"I just wish they didn't want to take their frustrations out on us," said Jack.

Fred and Jack and been lost in their thoughts and found themselves near the back of the column. When they reached the point in the road where the others in the column had stopped, they'd just sat down for a rest when the guards told them it was time to move on again.

"Come on," said Fred. "We need to be nearer the front of the column if we're going to make the most of these rest stops."

Though they were tired, they quickened their pace to overtake those around them.

As they neared the front, they could hear the Scots still singing Keep Right on to the End of the Road.

A truck of German troops passed. One hung out the back and shouted: "You're going to hang out your washing on the Siegfried line, eh tommies?" Fred now hated that song too.

"What happened to the Million Man Army the French were supposed to have?" asked Jack, as annoyed by the truck of Germans as Fred was.

*

"Well, that wasn't that bad," Fred commented, cleaning out the tin that had contained his evening meal.

"I know," said Jack. "Chunks of meat. A real treat."

As they prepared to settle down in their sleeping quarters, which had turned out to be a pigsty, they watched German troops bring more French prisoners into the temporary camp.

"There're more and more every day," said Jack.

Fred nodded.

"Good night, Corporal," he said as he lay down. Even though he was in a pigsty, when Fred lay down to sleep, it felt like a burden had been lifted from his shoulders.

Saturday, 15th June 1940 - Forges-les-Eaux to Formerie, France

"Sarge! Sarge!"

Fred struggled to pull himself up to a sitting position. It was becoming more and more difficult to rise in the morning. He rubbed his eyes to see who had awakened him. It was Fusilier Martin.

"Yes Fusilier, what is it?

"Some bugger has stolen my coat, sir."

"Damn it," said Jack, checking around him. "My bag's gone."

Fred checked his few belongings, but what little he had seemed present and correct. He looked around at the bustle of men, but with thousands in the column, the chances of finding the stolen items were next to impossible. The perpetrator would make sure they kept far from what was left of his platoon. There was nothing they could do. They just had to get up and follow the rest of the column back onto the road.

As the troops marched through the French countryside, they passed clamps, piles of vegetables covered by earth as a way of preserving the crop. Fred could see a clamp up in the distance. He could see the POWs in the column ahead, helping themselves as they passed the clamps, eating the vegetables raw. The column marched on the right side of the road and the guards on the left, which made it possible for some of the men to sneak into the fields to steal produce. However, by the time Fred's section reached the clamp, the men in front of him had robbed it of all the vegetables. He noticed some discarded vegetables by the roadside, but closer examination revealed they were just rotten onions, turnips gone off, and blighted potatoes.

When the column passed through a village, Fred watched with delight as a woman putting out a pail of water for the prisoners to drink. Fred was thirsty, as he hadn't had anything since they left that morning. However, before he could get to the bucket, a German guard ahead of him kicked it over as he passed. Fred wanted to punch the guard in the face, but thought better of it.

Other women in the village were trying to hold out bread, but the German guards were pushing them aside.

"They can't do that," Jack complained.

"What are we supposed to do?" said Fred. "The Germans have rifles and bayonets, which they won't hesitate to use. You can't even hit 'em with your tin plate now your bag's gone."

Fred had never felt hunger and thirst like this before. It was torture. The meagre meals the Germans had given them were never enough to make up for the energy they had to expend marching all day. Fred felt the tinned potatoes in his pocket and thought he wouldn't be able to resist much longer.

"See what I mean about taking their frustrations out on us," said Jack.

"Inhumanity is just routine for them," said Fred. "And don't forget that, until we're registered with the Red Cross, they can shoot anyone they want and say the men were killed in action."

Just past the village, they passed a trough surrounded by dead pigeons the British soldiers had pulled out of it to have a drink. Fred tried not to think of the filth as he quenched his thirst along with the others.

After what seemed like an eternity, the Germans halted the column for what they said was a lunch break. One of the guards walked through Fred's platoon, handing each man his lunch ration.

"What's this?" asked Jack staring at the six red beans the German had just dropped in his palm. "Are we meant to march on this?"

The German ignored him and continued giving half a dozen beans to each man.

"Look on the bright side," said Fred. "We don't always get lunch."

Fred noticed that his remaining men were quiet as they marched on that afternoon

"London is being flattened by the Luftwaffe," a guard taunted them as he walked alongside, but the men bit their lips and continued to march in silence.

In the evening, when they arrived at the camp, they were met by a group of guards shouting instructions.

"British over there, do not sit down," they shouted. "French first over here."

"Why do the French get to go first?" Jack complained.

"And why can't we sit down?" said Fred.

Fred's men watched as the Germans served the French what looked like some kind of soup into whatever receptacles on which the French could lay their hands.

As the line of French prisoners was getting smaller, a German officer called Fred and the other British NCOs over to speak to him.

"Dinner is pea soup," said the German. "There is not enough for all, so you will draw lots to see which of your men will eat."

"What? You've got to be joking," said a Scottish Sergeant from the Gordon Highlanders. Fred recognised him as the Sergeant who had taken a rifle butt on the chin on their first day out of St Valery.

"Lots," said the officer, turning on his heels and walking back to the queue of French prisoners.

"This is outrageous," said the Scot.

"It's against the Geneva convention," said another. "But there's not a lot we can do about it right now. If there isn't enough to go around and we don't draw lots, we run the risk of a riot on our hands."

"Let them riot," said the Scot.

"And give the Germans an excuse to massacre them?" came the reply.

The Scot had to concede the other Sergeant was right. All the NCOs agreed to draw lots among the men, and when the Germans gave them a rough estimate as to how much food would be left, each Sergeant was told how many of their men would be allowed to eat that day.

Sunday, 16th June 1940 - Formerie, France

"Why are they not marching us out?" asked Jack as he woke from his slumber.

"I think it must be a rest day," said Fred. "It's Sunday, you know."

"Is it?" Jack eyed Fred up and down. "You're all wet."

"Aye. While you had your beauty sleep, I went and had a wash in that stream over there. Ain't half cold, but I feel better for it, I can tell you. I also got these."

Fred dropped a bunch of dandelions down in front of Jack.

"Why, thanks. You shouldn't 'ave."

"They're to eat, you daft bugger. With these."

Fred pulled his tin of potatoes out of his pocket.

"I forgot about those," said Jack. "Mine was nicked. It was in the bag."

"Just as well I kept mine in my pocket then. It doesn't look like Jerry's planning to do any cooking today."

"Nice of them to give us a rest on a Sunday."

"I think it's them that's having a rest," said Fred. "I had a look around. I reckon there must be near two and a half thousand of us in this field."

While Fred was trying to break into the tin of potatoes, Jack noticed some French women calling to him from the fence of the field where they were camped.

"Martin, go and see what they want."

"Yes Corp," said Fusilier Martin, getting up.

"I'll go," said Bobby, leaping to his feet.

"Alright," said Jack. "But try not to get any of them pregnant."

"What do they want?" Jack said a moment later when Bobby bounded back, flushed with excitement from his discourse with members of the opposite gender.

"They're selling old sacks."

"How much do they want?" asked Jack.

"Fifty francs."

"What?" said Fred in surprise, almost cutting himself on the tin.

"I'll pay," said Fusilier Taylor. "I can make them into a coat. I almost froze to death last night."

"Well, I suppose it's not like he has anything else to spend his money on," said Fred as he watched the fusilier walk over to the expectant girls.

"What is that infernal racket?" asked Jack, referring to the sound of singing, which was drifting their way from a gathering on the other side of the field.

"They're holding church services," said Fred. "You want to go?"

"I'm fine, thanks. Much as I like a good singsong, the Great Almighty is not in my good books at the moment."

Monday, 17th June 1940 - Formerie to Lignières-Châtelain, France

The column had been marching for a while when it passed through another village.

"Look at that," said Jack in disbelief.

Fred saw that the German guards were allowing the villagers to give gifts of food and water to the French prisoners, while any attempts to help the British POWs was prevented.

"I can't believe it," said Fred.

"I can," said Jack. "The bastards."

At the far side of the village, they found a pond. The British POWs had moved the water lilies out of the way so they could drink. Fred and his men joined them.

*

At the end of the day, they found themselves billeted in another open field. The Germans maintained the same routine of dishing out their version of soup to the French prisoners first, and Fred noticed some British soldiers pushing in with the French to get their share, rather than wait for whatever scraps were left.

"Sarge, look what I found," said Bobby, running up to the men and handing them some British Army biscuits each.

"Where on earth did you get those?" asked Fred.

"Don't ask," said Bobby.

"OK, I won't."

"Hey look at that," said Jack. He was pointing to a group of French soldiers who appeared to be slaughtering a cow.

"Fusilier Martin, come with me," said Fred, already on his way over to the group.

"Tell them we would like to buy some of the cow," said Fred.

"*Nous aimerions acheter une partie de la vache.*"

The French eyed them with suspicion.

"*Combien d'argent as tu?*" one of them replied.

"They want to know how much money we have."

"Tell him we are willing to pay 100 francs."

"Nous sommes prêts à payer 100 francs."

"Pour cela, vous pouvez avoir les tripes."

"What did he say?"

"He said 100 francs will buy us the tripe."

"Ask him if he is willing to sell any other part of the cow."

"Êtes-vous prêt à vendre une autre partie si la vache?"

"Non. Seulement les tripes."

"No. He will sell the tripe."

"Tell him the tripe is worth twenty-five."

"Les tripes ne vaut que vingt-cinq."

"Cela vaut cent, mais en signe de bonne volonté je vous le laisserai pour soix-ante-quinze."

"He said he will let you have it for seventy-five."

"How about fifty?"

"Cinquante?"

"D'accord."

"It's a deal."

Fred paid the man the fifty francs and took the tripe back to the men, who were trying to get a fire started. Fred placed the tripe in his mess tin and took it to the stream to wash.

When he returned, he found the Germans were searching everyone.

"What's going on?" he asked.

"They are confiscating 'warlike articles,'" said Jack. "Knives and the like."

"Oi! I use that as a soup bowl," said Fusilier Martin as a guard pulled his tin hat out of his hands.

Fred and Jack moved to assist the private, but found themselves facing the wrong end of a couple of German bayonets.

"At least they didn't consider my mess tin to be a 'warlike article,'" said Fred when the Germans had gone.

By the time they had cooked, divided out, and eaten the tripe, it was dark, and the German guards made them put out the fire. As Fred washed out his mess tin in the stream, he understood why. In the distance, he could hear the unmistakable hum of the RAF.

"The RAF is busy," he said to Jack when he returned to the others.

"I've decided I need water, food, cigarettes, and ladies, in that order," said Jack. "Without being disrespectful to the ladies."

They lay in the field and listened to the RAF's bombs exploding in the distance.

Monday, 17th June 1940 - Monkwearmouth, England

Wash day. Leah turned the wireless on at seven o'clock. When it warmed up, she thought the newsreader had said that France had ceased fire. What would happen to Fred and the rest of the BEF? Would they become prisoners of Hitler or would the Germans kill them? If they didn't, would they feed them? Her head felt like broken glass. She wanted to cry. She wanted to scream. She looked at Jim, making a mess, eating his breakfast, and felt so cold inside. She went to the front door and opened it, standing in the bright sunshine, but it did nothing to warm her. She sat on the step, not caring whether the neighbours saw her. She felt all courage and strength had left her. She heard Jim in the kitchenette, and knew she'd somehow have to find enough strength in her legs to carry her back inside.

She got some *sal volatile* out of the cupboard, slipped off her overall, splashed water on her neck, and let her hands steep in cold water. She thought about Fred and the fact that the Germans might even deprive him of water, and she began to cry, trying to hide her tears from Jim, who was still eating.

The cries of little Beattie, getting air in her pram in the yard, brought Leah back to reality, and she went to lift her out of the pram and into the sunlight. Seeing her daughter and feeling the sunlight on her arms helped relieve her tension, and she began to feel that there might be hope and Fred might be all right.

There was a knock on the door. Leah straightened herself and carried Beattie with her to see who it was. It was Mrs Pearson.

"I just heard the news," she said. "I thought you might want a strong cup of tea. Shall I put the kettle on?"

Leah let her in and followed her through to the kitchen.

"I was thinking of getting a hen," Mrs Pearson said as she filled the kettle with water. "You know, for the eggs. But I worry that Mr Chamberlain might scare her too much, and she might never lay."

Leah welcomed Mrs Pearson's interference. It took her mind off her own problems and loneliness. She needed to find the strength to boil all of Beattie's nappies, and a strong cup of tea and a chat with her busybody neighbour might be just what she needed.

Tuesday, 18th June 1940 - Lignières-Châtelain to Airaines , France

As the day's march began, Fred estimated that they must be somewhere near the middle of the column. He saw the Germans ahead scattering biscuits to the prisoners, but by the time Fred and his men reached that point, all the biscuits had gone.

Further on, the column passed another clamp of stored vegetables. Fred arrived there to find Fusiliers Martin and Jones munching on raw vegetables, but there was nothing left for him or Jack.

He noticed that marigolds were growing by the roadside. He waited until the guards on their bicycles were out of sight, then gathered as many as he could before jumping back into the column and handing them out to the other men.

"They say we should reach the railhead today," said Fusilier Martin.

"They say that every day," said Jack.

"Well, we'll reach it one day," said Martin.

"Aye, one day," said Fred.

He looked down at the road and couldn't believe it when he spotted a bit of crushed rhubarb, which seemed to have gone unobserved by everyone in the column ahead of him. He thought it would give him diarrhoea, but he was so hungry he was willing to risk it. The raw rhubarb tasted like nectar, even though back home he'd have turned his nose up at the thought of eating something he'd found on the road.

"I need a haircut," Fred complained as he blew the hair out of his eyes during one of their precious rest stops.

"I'll cut your hair for you," said Bobby, producing a pair of scissors.

"Where the hell did you get those from?" asked Fred. Then he remembered how Fusilier Jones' would respond. "I know. Don't ask."

Bobby Jones just grinned as he gave Fred and the others quick, rudimentary trims.

At the end of the day, they arrived at a disused prison. It soon became clear they weren't the first group of POWs to use it. It was filthy, with human excrement everywhere, and almost no place to sit. As usual, there was very little in the way of food or water. The building itself was packed, and Fred's group had to find a space to sleep on the stony ground outside.

In the middle of the night a storm broke, and they soon became soaked. Fred watched other men around him drinking from the puddles that had gathered. He opened his mouth to the rain and drank the water that he knew would be clean. He also used the rain to wash his face and his hair.

Wednesday, 19th June 1940 - Airaines to Domart St Leger , France

The sight of Fusiliers Martin and Jones leaping into hedgerows to relieve their diarrhoea punctuated the day's march.

"I bet it was those raw vegetables you ate yesterday," said Fred.

"Serves you right for not saving any for your superiors," said Jack, busy munching on a handful of grass he had gathered from the side of the road.

"What are you doing?" asked Fred.

"It's not bad you know," said Jack, munching away.

"Look what I found," said Bobby as he returned from one of his emergency rest stops. He held up two French Army jackets and handed one of them to Fusilier Martin.

"Where the hell did you get those?" asked Martin.

"Don't ask," said Bobby.

Fred pretended he hadn't noticed.

At the next village, some of the women managed to give them sugar and raw rhubarb without the guards noticing. To Fred, it tasted even better than the piece he had found on the road. They were also able to get postcards and stamps, for a price, and written missives were despatched with hope in the next post box they found. Fred had no idea whether they would make it back home.

At the far end of the village, they found a rubbish heap and decided to explore it. Fred found a tin of salmon before the guards moved them on.

When they arrived at the field where they were to spend the evening, the Germans were dividing the British and French as usual.

Fusiliers Martin and Jones pulled their French Army jackets tight over their uniforms and went to join the French queuing for food.

Fred was waiting to see what would be left after the French had been served when he heard a commotion in the queue. Wandering over to see what was happening, he saw German guards separating Jones, Martin, and two French soldiers. The guards sent the two fusiliers back to their compatriots without their jackets.

"What happened?" asked Jack when they returned.

"They saw our shirts under the jackets," said Martin.

"The greedy bastards could have kept quiet and let us get our grub," Bobby complained.

"Oh well," said Fred. "We'll just have to see what's left."

What was left turned out to be a ladleful of thin soup each.

"Not much," said Fred. "I reckon we must have marched 16 miles today and all we get is this."

Jack was too tired to complain.

"At least we have the tin of salmon," said Fred sharing out the contents among the platoon.

"I'm going for a piss," Jack said when he had devoured his tiny share of the tin.

When he came back, he was smiling.

"What happened to you?" asked Fred.

"My piss is green," Jack laughed.

"It must be all that bloody grass you've been eating," said Fred. "I think I'll go and see what colour mine is."

While he was relieving himself by a fence, Fred noticed that there was a nearby well and some British POWs were trying to get water out of it. A German guard marched over and began challenging them. Fred watched in amazement as the POWs grabbed the guard and pushed him down the well. Fred looked around to see whether any of the other guards had noticed, but nobody seemed to have seen what had happened. The POWs walked back to their group and Fred buttoned himself up before going back to tell Jack.

Thursday, 20th June 1940 - Domart St Leger to Doullens, France

Fred could still taste the acorn coffee from breakfast. He felt he was getting used to walking the best part of twenty miles every day. He could see Fusiliers Martin and Jones ahead of him in a deep conspiratorial discussion about something. They were approaching a house, and Fred could see that there was an Alsatian dog chained to a wall. Martin and Jones checked to see none of the guards were watching and nodded at each other. Within the next moment, they had charged into the house and sprinted back out again, carrying a loaf of bread each, chased by an angry woman. Seconds later, they had hidden in the mass of the column, to the chagrin of the woman and the irritated guards to whom she was complaining. Fred again found himself pretending he hadn't noticed.

Later that day, one of the Cameron Highlanders wasn't so lucky. They were passing a field of sugar beet, and the Highlander, unable to resist, ran into the field to grab some of the beets. Perhaps thinking the POW was trying to escape, one of the guards raised his rifle and fired. The Highlander slumped into a heap in the middle of the field, dead.

After the incident on the road from St Valery, Fred had not often contemplated the idea of escape. He felt an obligation to take care of his men, but incidents like this made all of them think twice about running away. Even if he wanted to, he wasn't sure his legs would carry him. He thought it was better to live for his country than to die for it.

*

At that evening's stop, there were tarpaulin shelters. The Germans searched everyone again, but at least they gave them meat and soup, which they ate together with biscuits that Bobby had managed to procure from a BEF store somewhere.

As they ate their meal, the men in Fred's platoon saw villagers gathering by the fence and were able to buy a little butter, chocolate, and wine, of all things.

Feeling a bit better after the small quantity of wine, Fred washed himself and his clothes and settled down with the others under the tarpaulin, safe in the knowledge that he wouldn't be soaked that night.

Friday, 21st June 1940 - Doullens to Saint Pol, France

The men were so thirsty, they drank out of water butts. Fred warned them they'd be ill, but they were so thirsty, they ignored him.

As they passed through a small mining town, the inhabitants, with food of all descriptions, greeted them. Sandwiches, French rolls, cigarettes and tobacco. The rest mobbed any POWs lucky enough to receive a gift. The Germans used mounted guards to keep the residents away. At one point, they started shooting at the feet of the locals.

Fred watched the bravery of the French women as the German guards pushed and jostled them. He thought they showed much more spirit than the Frenchmen Fred had encountered on the front line. The French women of this town tried, as the women in the villages before, to put buckets of water out for the men, but the German guards just kicked them over.

"We treat our animals better than this," said Jack.

Fred watched as a tall Highlander was reaching out to take some food from one of the French women. A German guard knocked his hand out of the way with his rifle butt. The Scot turned around and gave the German a perfect right hook, which sent the guard flying through the air into the ground a few yards away.

"Get away, take yer 'at off, go to another part of the column!" his friends yelled at him.

"No way," he said and carried on marching. About half an hour later, the guard came up to him and shot him through the chest.

"All because he was too proud to take his hat off," said Jack.

The guards left his body by the roadside. It was the second time on the march that Fred and Jack had to step over a dead body along with the others.

The final destination of the day's march was an athletics track where the Germans were distributing British greatcoats and underclothes. Fred guessed there must have been about 3,000 POWs in the grounds.

On the way into the arena, Fred bought a cooked egg from a French woman and offered it to his men.

"No, thanks," said Bobby.

"You eat it, Sarge," said Fusilier Martin.

"Go on, you have it," said Jack.

Feeling guilty, Fred ate the egg and marvelled at how good it tasted.

Young girls ran up to them with bottles of tea and asked for kisses. Bobby was happy to oblige.

The town had provided two meals of good vegetable soup, and while they were eating, Fred and Jack noticed a small man with nothing. No great-coat, tin, or anything. They saw him collapse to the ground. As professional soldiers, Fred and Jack were fitter than most so, between them, they carried the man down to where the Germans were dishing out the soup and made sure he had something to eat.

That night they slept on the steps of the grandstand. It reminded Fred of Gosforth Park. How long ago those days seemed now.

Saturday, 22nd June & Sunday, 23rd June 1940 - Saint Pol to Bethune, France

At the end of an 18-mile march, they found themselves being ushered into another civil jail, but compared to the previous prison, this one seemed like the Ritz with cold showers, liberal rations, and chances to buy food, drink and toilet articles such as scissors for a much-needed manicure. They also had the opportunity to write and post letters with no guarantee the letters would reach their destination, of course.

"It's just as well you've had a wash and a brush-up," Fred told Jack. "Because, after ten days of marching, you were starting to look like a creature from another world."

"Thanks," said Jack. "I'll take that as a compliment."

Fred marvelled how the men hadn't become ill, despite drinking out of the water butts, as Fred had expected.

Sunday, 23rd June 1940 – Billingham, England

"Ah, there you are," said Beattie seeing her sister, Leah, and nephew, Jim, stood on the doorstep in the pouring rain. "Come in before you catch your death of cold."

Leah and Jim shuffled into the hall and Beattie took their coats before showing them into the living room.

"The kettle's on," she said. "I'll make you a nice cup of tea. And how about you Jim? Would you like some lemonade?"

Jim nodded.

Moments later, Beattie return with the a tray of tea and her husband, Ivor who was carrying a glass of lemonade which he handed to a grateful Jim.

"There you go young man," he said. "Get that inside you, it'll cheer you up."

"It's raining cats and dogs out there isn't it?" said Beattie. "How are you getting on? Any word from Fred?"

Leah shook her head.

"Jim is certainly growing up fast isn't he?" Beattie continued. "And how is my little namesake..."

Beattie looked at Ivor. Ivor looked at Beattie. They both looked at Leah.

"Leah? Where is Beatrice?" a hint of panic was creeping into her voice. "Leah? Beatrice? Where is she?"

Leah looked out of the window.

"Oh Christ!" said Ivor, leaping out of his chair and rushing to the front door, Beattie hot on his heels.

He pulled the front door open wide, popped his head outside and saw Beatrice's pram sitting in the rain.

"She's here," he said, the relief evident as he wheeled the dripping pram into the hall.

"Oh, heavens," said Beattie, scooping the damp infant up into her arms and looking through into her sister, Leah, sat in the sitting room, staring into the middle distance.

Monday, 24th June 1940 - Bethune to Seclin, France.

They had been marching for 3 hours without a halt on a broiling hot day. The men were too tired to talk. They felt very dirty despite the cold showers they'd had the day before.

When they halted at the end of the day in the grounds of a school, locals sold them white heart cherries and other foods. The women made thin barley soup in the evening.

Fusilier Martin, having no receptacle to collect his soup ration after they took his tin hat away, asked them to put it in his boot.

Another POW, Fred noticed, held out his cupped hands, and that was his ration for the day.

Fred and Jack saw the small man again. Their exploit last time had advanced them to the front of the soup line, so they told him to pretend to faint again and repeated the same procedure.

"You know, we didn't ask that man's name," said Fred later, as they were trying to enjoy their thin barley soup.

"This looks like dirty water cooked in a pig trough," said Jack.

Fred and his men found space in a room upstairs, not far from the toilets. The existence of proper toilets was a delight, and Fred and his men took the opportunity to relieve themselves of everything that had been building up inside for some time. All of the POWs had the same desire, and before long, matter entering the system exceeded its ability to absorb the contents, which it began to disgorge back out again. It wasn't long before a steady stream of this matter was flowing into the room where Fred and his men were trying to bed down. Fred ordered a strategic withdrawal, and they slept on straw in the crowded schoolyard instead.

Tuesday, 25th June 1940 - Seclin, France to Tournai, Belgium.

As they left the schoolyard, the Germans gave them green and mildewed bread loaves, which had to be shared one among ten.

Fred missed his cigarettes and was jealous of Jack, who smoked a pipe, because Jack was still getting the taste of nicotine from his empty pipe in the corner of his mouth.

He was still thinking about cigarettes when one of the POWs collapsed. A German guard rushed over and started waving his pistol at the fallen man. Jack and Fred rushed over and picked up the POW, helping him to walk for a bit.

"*Lassen Sie ihn am Straßenrand, wo er von einem Lastwagen abgeholt werden würde, der für die Nachzügler kommen würde.*" said a German guard, marching over to them.

"We don't speak German," said Fred.

"Leave him at the roadside, there will be a truck that will come," said the German.

They left the man, thinking it would be better for him to travel the rest of the way by truck.

As they continued, Fred noticed farmers stood protecting their crops and clamps with shotguns. Word had spread.

Other than the farmers, there didn't appear to be many Belgians about. Quite a contrast to the crowds of French women who had tried to help the POWs.

"Where is everyone?" asked Jack.

"Maybe they feel guilty," said Fred, referring to the Belgium Government's initial decision to remain neutral, which Germany had ignored when they invaded.

*

"I didn't see any trucks passing with stragglers, did you?" asked Jack when they had arrived at the field where they were to spend the night. Fred had found him by the entrance to the field staring back along the road in the direction they had just come.

"Come on, Jack," said Fred. "It's starting to get dark."

The Scottish sergeant, whom Fred remembered from the times they had to draw lots for food, joined them. He was the same sergeant who had taken a rifle butt to the chin on the first day of the march.

"What're you fellas looking for?" the Scot asked them. "You waiting for a bus?"

"Kind of," said Jack.

"Ah, a fellow countryman," said the Sergeant, recognising Jack's accent. "How on Earth did you end up in an English regiment?"

Fred ignored the jibe and told the sergeant about the man they helped by the side of the road.

"Ah, I see," said the Scot. "There are no trucks. I'm afraid your friend has been shot."

"He can't have been," said Jack.

"Come on, let's go," said Fred.

"The bastards," said Jack.

"I doubt it's any consolation," said the Scot. "But there's nothing could have been done to change the outcome."

Wednesday, 26th June 1940 - Tournai to Renaix, Belgium

They trekked through Belgium where, as before, women laid out buckets of water and held out bread to them as they passed, but the guards saw to it that they didn't get any.

After a march of 16 miles, the Germans led them into a crowded camp in a disused factory.

As they got near the entrance, villagers had gathered to try to sell products to the prisoners. Fred had a look to see what was on offer, but all he managed to buy was lemonade and cherries.

After their usual ladle of thin soup, they looked for a place to sleep. Everything was filthy, but after a search, they found space on some storage racks, which were still quite dirty.

"I've lost all the bits of fat I used to carry around with me," Fred told Jack, who didn't seem very interested.

"I feel like just gristle and bone," Fred continued. "But I also feel as hard as iron."

Jack said nothing, so Fred just put his head down and soon fell asleep.

Thursday, 27th June 1940 - Renaix to Ninove, Belgium

Fred was glad to get away from the dirty factory. As they marched, he looked at the uniforms of his men, how creased and dirty they were. It reminded him of the occasions he had given his men a hard time over the cleanliness of their kit.

"Corporal Cooper? Look at the state of your uniform" Fred said to Jack, loud enough for the other men to hear him. "You're letting your standards slip. When was the last time you washed and ironed it?"

Jack was silent, but the joke wasn't wasted on the men, who appreciated some light relief.

Fred could see how demoralised Jack was becoming, and he was relieved when, in the next village they passed through, there was a group of locals chanting good luck. Fred watched the men straighten-up. He could see it was giving them the motivation to continue.

At the end of the day, the Germans led them into an overcrowded barracks, the courtyard filled with thousands of pairs of clogs.

While they waited in the usual weary queue for a usual daily meal, Fred observed Jack, whose mood had not improved.

They had just finished their thin soup when Fusilier Martin ran up to them.

"Sarge, the officers are here," he said, out of breath.

"Show me," said Fred.

Martin led him to the other side of the barracks and took him straight to Captain Fawkes.

"Sergeant," the Captain said, extending a hand for Fred to shake. "Good to see you. If only it were under better circumstances."

"Is Major Potts here, sir?" asked Fred.

"No. He made an escape attempt with Captain Besley and we haven't seen either of them since, so we're keeping our fingers crossed."

Fred hoped the Major had made it. That night, he considered the possibility of his own escape again. He thought of Leah, Jim, and Beattie, as well as the soldier he had seen gunned down in the sugar beet field. There was always the chance the Germans would repatriate him. He convinced himself that his prime responsibility was to his men, and he should concern himself with looking after them rather than entertaining thoughts of escape. In any case, Jack was in no state to go with him, and Fred felt an obligation to ensure his corporal was all right

Friday, 28th June 1940 - Ninove to Aalst, Belgium

"The people ignored us today," commented Fred as they settled into the barracks the Germans had herded them into for the night. "At least these barracks are clean."

"Give to me the life I love, let the love go by me. Give the jolly heavens above, and the byway nigh me," Jack recited.

"What's that?"

"*The Vagabond*. We had to learn it in school. It seems apt now," said Jack. "Bed in a bush with stars to see, bread I can dip in the river ..."

Jack trailed off, and Fred was happy that he was once again as talkative as he'd been since they'd left the man on the side of the road, days before. Fred just put his head down and soon fell asleep.

In the middle of the night, Fred awoke. He felt a breeze coming from somewhere, so he sat up and saw one of the windows was open. He got up and walked over to the window to shut it. He poked his head out to get a look at his surroundings, but leapt backwards when a shot rang out, ricocheting off the roof just above his head. The shot woke half the inhabitants of the barracks, and Fred crawled on his knees, reaching up to shut the window without showing his head through the aperture.

"Jesus Christ. What was that?" asked Jack. "Were you trying to escape or something?"

It was the most Fred had heard Jack say in days.

"No, I would never abandon you," said Fred. "I was just trying to shut the bloody window, and Jerry shot at me."

"Now what would you want to try and do a thing like that for?" asked Jack.

"There was a terrible draft," said Fred. "It woke me up."

Saturday, 29th June 1940 - Aalst to Sint-Niklaas, Belgium

The Scots at the front of the column continued to sing, and by now, Fred had learned the words.

Keep Right on to the End of the Road
Keep right on to the End
Though the way be long, let your heart be strong.
Keep right on to the End.
Though you're tired and weary, still journey on
Till you come to your happy abode, when all you
Love and are dreaming of will be there, at the end of the road.

At the end of the long hot day's march, Fred and his men arrived at a disused silk factory, where locals selling ice cream greeted them. Fred had never had much of a sweet tooth, unlike Leah, but he thought this was the best thing he had tasted since he'd been in Europe. It tasted almost as good as the Burgess ice cream he could buy in Beverley. That was the best ice cream in the world, he thought, remembering the day he took Leah to the racecourse before Jim was born.

Another treat awaited him in the silk factory. He managed to get near the front of the queue for a Belgian barber who had set up shop for the POWs. Fred managed to get not just a cut and shave, but shampoo as well.

The rations were good, and civilians had set up stalls for the sale of custard pies and fruit, all at inflated prices.

Fred bought some tinned food with the objective of rationing it until they reached their final destination, wherever that would be.

The Germans were taking down particulars on official forms. Fred hoped this meant that the Germans would now report them as prisoners of war, and Leah would know where he was, at last.

Sunday, 30th June - Sint-Niklaas, Belgium

The next day, a Sunday, was the Germans' day off, and so the POWs were permitted a day off as well.

Fred washed his clothes, and while they dried, he joined Jack enjoying what Fred considered a hard-earned rest by lying in the sun.

He also wrote more letters home, which he hoped to post with the help of the civilian staff of the well-run canteen.

When his clothes were dry and he had finished his letters, he dragged Jack to the canteen, where they bought food and Fred negotiated for the posting of his letters.

"There's far more of them than us now," said Fred, referring to the French POWs who now far outnumbered the British.

Jack had returned to his old habit of not reacting to anything Fred said, so Fred just left it.

Monday, 1st July 1940 - Sint-Niklaas, Belgium to Hulst, Holland

When, at the beginning of the day, Fusilier Martin had told the men that today was the day they would reach the long-promised railhead, Fred just raised his eyebrows. He had long stopped believing the gossip that Fusilier Martin shared with them. However, here he was, 18 miles later, at the long-promised railhead at Hulst. Fred wasn't sure whether it was because he was in a better mood because of having reached the railhead, but he thought the Dutch had seemed very kind to them.

Tuesday, 2nd July 1940 - Hulst to Walscorden, Holland.

It was a broiling hot day, which became even worse by being crammed in a crowded tram steam way for the journey to Walscorden

It looked like the entire townsfolk had blocked the train's passage. They were cheering and throwing food, cigarettes, and tobacco up to the POWs. They also had large turrets of milk and soup, which they had prepared for the wounded. There were also people handing out pieces of yellow paper. Fred took one and saw there was a message in English and French.

To an unknown French or English friend, when you are at home in England again, do not forget us then and will you then write to us please
Signed
J. J. Se Rudder, Prins Hendrikstreet 17, Axel, Holland.

The train was passing through an area filled with water, canals and rivers. It stopped at a jetty. It was a relief for Fred to get off the tram and, at first, the jetty was obscured by the green grass of the dykes, which separated the polder from the river. Daisies were growing on the grassy banks, and Fred felt it might not have been a bad place to visit, had it not been under such terrible circumstances. He wished he had a camera or a sketchbook and pencil so that he could record what he saw to show Leah when he got home. If he ever got home.

"I just heard that 60,000 German troops were heading to Britain, but were foiled by a death ray," said Fusilier Martin when he returned from his gossip-mongering with the other privates.

"His stories get more and more far-fetched by the day," Fred commented to Jack, but Jack was not responding as usual.

Fred noticed that, by now, some of the POWs had worn out their shoes and they had been walking barefoot. Despite their lack of belongings, most of the POWs had small tin cups hanging on their side for the little food the Germans gave them or they could get by other means. The lack of food meant that the POWs could barely march, let alone plan to escape, and Fred assumed that this must be the reason why they weren't that heavily guarded any more.

A guard who was distributing bread interrupted his thoughts. He gave each man a piece of bread. Fred examined his. It was dry and covered in mouldy cracks.

"Look at this," Fusilier Martin protested.

"It's better than no bread," said Fred.

*

After a wait of what Fred estimated must have been seven or eight hours, the Germans started loading them onto coal barges. At first, some of the POWs refused to go down into the hold, but the Germans turned fire hoses onto them until they complied.

When it was the turn of Fred and his men to descend into the hold of the barge, they found it to be pitch black and everything covered in coal dust. It seemed full when they entered, but the Germans kept loading more and more men until there was no room to sit down.

Fred wondered whether this is what it was like for the black slaves, which the Europeans had shipped from Africa to America.

Wednesday, 3rd July 1940 - Wesel, Germany

Fred was wondering what the Germans expected them to do if they needed to go to the toilet. He had seen guards leading POWs, who had communicated their desperate need to answer a call from nature, up out of the hold and returned a few minutes later, with a mixed expression of satisfaction and incredulity as they recounted their experience to their colleagues.

The point arrived when Fred could not wait any longer, and he too needed to communicate his need to the guards. They led him out of the hold. As he emerged into the daylight, Fred realised that coal soot was covering him from head to toe. A guard led him to the edge of the deck where a wooden structure, not much more than a pole, hung over the side. It was at this point he realised that they expected him to use this structure to dangle his rear end over the canal while he did his business.

The barge was moving through a built-up area, and Fred was reluctant to pull down his trousers while people walking along the side of the water could see everything. However, the desperation of his need and the shouts of the guards to hurry up convinced him to get on with it.

When he had finished, and the guards had returned him to the hold, he described his experience to Jack.

"It just shows the complete disrespect they have for us," Jack complained.

Soon, it was Fusilier Martin's turn to go, and when he returned he was soaked to the skin.

"What happened to you?" Fred asked.

"I fell in," Martin replied. "They had to fish me out."

Fred's laughter was interrupted by the appearance of a guard with a bucket of potatoes which he began distributing, one per man.

Many of the POWs began peeling their potatoes using knives they had somehow procured from one of the locals or had managed to hide from the German guards.

Not only did Fred and Jack not peel their potatoes, since they couldn't have peeled them if they wanted to, they went around collecting the peelings off the floor, which the other POWs had discarded.

"It's the best bit," said Fred. Maybe it was because they were professional soldiers rather than enlisted men, but Fred and Jack knew enough to know they had no idea where their next meal was coming from and that they might be glad of the peelings before long.

Fred had not long eaten his own potato and had stuffed the peelings in a pocket when he began to feel itchy. Once he started to itch, the feeling got worse. He noticed that Jack, too, had begun to itch and was scratching his scalp.

"Let me have a look," he said and began to examine Jack's hair. "Oh God. We've got lice."

Thursday, 4th July 1940 - Hemer, Germany

When the barge stopped, they realised they were in Germany because, as they emerged from the hold into the daylight and got their first view of the town, they saw that there were swastikas everywhere.

When they disembarked, they saw that black soot covered every one of the POWs. Fred wondered whether he should repeat his joke about the condition of the men's uniforms but, on examining their faces, thought better of it.

The Germans ushered the men into a containment area where they gave them bread, rice, and bowls of potato soup.

Fred noticed that Taylor was looking very weak. Fred encouraged him to eat all of his soup.

Friday, 5th July 1940 - Hemer, Germany

After a welcome rest day, in which they did their best to rid themselves of soot and lice with mixed success, the Germans paraded Fred and the rest of the POWs through the town to the railway station. German women were trying to kick and spit at them as they passed. There were also old men and Hitler Youth lining the street.

The POWs were hot, sweaty, exhausted, starving men trying to hold onto their sanity. Fred kept thinking of Leah and what might happen to her when the Germans got to Sunderland. At least here in Germany, despite all the deprivations, Fred's mates surrounded him.

When they arrived at the railway station, groups of German soldiers were waiting for trains to take them to the front.

"Pack up your troubles in your old kit bag," some of the Germans jeered at the POWs.

Fred thought this was ironic, as he had abandoned his kit bag weeks ago.

"Keep smiling, lads," said Fred. "One day we'll get our own back."

The men did their best to smile and not to let the Germans think they were getting to them. Even Jack and Fusilier Taylor were doing their best to force a grin. Then, all of a sudden, the air raid sirens went off and the local population scattered. Fred thanked the RAF.

*

Once the threat of the air raid had passed, the Germans started to cram the POWs into railway wagons. They packed eighty men into Fred's carriage, and four small, square, rectangular openings covered with barbed wire provided ventilation.

Once the POWs were in, the guards locked the doors. There was no escape, not much room to move around, and not much air to breathe.

Fred felt lucky that he was near one of the vents and could breathe some fresh air. He felt much less lucky when a POW at the other end of the wagon, needing the toilet, urinated into a steel helmet and emptied the contents out of one of the ventilation holes. It blew back in Fred's vent, into his face.

Progress was slow. The train was stopping and starting all the time. Fred crouched on the bare boards with his knees drawn under his chin. He could feel every vibration. Occasionally he had to stand up to relieve cramp, but when he did, he couldn't sit down again for a while, because everyone had shifted to absorb the space.

He felt ill. His stomach ached, and he was desperate to empty his bowels. It seemed that everyone had upset stomachs.

"It must have been that terrible food they gave us in the camp yesterday," said Fred.

"If I'm going to die, I'm going to die," said Jack.

"I can't die," said Fred. "I have to get back to Leah and Jim and Beattie."

The train stopped yet again, and they could hear the sound of the guards opening and closing doors in the other carriages. A few moments later, the door of their own wagon opened, and a guard pushed in a bucket of water and some loaves of bread. There was a frenzied struggle as POWs writhed against each other to get a piece of what passed for food. Only those near the door managed to get any at all.

Saturday, 6th July 1940 - Somewhere in Germany

The train had stopped at a halt and, as Fred looked out of the vent, he could see families staring at the train. They were all wearing their Sunday best and seemed to be on their way to church.

Fred's stomach was getting worse, and he knew it was just a matter of time before he couldn't contain the contents of his bowels anymore. He didn't have a steel helmet like a few of the other POWs. Then he had an idea. He apologised to those surrounding him, warned them what was about to happen, and then, taking his handkerchief, he pulled down his trousers and did his best to capture the loose faeces in the cloth before disposing of it out of the vent and pulling his trousers back up. He avoided eye contact with any of the men for a long time afterwards.

In the end, he had no choice when Fusilier Martin called to him.

"Sarge, It's Taylor. He won't wake up."

Fred did his best to get over to the man.

"He's dead," said Fred having checked and rechecked for signs of life. "Is there anything we can wrap him up in?"

After a bit of commotion, some of the POWs volunteered sackcloth and string. Fred and his men did their best to wrap him up. They tried to call the attention of the guards every time the train stopped, but in the end, they just had to accept the fact that they would be sharing the rest of their journey with a dead body.

At night, there was no space to lie down. Fred tried to sleep with his back resting against Jack, but he felt it very difficult to sleep. All he could hear was a constant bumpty-bump.

Sunday, 7th July 1940 - Somewhere in Germany or Poland

In the morning, another POW failed to wake up. Somehow, the POWs found more sackcloth and twine, and they managed to wrap him up and put the two corpses together.

Fred wondered how much longer they could travel like this.

Monday, 8th July - Torun, Poland

The POWs blinked in the bright sunlight as they emerged from the dark carriages.

The German guards shouted *'raus raus'*, but as the men jumped from the train, they just crumpled to the ground.

There was a sign at the end of the platform, which read *'Torun'*.

"Where the hell is that?" Fred asked.

"Haven't the foggiest," said Jack. "Well, I guess this is the end of our Cook's Tour of Europe."

They removed the bodies of the dead men and lay them on the ground.

When his eyes adjusted to the light, Fred could see two massive gates made of wood laced with barbed wire. The gates appeared to be the entrance to a large area of flat land surrounded by a double fence of barbed wire. Each corner of this compound held a raised machine gun post manned by German guards. Two guards also operated the gates, one of whom opened them to let the POWs through.

"It's no Butlins Holiday camp," said Fred.

"Eingeben," shouted the guard, gesticulating for the POWs to enter the camp.

As they walked past the gate, the other guard counted them all in. Fred became aware of a commotion inside the compound, where it seemed there were already prisoners.

Some of the German guards were flicking cigarette butts towards the men and then stamping on them as the men tried to pick them up.

"Don't pick them up," Fred told his men. "Don't let them think they've got the upper hand."

Fred himself was dying for a smoke.

When they arrived in the compound, they were marched past some empty-looking huts towards a large marquee, where they found that Norwegian soldiers had already prepared soup for them, but before they could get to the food, a British Major in a pressed uniform and a polished Sam Browne belt approached them.

"You people are filthy! You get nothing till you get yourself cleaned up," he said with disgust.

It was all Fred could manage to keep himself composed. He and his men hadn't eaten in four days, and he wasn't about to let this little twit get in between them and the food he could see the Norwegians preparing in the tent behind the Major.

"With all due respect, sir," said Fred, trying to keep calm. "My corporal here wants nothing more than to punch you in the mouth as hard as he can. And believe me, if he did, you'd be spending the rest of the day picking your teeth out of the back of your neck. Therefore, I advise you not to attempt to prevent my men or me from going over there and getting some grub. Because, if you do, I would be powerless from stopping my subordinate here from carrying out his violent wishes."

The Major needed one glance at Jack's face, which even to Fred looked murderous, and began to stammer something inaudible as he shuffled out of their way. Fusilier Martin was so weak they had to help him to the tent where the soup was being served.

Fred and his men devoured the soup with relish, all except Fusilier Martin, who ate the soup as fast as the others, but then threw it all back up again.

"Some soup will have stayed inside," Fred tried to console him.

Once Fred had recovered from the overwhelming urge to get as much soup into his mouth as he could, he began to look around the tent-covered compound. When they had finished eating, they were ushered into the first of the tents.

The Germans processed them very efficiently. They had metal identity dog tags made, the guards took photographs and fingerprints, and noted their occupations, as well as the colour of their eyes.

"Smile for the camera to show Jerry we're not beat," said Fred as the men had their photographs taken holding a chalkboard with their number. They all did. Even Jack, for whom the strain on his cheek muscles seemed to cause some pain.

They were told to fill in a Red Cross form, and Fred thought that if Leah didn't yet have news that he was a POW, she was bound to now.

"Put your rank down as Sergeant," Fred told Jack.

"What?"

"I'm promoting you."

"You can't do that."

"I can. As the most senior rank in D company, I hereby promote you."

"Why?"

"Because as an NCO you will be exempt from manual labour under the Geneva Convention."

"But I might be happy to work if it gets me out of this dump."

"If you'd heard the stories I've heard from those who were taken prisoners in the last war, you'd be taking my advice."

Jack looked at Fred for a moment and then wrote 'Sergeant' on his form.

The guards took any spare clothing away and took the POWs into the main building, which appeared to be an old fort. They took Fred and his men downstairs and told them to strip. They gave each man a small rough towel and some soap. Fred and his men entered the barbershop three at a time.

"I'd like a short back and sides please," said Fred. "Not too much off the top."

The guards shaved their whole bodies and then told them to stand under a showerhead. A guard turned the water on and off, and then they rubbed the soap over their body leaving a cover of fine pumice and an indescribable smell.

"Wasser!" a guard shouted, and the water came back on to rinse them off.

They sat outside the shower room on a hard wooden bench, and Fred noticed the absence of fat on his buttocks.

A guard handed him a uniform.

"It smells like a damp dog," he said, inspecting the tatty garment. "Hang on a minute, there are still lice in the seams."

"This isn't my uniform," said Jack. "Even a poverty-stricken rag and bone man wouldn't want this piece of tat."

The guard returned and gave each a pair of wooden clogs with square pieces of cloth instead of socks.

Once they had dressed, the guards led them to a large hut, which they came to know as Fort 17. Fort 17 turned out to house 1,000 men. Fred had lost a lot of weight but, despite still having the shits, he felt as hard as nails from his ordeal.

When he went to bed, he took off his clogs, which had been causing him discomfort ever since he had put them on this morning. He was astonished to discover that they had already made his feet bleed.

Tuesday, 9th July - Torun, Poland

The routine began. At 9 am, the guards told them to go out on the parade ground and get into groups of five so that the guards could count them. The Germans seemed to keep getting the count wrong and having to start over again. In the end, one of the British sergeants offered to help, and by 11 am, the Germans had a count they were satisfied with and dismissed the roll call.

Fred looked around at the men. They looked like they had given up. He worried about their welfare. If they just sat around feeling sorry for themselves all day, who knows how long they would last?

He waited until after lunch, which happened at one o'clock. It consisted of soup, which looked like water that had once known some vegetables.

After this, he could not look at the depressed faces of his men any longer.

"Right men, on yer feet."

Nothing.

"On your feet now. That is an order," he yelled and looked to Jack for support.

Jack got to his feet and one by one, his men followed him. They looked like they were cursing Fred for not letting them rest.

"Attention!" he yelled, and the scruffy POWs straightened themselves a little. "By the right, quick march."

Fred set off around the compound with his men in tow, marching as best they could, Bobby and Jack supporting Fusilier Martin and already lagging behind.

The POWs from other platoons looked on as if they were barmy, but Fred knew that if he didn't keep the men moving, they would soon atrophy.

He took them on one circuit of the compound for their first day. When they returned to the hut, the entertained spectators gave them a round of applause. Fusilier Martin and his two helpers, who limped in some minutes later, received the biggest applause.

"Well done, men," Fred told his platoon. "We'll show Jerry he hasn't got us beat."

The men didn't seem to be cursing him any more, but appeared to appreciate the motivation they'd needed to get up and move about.

A guard arrived and began handing out postcards to each of them, which they took in turns to complete before handing them back for the Germans to send.

The Germans then divided the men into groups of thirty and gave each group six 7½-inch loaves. The man given the responsibility for cutting the bread had to be very careful to cut each slice an inch and a half, because he would have the last slice.

After they had eaten, the guards took them from their temporary accommodation in the hut to their permanent accommodation in subterranean rooms under the fort. The rooms were dark, and the guards put Fred's group of thirty in one room together. The room had an arched ceiling which made it look like a tunnel. It was about six yards wide and eighteen yards long. The beds were three shelves six and a half feet wide, with a yard between the bottom and the middle bunk, and the middle and the top bunk. There were small windows at the top which the guards ordered the men to cover at night with blackout blinds. Fred had a position on the top bunk, and that night he discovered it was the best place to be. He liked the fact that it was lighter and airier on the top bunk, but the events of their first night in that room proved to him why the top bunk was the best place to be.

In the middle of the night, Fred woke up twice. The first occasion was when Bobby, on the bottom bunk, cried out because Fusilier Martin, above him, had vomited, sending semi-digested bread and bile cascading down on-to the fusilier below. The second was when Jack, also on a bottom bunk, cried out in disgust because the man in the bunk above had lost control of his bladder.

Wednesday, 10th July - Torun, Poland

Fred awoke with a headache. He took the cover off the window and breathed in the fresh air.

"How did you sleep last night?" Fred asked Jack.

"Terrible. With you tossing and turning above me, and people throwing up and pissing themselves."

Fred looked to see that the rest of the platoon couldn't hear them.

"And then there was all the coughing, farting, snoring, moaning, burping," Jack continued. "And I've got a bloody headache. There's no air in this dungeon."

Fred was glad that Jack seemed to be getting back to his old self again.

Apart from what little light came through the windows, the light in their room came from a bare bulb at the end of the corridor outside the room. It was a dark, damp cellar with straw covering the floor.

The Germans were serving coffee made from acorns. As Fred drank his coffee, he watched the men, sitting with their shirts off, cracking lice between their fingernails.

When they had finished their coffee, Fred and Jack climbed up the hill to the toilet, which was two trestles and a plank of wood over a hole.

Over loudspeakers, the Germans were announcing the tonnage of ships their submarines had sunk.

"It's depressing having to listen to all these figures of boats being sunk," said Fred.

"I've been thinking about that. If you add up all the figures they keep announcing over the loudspeakers, that's more tonnage than the allies have ever had afloat."

Fred thought about it for a moment.

"Yes, you're right," he said at last. "Those figures are ridiculous."

Fred noticed that there were rabbits in the moat of the fort and pointed them out to Jack.

"We should try to snare one. It'd make a stew," said Jack.

"In Germany, the snare is illegal and the punishment is heavy," said a guard who was eavesdropping.

Fred and Jack weren't sure whether he was telling the truth, but thought it best not to risk it.

At lunchtime, it was all they could do to find the energy to pull themselves off the straw-covered floor and stagger into the corridor to get a litre of thin soup, with evidence of peas this time. Those with a receptacle could collect food, others had to use their cupped hands.

At 4pm, the guards gave the group six 1.5 kg mouldy loaves of black bread, each, of which Fred shared among five men. They ate it with a little margarine and honey. The bread tasted like the baker had used sawdust to bulk it up but, even so, after the march, it seemed like a feast.

Fred ordered the men to wash and shave. He knew that some of the men appreciated his efforts to keep them moving, but also realised were many others who resented his authority now that they felt they'd done their bit.

Wednesday, 31st July 1940 - Monkwearmouth, England

Leah sat on the stairs and read the letter she had just received from the Regimental Paymaster.

I have to refer with regret to the notification you will have received that your husband is at present held to be missing, in order to inform you of the allowances which are payable to you during the period you are awaiting further information. During the period a soldier is missing, allowances are payable for seventeen weeks as follows: - 4 shillings per week. If at the end of this period, no further news of your husband is available, allowances will continue, but such allowances will be authorised by the War Office.

She stared at the letter in disbelief. 'Missing'. They didn't know where he was. She felt mad. She had to get out of the house. She went to get Jim ready.

*

Leah pushed the pram along the High Street with one hand, Jim hanging on to the other. She looked in the window of Stephenson's confectioners and thought what a waste of sugar it was when anyone could have used the sugar for jam. She felt angry with the Government who had lost her husband and allowed this waste of sugar. She thought Churchill and his cabinet should come and live in Monkwearmouth and see what life was like for real women, real women like Leah on a fixed income who saw ordinary things wasted and no shortage of unnecessary things. Leah looked at the women walking along the High Street and could see the haves and have-nots. The haves with their silk stockings and dressed hair.

The High Street was just making her feel worse, so she decided to go back to Monkwearmouth and show her father the letter.

Thursday, 1st August 1940 - Torun, Poland

Fred wasn't sure what to do. His men were still losing weight. Some had sores on their skin and had lost teeth.

Dizziness and blackouts were common. Whenever the men lay down for a rest, they had to get up slowly, onto one knee at a time, and then raise themselves into an upright position. Anyone who attempted the procedure too quickly was liable to faint.

Fred felt sorry for them and tried to keep them moving and looking after themselves, but he knew, more than anything else, that he had to look after himself to get back to Leah, Jim, and Beattie.

For lunch, the guards had given them the usual thin pea soup, but today it came with rancid sauerkraut. Now it was teatime, and it was Jack's turn to cut the bread.

"It seems that there's mouldy potato at the bottom today," he said as he tried to cut the slices as accurately as possible.

Fred noticed the professional soldiers like himself and Jack were faring better than the enlisted men.

The guards gave them jam and liver sausage to go with their mouldy bread, a rare treat.

"Come and get it," said Jack.

Fusilier Martin bent over to tie his bootlaces and collapsed onto the straw-covered floor. The surrounding men rushed to get him back into the bottom bunk.

"He's been complaining about seeing spots in front of his eyes," Bobby told Fred.

"Try and get him to eat some of this bread. There's liver sausage today. That'll help if he can keep it down."

Jack and Fred made sure everyone got an even share of food, so there would be no arguments or fights, of which they had heard stories from some of the other rooms.

Monday, 5th August 1940 - Monkwearmouth, England

Leah couldn't believe it when the postcard arrived. She had to read it over and over to make sure it was true. She got the children ready as fast as she could and rushed to Dame Dorothy Street to show the postcard to her father. She recognised Fred's handwriting, his way of saying things. She felt so elated. Even though he was in a prisoner of war camp, at least he was alive and not lying dead in a ditch by the side of a French field, as Leah had dreamt so many times.

Tuesday, 6th August 1940 - Torun, Poland

As he made his way into the corridor, Fred was surprised to find that, for lunch, there was an accompaniment of smelly cheese to go along with the thin pea soup.

Fred, like the rest of the men, was struggling with boredom. When he had finished his meagre lunch, he looked around at the other men and noticed Bobby was reading a tatty-looking book.

"Fusilier Jones?" Fred said as he climbed down from his bunk. "Do you think you could lend me that book when you're finished? I could do with a good read."

"I'm afraid that's not possible, Sarge," said Bobby, holding up the book, which looked like half the pages were missing. "I've been using the pages as toilet paper. It's a race between my bowels and my intellect as to which finishes the book first."

"Sarge," said Fusilier Martin, who was now in the bunk below Bobby. "I heard that Jerry`s used poison gas over British cities."

Fred was pleased that Walter Martin was getting back to his usual gossip-gathering self, but he also hoped that this piece of news was as fantastic as the death ray story, and that Leah and the children wouldn't have to use their gas masks for real.

Fred was a little envious that Bobby Jones had his own supply of toilet paper. Fred's bout of the shits had returned, and he walked up the hill to join the queue for the latrine. The latrine had space for six men, and with over 1,500 in the camp, it meant there was always a queue. Fred arrived at the front just as he thought he could hold it no longer, but once he had evacuated his bowels and emerged from the latrine, he felt the sudden sensation that he was going to need to go again, so just joined the back of the queue once more.

Friday, 9th August 1940 - Monkwearmouth, England

Leah was listening to *Music While You Work* when the air raid siren sounded. She picked up Beattie, grabbed Jim by the hand, and rushed out of the house and down the street to the communal brick shelter.

There was an old clippie mat and a curtain at the entrance to make the shelter feel more homely, but as soon as she was past the curtain, she could smell the mould.

Mrs Pearson followed them in. She was carrying a large pot of tea in one hand and a mug in the other, with her gas mask slung over her shoulder. It was then that Leah realised she had left the gas masks at home.

Leah found a space on one of the wooden bunk beds and sat down. Noticing the curtain, which protected the bucket WC in the corner, she wished she had used the toilet before she left the house, but that thought was short-lived as she soon heard the whistling of the bombs coming down.

Mrs Pearson poured tea into the mug and passed it around.

"I'd just made it, and it seemed a shame to waste it," she explained.

Leah wondered why an old woman living alone would require such a large pot of tea, but she kept her observations to herself. Other neighbours used to comment that Mrs Pearson seemed to have a sixth sense, which she used to detect when a raid was coming before the warning sounded.

With the door of the shelter closed, it soon began to smell of a combination of mould, smoke, and body odour, but all Leah could think about was that she didn't want to die. The bombs seemed to be landing nearby.

Mrs Pearson started to sing

There'll always be an England
While there's a country lane
Wherever there's a cottage small
Beside a field of grain

It didn't take much for the rest of the people sharing the shelter to join in.

There'll always be an England
While there's a busy street
Wherever there's a turning wheel
A million marching feet

Someone joined in with a mouth organ, but when they heard the whistling of the next bomb, the singing stopped until it was clear that it had landed elsewhere, at which point the singing and playing commenced once more.

Wherever there's a turning wheel
A million marching feet
Red, white and blue
What does it mean to you?

When the all-clear sounded, Leah was glad to get out into the fresh air, even if the smell of burning buildings was tainting it.

*

After he had closed the shop, Leah's father came for tea and brought news of the consequences of the raid.

"They hit the Laing's shipyard," he explained. "The Station Hotel, a railway bridge. Two youngsters were killed, Irene Mooney and Thompson Reed. Dozens of injuries."

Leah shook her head in sympathy with the unfortunate.

"They got the bastards who did it, 'scuse my French," her father continued. "People saw him shot down over the sea. He won't be dropping bombs on anyone for a while."

"Thank goodness," said Leah. "I did such a stupid thing. I left the gas masks in the house. Imagine if they'd ..."

"Well, they didn't though, did they?"

"No, but they might have done."

Her father sighed.

"You have to stop being so hard on yourself, luv," he said. "You're doing the best that you can. Everyone is. That's all we can do."

Friday, 6th September 1940 - Monkwearmouth, England

It seemed a regular thing now, Leah going to visit her father in the shop to find out the gossip about the previous night's air raid.

"Tell me, what happened?" she asked when the last customer had left. Jim was playing with potatoes and Beattie sleeping.

Her father waved for her to be patient while he finished coughing and then turned to her with excitement.

"They shot down another one of those blasted bombers. It crashed in Henson. On Suffolk Street."

"Was anyone killed?"

"A woman was killed. About a dozen injured, the woman's husband severely. Their daughter was injured too. 15 years old."

"Such a shame."

"It hit their air raid shelter."

"No!"

"Set two houses on fire. It was a Heinkel, shot down by the anti-aircraft guns. About half eleven."

"The shelters are no good then?"

"Not if it's a direct hit. But you're much safer than in a house."

"Are you sure?"

"They say there were crowds in the streets and people standing in doorways cheering when the bomber was shot down."

"Why weren't they in the shelters?"

"That's what I asked. No one seems to know."

Leah slumped down in a chair.

"You all right, pet?" her father examined her.

"I'm just a bit tired, that's all. I get them both to bed before the news, and then I'm in bed myself by 9.30. But I sleep about 3 hours a night. I just lay in bed listening for the planes. They sound like they're circling around looking for us. I just feel so tense, and if I doze off, I wake up with a start thinking 'what's that?'"

"Have you taken anything?"

"I don't want to start taking aspirin. I've tried chewing gum, deep breathing, and counting. I think I'll try stuffing cotton wool in my ears."

"Worth a try."

"What do you think about these rumours of invasions at Southend?"

"I don't think there's anything in it. We would have heard it on the news."

"Maybe the Government is keeping it quiet."

James laughed.

"You worry too much. And I wish you wouldn't come out in the rain. I can pop down and see you when I've closed up."

"I needed to get out. And you shouldn't be out in the rain with your chest."

Thursday, 26th September 1940 - Torun, Poland.

It was Fred's birthday, and it seemed that the Germans made a special effort for his birthday tea. They'd given the men mouldy bread and black potatoes.

"Even pigs would turn their noses up at these," said Jack.

"At least it's still edible," said Fred.

"Just."

There was a bad atmosphere in the camp, because the food stealing had become worse. POWs who had stored part of their lunch for later had stopped the practice because, after a trip to the latrine, they would return to find their stash gone. Accusations and suspicions were rife, and Fred had to defuse tense situations on a daily basis.

He had received a birthday present from the Germans, of sorts. The lack of clothing was becoming more and more problematic, so the Germans decided to address the situation by giving the POWs clothes from other armies.

Earlier that day the guards had gathered them in the compound. The Germans reversed up a truck and just threw the uniforms out the back at the POWs. Fred thought the platoon looked like a pantomime army by the end of it.

The Red Cross had organised a system where the POWs could communicate with home. The guards gave them four postcards and two letter cards each month. The Germans prohibited writing about the camp or military details.

Fred sat on his bunk and wrote home to Leah, explaining the details of his birthday and wishing her a happy birthday and wedding anniversary, which was just a month away now.

Monday, 21st October 1940 - Monkwearmouth, England

Leah consoled herself that at least she had received a postcard from Fred wishing her a happy birthday and wedding anniversary. She might not be able to have him at home, but at least she knew he was alive and in relative safety. She felt very emotional. Tears were very near the surface all the time she was doing the washing. Wash day couldn't wait just because it was her birthday.

Now that she had the children into bed, she could put her feet up. She looked at the beautifully embroidered handkerchief that Beattie had given her over the weekend when she visited with her husband, Isaac. It must have taken her hours to do. She looked at the cards on the mantelpiece and felt a little less alone, though she did wish that Fred were here to share her birthday with her.

The Government had chosen her birthday as the day to introduce the new purchase tax they had announced in the last budget. It applied to everything except food and children's clothes. She was fed up. Jerry had better not get any ideas of dropping any bombs tonight.

Tuesday, 22nd October 1940 - Torun, Poland

Fred sat on the edge of Walter Martin's bed, dabbing his lips with a damp cloth when the Fusilier opened his eyes.

"Where am I?" he asked.

"You're in the infirmary," said Fred, looking around the hut. "Or what passes for it."

"The infirmary?"

"You've been here for five days," said Fred. "We had to tie you to the bed for most of that. The doc says it was gastroenteritis. But the worst should be passed by now."

"I thought I was in heaven."

"No, I'm afraid you're still in the land of the living, for now. My advice would be to get out of here before they carry you out. Why don't you join a work party?"

"I can barely stand, let alone work. I don't think I can take any more, Sarge."

"Look, Martin. This place is no good for you. Our room has water running down the walls and fungus growing everywhere. I've arranged to get you into a small work party."

"Are you going too, Sarge?"

"No. As an NCO, I am exempted from work by the Geneva Convention, so instead of joining you lot on jollies outside the camp, I have to stay here and sort out the clothing supplies and Red Cross parcels."

For Fred, life in the camp was not far removed from his previous life in Army barracks. He felt for the enlisted men, who were unused to life with such strict routines.

"I just want this damn war to be over," said Fusilier Martin. "I don't think I can stand another week in this place, Sarge."

"We all want it to be over. Maybe by Christmas, eh?"

Fred left Walter, promising that tomorrow he would go on one of the work parties.

The Germans were unloading a truck of Red Cross parcels, and Fred wanted to help the other NCOs observe that the parcels arrived with their rightful recipients and none 'went missing.' The Red Cross parcels contained meat, jellies, margarine, custard puddings, chocolate, and biscuits.

Wednesday, 25th December 1940 - Torun, Poland.

He's the little boy that Santa Claus forgot
And goodness knows, he didn't want a lot
He sent a note to Santa
For some soldiers and a drum
It broke his little heart
When he found Santa hadn't come

As Fusilier Bobby Jones sang, Fred thought about what a good voice the young soldier had. As he listened to the words, he began thinking of Leah and the children at home.

In the street he envies all those lucky boys
Then wanders home to last year's broken toys
I'm so sorry for that laddie
He hasn't got a daddy
The little boy that Santa Claus forgot

Fred thought of Jim and how he must be feeling at Christmas, with no daddy there for him. Fred turned away from Bobby and faced the wall, trying to stifle the tears which were welling up in his eyes.

You know, Christmas comes but once a year for every girl and boy
The laughter and the joy they find in each brand new toy
I'll tell you of a little boy that lives across the way
This little fella's Christmas is just another day
He's the little boy that Santa Claus forgot
And goodness knows, he didn't want a lot.

Fred began to weep. He missed Leah. He missed his children. He missed their company. Of course, he missed sex too, but he and the men never discussed this in the camp. It would only serve to make the men more frustrated.

Tuesday, 4th February, 1941 - Sunderland, England

"It was my father who insisted I come and see you," Leah said.

The doctor nodded, waiting for Leah to expand on her statement.

"He worries about me. Says I'm too nervy."

The doctor nodded again and began scribbling on his notes. Leah looked around and saw a framed photo of the doctor with a woman who must be his wife, holding a baby."

"You have a child," said Leah with a hint of surprise, which she regretted as soon as she spoke.

The doctor looked up and followed her gaze to the photo.

"Yes. She'll be a year in a couple of weeks."

"Same as Beattie."

"Yes."

The doctor finished writing his notes.

"Mrs Wooll, would you say you have many friends?"

"We've moved around such a lot. We live very close to my father, so I see him every day, and there's Mrs Pearson next door, who is very chatty."

"What about women your own age?"

Leah thought about it for a moment and then shook her head.

"I would recommend that you try to make some friends your own age. Do you go to church?"

"St Peters."

"Perhaps they have a Mothers' Union you could go to. They do very good work. It would keep you busy."

"I am busy. I have two children to look after. I have to cook and clean. I have no one to help me."

"I understand that. I just think it'll do you a bit of good to have the company of women your own age. We are living in difficult times, Mrs Wooll, and the more support we can find in those around us, the better."

Wednesday, 5th February 1941 - Torun, Poland

"What's going on?" Fred asked his corporal.

Jack leant close to whisper so they couldn't be overheard.

"The goons discovered the escape plan we were working on."

"The goons?"

"That's what the men call the Jerry guards."

"Well, these things happen. You can't expect to keep everything a secret."

"It's not just that," said Jack. "It all happened a bit too easily."

"What do you mean?"

"We think we might have a traitor among us."

Fred gave Jack a look of incredulity.

"I know," said Jack. "But we've got a plan to catch the bastard, whoever he is."

Fred could hear *Fahren Gehgan Engeland* over the camp tannoy system and wondered whether the German Navy was sailing for England. At least it made a change from the news that everyone back home in England was starving because the German U boats were sinking so many supply ships. Fred knew it was just propaganda. If it were true, they wouldn't be receiving a steady stream of Red Cross parcels.

Monday, 3rd March 1941 - Monkwearmouth, England

It wasn't long after blackout when the air raid warning sounded, and Leah had to wake the children, put their coats on, grab their gas masks, and get them down to the communal shelter.

Leah thought about the baby killed in a raid a couple of weeks ago. She held Beattie close. Her daughter was getting heavy, as it would be her first birthday on Saturday. Leah had been trying to organise a birthday tea. Her sister had said she might come up from Billingham, her brother Jim would probably come if he wasn't on a shift at the pit, and her dad would come once he'd closed the shop.

By the time she laid Jim and Beattie down on the wooden bunk, someone had already begun to sing *Daisy Daisy,* but they soon stopped when they heard the whistle of the first bomb. It must have landed nearby, because it shook the shelter and all the children began to cry. There were six explosions nearby, and each sounded almost as close as the one which had shaken the shelter.

It was half midnight by the time they sounded the all-clear, and Jim and Beattie had gone back to sleep, so Leah had to wake them again to take them back to their beds. The air in the street was thick with smoke, and it looked like Thompson's Yard had taken a hit as well as the dock on the other side of the river. Leah felt like running away, but she had no idea where she could go to or how she would survive. Her lack of sleep was catching up with her. If she couldn't run away, then maybe she could lock herself away from everyone and everything. She found even the smallest tasks difficult, such as making decisions when shopping.

Tuesday, 4th March 1941 - Torun, Poland

Fred thought he had been one of the first up, but when he got up the hill, there was already a long queue for the latrines. No sooner had he joined the line than there was a commotion at the front.

Guards came running, and a crowd gathered to get a look at what a POW had discovered at the bottom of one of the latrines. In the bottom of the pit lay a human figure.

"They've found a body," Fred told Jack as he joined him in the queue.

"I'll come back later then," said Jack.

"What do you mean? Don't you want to find out who it is?"

"I know who it is."

"You know? You don't have anything to do with this, do you, Jack?"

"I didn't kill him if, that's what you mean. But I know why he was killed."

"Why?"

"You remember when the goons uncovered that escape plan, I told you they thought there was a traitor in the camp?"

"Yes."

"Well, we decided that to uncover the traitor, we would give each person on the escape committee different information about the new escape. Whichever version of the plan the goons uncovered would tell us who the traitor was. That's how that man ended up at the bottom of that pit."

Jack walked back down the hill, leaving Fred to watch the guards lift the body of the dead POW out of the shit.

Thursday, 3rd April 1941 - Monkwearmouth

"Leah, your hand is shaking," said her father.

"Is it?" she said, looking at her hand and trying to steady it. "It's the raids. The children scream. They worry me."

"We need to get you out to the country. Do you think you could stay with Beattie and Isaac in Billingham?"

"They don't have space," said Leah. "And anyway, the ICI factory is just as much a target for the Germans as the docks are here."

"What about Fred's family?"

"Hull gets bombed more than we do."

"Yes, but they live in Beverley, don't they? I bet it's peaceful there."

"Live with Fred's family? No thanks."

"What's wrong with his family? I met his mum and dad, and they seemed nice enough."

"His mum would be too helpful. She'd drive me mad. Anyway, she's already looking after Fred's nephew and she has a soldier and his wife billeted there."

"How come?"

"The Army has been asking people to make their spare rooms available."

"No, I mean how come she's looking after Fred's nephew?"

"When Fred's brother and his wife bought a place and moved out of his mother's house, Ron wouldn't go with them."

"Ron?"

"Fred's nephew. Their son."

"Oh yes, I remember Fred saying something about that."

James coughed into a large handkerchief.

"Why don't you go and see the doctor?" he said. "Maybe he can give you something for your nerves."

"I can't afford to keep going to the doctor every five minutes."

James sighed.

"Well, you can't keep on like this," he said.

"I'll get another bottle of Sanatogen."

"How about something stronger? "

"What are you suggesting? Gin?"

They stared at each other for a moment, then burst out laughing. James' laugh turned into another cough.

Sunday, 6th April 1941 - Torun, Poland.

"Sarge, Sarge, you've got to come quick," Fusilier Jones beckoned Fred to follow him.

Fred was about to ask the fusilier what the matter was when he saw for himself. Upon the roof of the fort, Fred could see the figure of Walter Martin.

"What's he doing up there?" Fred asked, but then realised he didn't want to know the answer.

Fred broke into a run when he saw the guards approaching with their rifles raised.

"No!" Fred shouted, but it was too late. Fusilier Martin had jumped.

By the time Fred reached him, life had already left the private's body. Fred could feel the anger swelling up inside. He wanted to lash out at his captors, but he knew it would be pointless. He just had to swallow his rage and bide his time. One day he would have his moment. Until then, he would just have to wait and keep everything bottled up inside for the sake of Leah and the children.

He waited to ensure that the guards dealt with Martin's body with respect and then went back with the other men to their underground room.

He watched Fusilier Jones light a cigarette and hold it between his index and middle fingers, so that the two fingers formed a thin V.

Fred thought it was a stupid way to hold a cigarette and almost told Jones as much, before it dawned on him that he was getting upset about the most trivial of things and should just try to look at something else. He turned his back on the room and stared at the wall.

Saturday, 3rd May 1941 - Monkwearmouth, England

When Leah awoke, she heard the whistles of the first bomb beginning to fall.

It seemed to have landed very close, as the house shook from the explosion, but the next which followed straight after seemed even closer, and the next in quick succession was closer still. It was clear to Leah that the German bomber had dropped a series of bombs in a straight line and each successive one was landing closer and closer to her house. The noise was unbearable and the children were screaming. The next bomb seemed to be falling right on top of them. When it exploded, all the windows shattered, and a plume of soot fell from the chimney, covering them and the house in a blanket of black dust. Leah began screaming as loudly as the children. The next would be a direct hit, and she waited for the inevitable. This was how it was going to end. She would never see her children grow up or Fred return. In a guilty corner of her mind, Leah was relieved that the daily struggle with life would be over. She wondered if there was an afterlife and whether she would be allowed in or whether she was about to discover what eternal torment felt like. She wished she had opened the tin of fruit at teatime instead of putting it back in the larder to save for a special occasion.

The inevitable never arrived, and the bombs seemed to be falling further and further away. Leah held her children, then put their coats on them, took them downstairs, and out onto the street. It was then she realised that all of the houses on her side of the street had been bombed. Her house was the only one left standing.

She went as fast as she could to the communal air raid shelter and got the children onto the wooden bunk, cuddling them until they got to sleep. Then she sat and waited for the all-clear to sound. She felt guilty for the moment of relief she'd felt when she had thought they were all about to die. How could a mother feel relieved about the imminent death of her children? She wondered whether she was a bad person and contemplated where she might have found herself if the bomb had fallen on their house. Would St Peter have turned her away? Would he have separated her from her children for all eternity?

She looked for Mrs Pearson, but couldn't see her. Perhaps she'd been asleep in bed when the bomb had fallen and hadn't known anything. Mrs

Pearson didn't have a sixth sense after all. Perhaps she was with St Peter now. She felt a little bit sorry for St Peter. He wouldn't stand a chance faced with Mrs Pearson. At least the quality and quantity of tea in heaven would take a sudden and dramatic upturn.

Leah imagined heaven wouldn't be subject to rationing, and she felt another pang of guilt for thinking it might not have been so bad if the bomb had fallen on their house instead.

The all-clear sounded at about 4 am, but Leah let the children sleep until morning.

When it was light, the children and Leah, still shaking, emerged from the shelter and returned to their street to examine the damage.

She could hear a lot of commotion as she approached her street. People shouting and engines.

She approached her house, which looked still intact.

"We can't let you in there in case your house collapses," said a fireman who stepped between Leah and the house.

Leah didn't like the sound of that and led the children up towards Dame Dorothy Street and her father's grocery shop.

She thought of Mrs Pearson and Mr Chamberlain next door and hoped it had been quick and that they hadn't suffered.

"What about Dame Dorothy Street?" Leah asked a firefighter.

"It's all right as far as I know," he said, and Leah headed up the street in the direction of her father's shop to see for herself.

When she got there, her father was already dressed.

"What the hell happened to you lot? Have you been down the pit? I was just coming to see if you were all right," he said as they met each other in the doorway.

Leah laid Jim and Beattie on the floor so they wouldn't soil the furniture.

"Dad, they flattened the whole street. Ours is the only house on our side of the road left standing."

"Bloody hell. Let's put some water on and get you all cleaned up."

Wednesday, 28th May 1941 - Torun, Poland

"We are pleased to announce that a few days ago, on your Victoria Day, May 24, our ship, the Bismarck, sunk your boat, HMS Hood. Your biggest battlecruiser. The ship you thought was unsinkable."

Fred and the other POWs looked at each other in disbelief. It was true. They had thought the HMS Hood was unsinkable, yet here were the Germans telling them just that.

"You will go on the working party, too," a guard told Fred and Jack as they dismissed the 5 am roll call and ushered the men off to their work detail for the day. This left Fred, Jack and the rest of the NCOs in the camp sorting out Red Cross parcels if there were any, or trying to organise spare clothing, visiting the sick in the infirmary, and dealing with the monotonous administration of the POWs affairs. In a way, he was envious of the men, getting out of the camp and doing something different, getting some exercise. However, he wasn't going to let the goons have any more free labour than they were entitled to under the rules of war.

"I will not," said Fred for the umpteenth time. "Under the Geneva Convention, non-commissioned officers are not required to work."

Fred had lost count how many times he had repeated this phrase to the guards, but today, the guard in question nodded to one of his colleagues, who smiled. This looked ominous, but Fred wasn't going to let it worry him. The compound was emptying of POWs, and Fred made his way over to the latrines. As he did so, he noticed the guards outpacing him so they would arrive first at the queue.

"No toilet for you today," one of them said when he arrived.

Fred just shrugged, made an about-turn and headed towards the infirmary to begin his rounds. He wasn't about to let the goons intimidate him, but he also wasn't sure for how long he'd be able to contain the contents of his bowels.

Parcels were arriving on a daily basis. Some were from families of individual soldiers, and others were from the Red Cross, including some from Canada. The guards would try to barter for tea and coffee and, this way, Fred was often able to obtain fresh eggs, bread, and, sometimes, even butter. He was glad to have got hold of a needle and thread and attempted to darn what was

FRED & LEAH: A TRUE LIFE SECOND WORLD WAR DRAMA
OF LOVE, LOSS AND CAPTIVITY.

155

left of his socks which he remembered Jack describing as "more holey than godly."

When Fred felt he could contain his bowels no longer, he returned to the latrines, but the guards posted there met him with the same refusal.

Fred was beginning to wander back, wondering where he might be able to go to defecate, when an officer called him back.

"OK, Englishman. You may go to the toilet."

Fred smiled as he marched past the officer and into one of the latrines where he made himself as comfortable as he could on the plank, which hung over the pit of effluence. No sooner had Fred begun to loosen his bowels than the guards burst in and pulled him out of the latrine, forcing him to secure the contents of his bowels once more or risk soiling himself.

"Are you ready to go to work?" said the officer who was waiting for him outside the latrine.

"As a non-commissioned officer, I am exempted from work under the terms of the Geneva Convention," said Fred as he re-fastened his trousers and tried to ignore the pains in his abdomen.

The infirmary was full of men suffering from a mysterious illness. The men would try to retch and vomit, but only salt water would come into their mouths. The retching made their stomachs sore, and the men were infested with lice which made them scratch, creating sores. It had not been that long since the guards had deloused them, and they had access to soap, but the lice proliferated. Some men tied a length of string around their torso on which the lice would gather. They then removed and burnt the string. A grim business.

Thursday, 29th May 1941 - Roker, Sunderland, England

Beattie was crying again, and although Leah had been putting it off, she relented and picked up her daughter, who was getting heavy now. Leah looked around at her new home and at all of her belongings, which were still mostly in boxes. Her life seemed to consist of packing and unpacking. It was such a shame that the bomb had damaged their house in Normanby too badly for them to stay. But if it was unsafe, then it was unsafe, and there was nothing she could do about it. She felt thankful that she had managed to find another property so fast, with more and more bombed out families looking for alternative accommodation. They had managed to salvage a lot from the house, although soot had covered everything and it seemed to take forever to get it all clean.

At least they didn't have to move the furniture, which had belonged to the landlord, along with all the cutlery and crockery in the kitchen. Leah didn't like the crockery in this new place as much as in the last house, but a lot of that had been smashed by the bomb anyway.

She worried that some of Jim's toys might be beyond cleaning and she hoped he wouldn't notice if she had to get rid of any.

This new house was another small terrace in Roker. Not quite as close to her father's shop as the last place, but still within walking distance. The money she was still receiving from the Ministry of Defence was enough to cover it.

Her father had to manage the shop by himself for a couple of days while she got the house sorted, and she wished that the children would give her a moment's peace so she could get on with it all. If Fred's bottle of whiskey hadn't broken in the raid, she could have let Beattie suck a drop off her little finger, and that would have sent her off to sleep. It used to work a treat with Jim.

Sunday, 22nd June 1941 - Torun, Poland

Fred looked up and saw more German planes heading east. It had been like that all morning, but it wasn't until the afternoon that Fred heard the reason why.

"German troops attacked Russia," one of the goons explained. "Your men are to be taken from their sleep quarters to Fort 17, while your room is fumigated."

"At last," said Fred, glad that the Goons were taking the lice problem seriously. "Why the sudden change of heart?"

The guard look puzzled.

"Why now and not before?"

The guard leant closer to Fred and spoke quietly.

"Some of the lice have begun to disturb the German soldiers."

Fred stifled a laugh and ordered his men to collect up their meagre belongings so that they could move to their temporary home while the guards doused their room in sulphur.

Sunday, 29th June 1941 - Monkwearmouth, England

"You know, I did have twins," said Leah.

"What are you talking about?" asked her father. "I thought you had all this out with the doctor when you were in the hospital?"

"Well, I did. And I believed them. Then I thought, *what if they hid the other baby from me?*"

"Why on earth would they do that?" her father asked.

"That's what I've been trying to work out," she said.

"It seems a bit far-fetched to me," her father said.

"Everything seems far-fetched to you."

Leah sulked at her father's reluctance to take her seriously. While she sulked, she remembered the other train of thought, which had been passing through her mind.

"Do you remember when Fred was last here?" she asked.

James thought about it for a moment.

"Yes. When Beattie was born. He went back to France not long after the christening."

"Did he seem different to you?"

"Different? In what way? He was worried about leaving you and going back to France. The prospect of war can weigh heavy on a man."

Leah wondered whether she should tell her father what she had begun to suspect. - that the man who had visited them in the winter of 1940 was not her husband, but his twin brother impersonating her husband. Her father would never believe her. He would say she was just silly, like he had when she had told him about them stealing the children from her. He blamed it on stress and told her she needed a rest. He said it was the war that was doing it and asked her if she had enough Sanatogen?

Leah decided to keep quiet for now.

Sunday, 13th July 1941 - Torun, Poland

The guards had rounded up all the Polish prisoners, taken them out of the camp, and marched into the town. There was much debate in the camp about the reason for this and what was going to happen when they were there.

The speculation ended when a truckload of British greatcoats arrived. The men had been wearing uniforms from any country but their own since they had arrived in the camp, and Fred was pleased that his men would look like British soldiers once more.

Fred distributed the greatcoats to his platoon and was just handing out the last ones when the Polish prisoners were marched back into the camp. The Polish looked even more depressed than usual, and the British POWs approached them to try to find out what had happened.

"They ordered us to watch a Pole hanged," said one of the Polish prisoners whose English was quite good. "They said he slept with a German girl."

Sunday, 20th July 1941 - Monkwearmouth, England

"I've worked it out," said Leah. "I know why the doctor said I didn't have twins."

"Because you didn't, Leah," said her father. "We've been through all of this before."

"No, I worked it out. He told me I didn't have two because he wanted the other one himself, because his wife can't have children. I overheard Mrs Pearson talking about it."

"Mrs Pearson is dead. She died in the bomb that flattened your street."

"I know that," said Leah. "I overheard her saying that before she was killed."

"Then why didn't you say anything before now?" asked her father.

"Because I just remembered it," said Leah.

James looked at his daughter. He was worried about her. He didn't know what to do about all these fanciful notions which were swimming around in her head. She had gone to the doctor as he had asked. She couldn't keep on going back. Doctors cost money, and things were tight enough as it was. There was a war on, after all. James cursed the war under his breath and wished it would be over so that Fred would come back and he and Leah could go on a holiday to recover from all this madness.

Friday, 1 August 1941 - Monkwearmouth, England

"I found him. He has him," said Leah with excitement.

"Not now," said her father. "You have to help me serve these customers."

"I went to see him," she continued. "He denied it, of course. I know where he lives. I'll catch him when he's unaware."

"Don't do anything, Leah," her father warned her. "Give us a chance to close the shop, and we'll have a chat about it."

*

By the end of the day, Leah had thought better about sharing her plans with her father, and James didn't want to raise the subject, because he didn't want to encourage these daft notions his daughter had been entertaining. He hoped she had forgotten about it for the moment and the two of them tidied up the shop in silence.

Saturday, 2 August 1941 - Sunderland, England

"Mrs Wooll, I do not have your baby," said the doctor.

"You do. I want to see it," said Leah.

"I am asking you to leave, Mrs Wooll. If you don't leave, I shall have to call the police."

Leah stared at him trying to decide whether he was bluffing. She decided he was not and realised that she was going to have to approach this differently.

Sunday, 3 August 1941 - Sunderland, England

"Dad, I think I'm going to pop out for a bit of fresh air with the kids?"

"Of course," her father said in between wheezes. "There's not enough fresh air in the world for me, luv. Get it while you can. I'm a bit tired. Do you mind if I stay here?"

"You have a nap," said Leah, grabbing the children and rushing out of the door.

*

"My baby," Leah muttered as she walked along the pavement, dragging the trailing children with her. "My baby."

She slowed as she approached the doctor's house and, seeing a pram in the garden, stopped as soon as she was alongside. She looked into the pram and saw the lump under the blankets.

She grabbed the pram and wheeled it out of the garden and down the street, dragging Beattie with Jim holding into her pocket. Behind her, the curtains twitched.

*

"Where are they?" James asked when he opened the front door and saw the Police sergeant.

"Still at the station," said the sergeant. "They'll be going to the Institute. The doctor's already signed the papers."

"What did she do?" James asked.

"She stole a pram."

"A pram? An empty pram? Well that's not such a big deal, is it?" said James.

"Mr Stevenson," said the sergeant in a tone that suggested that his patience was wearing thin. "Your daughter has been warned on a number of occasions. She refuses to leave the doctor and his wife alone. What if there had been a baby in that pram?"

"It was the doctor's pram?"

The sergeant didn't answer.

"He can't lock her up just because she's annoying him."

"Mr Stevenson, it's not like it's a one-off."

"Let me talk to her," said James.

"I'm afraid it's too late for that," said the sergeant. "I just came to warn you that the Institute will be caring for the children until provision can be made."

"What? Can't they stay with me?"

"You'll have to have your house inspected. It's unlikely they'll let them stay with you, since you have the shop to run and everything. I've seen this situation before."

"So it's the workhouse, and that's that?"

James began to cough.

"What about your other daughters?" asked the sergeant.

"Beattie has her own little one down in Billingham, and she has to help Isaac run their shop. Bessie and Becca have children of their own."

"Then I'm afraid there's nothing for it."

"Fred has family in Beverley. Perhaps if I wrote to them and explained the situation," James wondered aloud.

"You could try," said the sergeant. "Their houses would have to be inspected, but assuming they were found to be suitable..."

Seeing James was daydreaming, the sergeant trailed off.

"Right. Well I'll leave you to think about it, then." said the sergeant, placing his helmet back on his head.

*

"Where's mi mam?" asked Jim.

"She's not well," said the nurse. "She's being looked after."

"I want mi mam," said Jim.

"I know you do. However, there's nothing we can do about it right now. You're going to stay in this big house until she's better or until we can work out some kind of alternative."

"This big house? Is it a palace?"

"Hardly," said the nurse glancing around. "But they'll look after you here. Do you understand?"

"I want mi mam."

"I know you do."

Beattie, sensing that something was wrong, began to whimper, and Jim held her hand.

"Now don't worry, you two. Everything is going to be all right. And I'll come to make sure you're OK. I promise."

Jim and Beattie didn't look as though they had been convinced.

*

"Mrs Wooll?"

A large nurse entered the room in which they had put Leah.

"I'm Nurse Robertson. I'm the head attendant on the ward."

"I want to go home. Where are my children?"

"They are being looked after. It's important that you try to calm down."

"You calm down! I want to see my children."

"Mrs Wooll, it is important that you realise that you won't be allowed to see your children until you begin to behave."

"What do you mean?"

"I mean that you can't go around stealing other people's prams."

"Other people's prams? She stole my child."

The nurse consulted her notes.

"You have two children. Frederick James, born 25th October 1937, and Beatrice Leah, born 8th March 1940."

Leah grunted her disapproval.

"It says here that your husband is a prisoner of war in Germany."

Leah sat and sulked.

"Mrs Wooll, I recommend that you become a little more cooperative, unless you wish to remain a patient in the mental wards of Highfield or some other institution for the rest of your days."

Tuesday, 5 August 1941 - Highfield Institute, Sunderland, England

"What do you mean we can't take them?" Lizzie was incensed. "They are my grandchildren."

"That may be the case," said the pedantic-looking official. "But we must follow the correct procedures. Your house will need to be inspected first."

Lizzie looked at her daughter, Bub, in disbelief and then back at the official.

"We've spent a fortune to come all the way up here."

"That is not my fault," the official sniped. "Perhaps it would have been wise to call first, and I could have explained the situation over the phone."

"But no matter how bad you might think my house is, I can guarantee you it is no worse than this place."

The official appeared taken aback.

"I assure you, Mrs Wooll, that your grandchildren are in safe hands. They will want for nothing while they reside at the Institution."

"Except their family," Bub commented.

Friday, 15 August 1941 - Torun, Poland

Fred was feeling a bit more optimistic. Three days ago, a consignment of Red Cross parcels had arrived. He had received two hundred cigarettes and two ounces of tobacco and had managed to swap his chocolate with a non-smoker for some more cigarettes. He envied the non-smoker, who had not only managed to accumulate chocolate, but had also swapped cigarettes with the more amiable goons for meat and eggs. Fred was jealous, but not enough to attempt to give up smoking.

Today another truck arrived, this time with Red Cross parcels from Canada, which contained powdered milk, more chocolate and canned meat.

Monday, 18 August 1941 - Cherry Knowle Mental Hospital, Sunderland

Leah sat and observed the doctor as he read her medical notes in front of her.

"So, you've been in Highfield Institution for a couple of weeks," he said as he glanced up at her. "It says here that your committal is to be charged to the ratepayers of Beverley. Is that where you are from? Do you have family there?"

"It's where my husband was from," said Leah. "He still has family there."

"Are you religious, Mrs Wooll?"

"Church of England."

"Good," the doctor said, as if turning it over and weighing it up in his mind.

Leah had no idea why her religion had a bearing on the doctor's opinion of her mental state.

"And it says here that your place of residence was 55 Cooper Street in Roker. Is that home?"

"It's rented. It's what I had to call home before they locked me up."

"Do you understand why you have been 'locked up,' as you say?"

"No."

"You stole a pram from Dr Beal."

"So?"

The doctor raised his eyebrows.

"It's a pram. That is no reason to take my children away and lock me up. It was nothing stealing Dr Beal's pram. Mrs Beal stole my baby, and I was trying to take it back."

"But, Mrs Wooll, you had one baby," he looks at his notes. "Beatrice."

"You would say that, wouldn't you? You're in cahoots with them."

Leah was irritated.

"Mrs Wooll ..."

"Mrs Beal has my child."

The doctor coughed. He was getting nowhere.

"Tell me about the air raid at your home ..." the doctor consulted his notes again. "... on the night of 3rd May."

"I know why you're asking me that," said Leah. "You think I'm having delusions because of the air raid, but before that, I was sure that I had four children and that two had been taken away from me."

"Tell me about the bomb anyway."

"We were in bed when the bomb burst, and later we went to a shelter. There were ten people killed in the vicinity and some damage done to my house."

"That was in May?"

"That's right."

"And it was a couple of weeks ago on 3rd August that you took the empty perambulator from the garden of the doctor's house?"

"Yes, I was annoyed that they wouldn't let me see my child."

"And a policeman went after you?"

Leah nodded.

"Where are my children?"

"James and Beatrice are being cared for at the Institution until alternative arrangements can be made."

"Alternative arrangements?"

"Yes. Now that you have been committed, they will try to rehome your children with one of your relatives, but their houses will have to be inspected first to ensure they are suitable for small children."

Sunday, 12th October 1941 - Beverley, England

"What did she say?" Lizzie, Fred's mother, asked.

"She said that our gate is too low for Beattie, but that Jim would be all right," said Minnie, Fred's sister.

"Why?"

"Well, she thinks that Jim is old enough to know that he shouldn't open the gate, but she won't let Beattie stay with us because we are on a busy road."

"What are we going to do? I already have the soldier and his wife. I'll have to ask them to move out. But that still leaves Ron, and he's not going to move out," said Lizzie. She was referring to her eldest grandchild, Ron, who had lived in her house since his birth. Ron's father, Lizzie's son, Harry, and his wife Flossy had been living with her when Ron was born. When they had moved out to the new house they had bought on Holme Church Lane, Ron had refused to go with them and had stayed with his grandmother ever since. The Army had billeted the soldier and his wife with Lizzie when she notified them that she had a spare room, but they would have to go.

"You'll have to take Beattie. Jim can stay here with Shirley," said Minnie, referring to the daughter of her sister, Bub.

Bub worked long hours as a maid and was unable to look after her daughter, and so had entrusted her to Minnie, who was unable to have any children of her own. When Minnie heard what had happened to Leah and that the children would be coming to Beverley, she'd relished the idea of more children to look after, but the words of the inspector meant that she wouldn't be able to have Beattie after all. That task would have to fall on Fred's mother, Lizzie, who already had one grandchild to look after due to Ron's refusal to move into the house where his parents, Harry and Flossy, were living.

"It seems a shame to split up Jim and Beattie," said Lizzie.

"Yes, but we don't have much choice," said Minnie. "Unless you want three children to look after. "

"No thanks," said Lizzie. "I'm 61, you know. I should be retired."

"I know, mum," said Minnie. "There is another problem though."

"Oh?"

"Beattie has developed whooping cough."

"Oh, no. Poor thing."

"They're talking about transferring her to Sunderland General Hospital. They won't release Jim until Beattie is well enough, and then they will release both of them together."

"That's terrible. Let's hope she gets better soon."

Monday, 17 November 1941 - Broadgate Hospital, Walkington, England

It was already dark by the time the nurses led Leah, weeping, into the ward. They led her into a room and brought her a cup of tea, and she was just feeling like she was starting to compose herself when a doctor came in and sat opposite her at the table.

"Hello. I'm Doctor North. Can you tell me your name?" he said. His voice was soft and polite.

"Leah Wooll."

Doctor North gave an approving nod.

"Leah, can you tell me about the events which led you to be brought here?"

"My babies were taken by a doctor in Sunderland."

"Now Leah, are you sure about that? Your children are in care in Sunderland, are they not?"

"Yes, I am quite sure. I gave birth to twin boys in 1937 and twin girls in 1940. One of each was spirited away."

"Spirited away?"

"They were taken from me and are being brought up by doctors who worked at the maternity hospital."

"Your husband is a prisoner of war, is he not?"

"Yes."

"When did you last see him?"

"In March 1940. But Doctor, here's the thing. He was being impersonated by his twin brother."

"His twin brother? When did you find out about this? All the twins."

"Last year. Around that time. In 1940."

"Are you surprised to find yourself here?"

"No. But everything that I have told you is true, Doctor."

"And how do you feel about the doctor whom you say took your baby?"

"Nothing."

"You don't feel any kind of resentment toward him?"

"No."

"Would you like your children ..." he consulted his notes, "... James and Beatrice, to join you?"

"My daughter is recovering from whooping cough. She's not fit to travel."

"Very sensible."

"My boy should wait in Sunderland until they can come home together."

"Alright. Well, the nurses here are going to look after you. You'll be very tired from your long journey and will want to get some rest. We'll talk over the next few days."

The doctor stood up and let the nurses lead Leah out of the room. He followed them out and found his colleague, Doctor Baker, waiting for him in the corridor.

"What do you think?"

"Well, she's a paranoid of sorts. She has two streams of consciousness," Doctor North said as he watched the nurses lead Leah away. "She must have been a bit mental in 1940 when she made the discoveries she claims. Still, she seems in moderate health. Just a couple of bruises on the shins."

"I'll interview her tomorrow when she's had time to rest," said Doctor Baker.

"Yes. Let's leave it to the end of the week before we start the treatment."

Tuesday, 18 November 1941 - Broadgate Hospital, Walkington, England

Leah sat in an armchair in the day room and stared at the ward sister's office where the charge nurse was chatting to Doctor Baker. As she stared, she felt herself filling with rage at the injustice of her captivity.

"I shouldn't be here," shouted Leah towards the office. The staff just ignored her.

"I wouldn't do that if I were you," said an old woman sat in the armchair opposite Leah.

"Who asked you?" snapped Leah.

"Nobody. But you should know that you'll get yourself in trouble acting up like that."

Leah looked at the old woman. She wasn't like the other patients she's encountered in Highfield and Cherry Knowle. This old woman's eyes were bright and alert, and darted between Leah and the staff in the office.

"What do you know?" Leah asked.

"Oh, believe me, I know."

"What are you in here for?"

"Nothing. I'm innocent like everyone else," the old woman laughed.

Leah looked puzzled.

"Most people don't think they should be here. Especially if they've been committed like you."

"What makes you think I'm committed? "

"Oh, you're committed all right. Otherwise, you wouldn't be screaming at the charge nurse like that. Even if you weren't screaming at the staff, I would be able to tell."

"How?"

"I have my ways. You'll be able to tell, too, if you stay here long enough. But you won't stay here if you keep acting like that."

"Oh no?"

"No, they'll be shifting you off to Ward 5."

"Ward 5?"

"That's where they keep all the disturbed patients. That's right. You see, you're in the good ward with us. We are curable. We can get better. But you go on the way you are, and they'll be giving you treatment, and after enough of those treatments, you'll be shipped off upstairs with the rest of the disturbed. The incurables. Very few come back once they end up there. In fact, I don't know of anyone who came back from Ward 5."

"You don't scare me."

"Oh no? I'm not trying to scare you. I'm trying to warn you. You carry on the way you are, dear, and you'll be buying yourself a one-way ticket to oblivion."

Leah burst out laughing.

"You're a right one, you are," Leah chuckled. "What's your name?"

"Aida. What's yours?"

"Leah. Leah Wooll."

"Pleased to meet you, Leah Wooll."

Aida stared towards the glass window of the office, the other side of which the charge nurse and Doctor Baker were chatting and laughing, and Leah thought she could detect loathing from the expression on Aida's face.

"You see the office?" Aida asked.

Leah nodded.

"They keep a list there of all the patients who are scheduled for treatment the next day," the old woman continued. "And if you make life difficult for the staff, your name will end up on it, as punishment."

"Treatment?"

"Electroconvulsive shock therapy. I see from your puzzled expression that you've yet to experience the delights of ECT."

"What is it?"

"My dear, they attach electrodes to your skull and turn on the juice."

"Electrocution?"

"For a second. You become unconscious, and when you wake up, you don't know where you are. It's meant to calm the mind."

"Does it hurt?"

"Oh no, it doesn't hurt. But after they've given you the first treatment, no one ever asks for a second."

Leah gaped at the old woman in astonishment and then at the charge nurse busy showing her paperwork to Doctor Baker. Leah wondered whether her name was already on the list.

"How do you know?"

"How do you know what?"

"If they've written your name down."

"You can go and have a look if you're sneaky enough to get a peek when a nurse isn't looking. The easiest way to tell is at breakfast time. If they bring you breakfast, then you're safe. But no breakfast, treatment."

The door of the ward opened, and Leah watched Doctor North enter. He headed straight over to the office where he joined in the conversation.

Leah and Aida saw them glancing towards them. They guessed the staff in the office were speaking about them.

"Are your ears burning?" asked Aida.

Saturday, 22 November 1941 - Broadgate Hospital, Walkington, England

Leah felt very anxious. She watched the nurses as they moved around the ward with the breakfast trays. With each tray, she willed the nurse to come her way, but each time the nurse changed direction and headed towards another patient. Leah watched as, one by one, the trays disappeared. Four large male attendants entered the ward. Then there were no trays left.

"Nurse, you've forgotten me," Leah shouted at the woman pushing the trolley.

"What's your name, luv?"

"Leah. Leah Wooll."

The woman consulted her list. Leah saw the four attendants talking to the Charge Nurse and the charge nurse pointing down the ward in her direction.

"Mrs Wooll ..." the woman was checking the list again. "No, sorry, luv. Speak to the charge nurse. She might have special plans for you this morning."

"No!" Leah screamed as she saw the four attendants coming towards her. She got up out of her chair and tried to make a run for it, but the attendants soon caught her.

The attendants dragged Leah through the corridors to the treatment room. All the way, she screamed and shouted her dissent. They held her down while they fastened straps to render her immobile, unable to struggle while they fixed the electrodes to her temples.

*

Leah looked around. She had no idea where she was or why she was there. She sat in a chair wearing a gown and a robe. There were other people in chairs around her. Some were sleeping. A couple were shouting, but at whom she could not see. She had no idea how she got there. She had no memories of having arrived. The last thing she remembered was being in her house in Normanby Street, putting the children to bed. The children? Where were the children? She wanted to get up and find them, but she felt nauseous. Her head ached. Her jaw ached. She looked around but couldn't see either her children or anyone who looked like they might know where they were. It seemed like some kind of hospital, and she realised that the chair in which she was sitting was a wheelchair. Was she ill? What had happened? Who was looking after the children? She looked for anyone who looked like they might work here, but everyone looked like a patient, sitting and staring at her. Some were not staring at her, but were still staring, at what she couldn't be sure. Leah tried to see what they were staring at, but she could not see anything. She began to panic. She needed to get out. She should be helping her father in his shop. How would she get to Dame Dorothy Street if she were stuck in here? She realised she was wearing a nightdress. How was she going to catch a bus to Dame Dorothy Street in her nightdress? She needed to find her clothes. Where were her clothes?

"Where are my clothes?" she shouted at anyone who might listen.

Tuesday, 2 December 1941 - Stalag XXA, Torun, Poland

"Sarge?"

"Yes, Jones?"

"How many aircraft carriers called the Ark Royal does the British Navy have?"

"Just the one, I think."

"That's funny. I was just listening to the tannoy, and the goons have just announced that they've just sunk the Ark Royal. That's the third one they've sunk since we've been in here."

Fusilier Jones was carrying some mail.

"There's one for you here, Sarge."

Fred took the letter, which the goons had taken the liberty to pre-open for him. 'Very kind of them,' he thought.

As he read the letter, his face fell. It was from his mother. It spoke of Leah's committal, and the fact that his daughter was in Sunderland General Hospital with whooping cough and his son still in the workhouse in Sunderland.

Jack observed Fred's expression.

"What is it, Sarge?" asked the new sergeant.

"Ah, nothing. It's from my mother. You know what mothers can be like. Always so melodramatic."

"I sent a letter to my wife," said Jack. "I asked her what she liked best about me ... is it my firm, trim, athletic body? Or rather, is it my astounding intellect?"

"What did she say?"

"When she replied she said ...'your sense of humour, dear.'"

Fred smiled. He appreciated his friend's attempts to cheer him up, but he felt so helpless stuck where he was in Poland. Maybe if he was able to get back to England and see Leah, he might be able to help her. She might snap out of it. But how long would he be stuck in this place? Maybe he should try to escape after all. But if they killed him trying to escape, then he would be no use to any of them.

"Do you remember any of those jokes Barnett used to tell?" Jack asked.

Fred thought about it for a while and then chuckled to himself.

"I do remember one," he said.

"Go on then."

"Alright then, here goes. A man was sitting in the pub when he noticed a pirate walk in the door. The pirate had a peg leg, a hook for one hand, and a patch over one eye. Feeling sorry for the pirate, the man said, 'Come over here, friend. You look like you've had a hard life and I'd like to buy you a drink.' The pirate came over and ordered rum. 'Just out of curiosity,' the man said, 'how did you lose your leg?' 'Arrrgh!' said the pirate,"

Jack's attempt at a pirate accent made Fred smile.

"'I lost that limb to a tiger shark in the Caribbean when I was thrown overboard for stealing a man's rum.' 'That's just terrible,' said the man. 'How did you lose your hand?' 'Arrrgh!' said the pirate, 'I lost that fighting cannibals off Madagascar under Admiral Nelson.' 'Oh my!" the man said, 'I can't even imagine! How did you lose your eye?' 'Arrrgh! A seagull pooped in it!' said the pirate. 'A seagull!' the man exclaimed. 'Is seagull poop dangerous?!' 'Nay, matey, it was me first day with the hook ...'"

Jack burst out laughing, and Fred returned another smile.

Wednesday, 3 December 1941 - Broadgate Hospital, Walkington, England

"Good morning. How was Mrs Wooll last night?" asked Doctor North.

"Very restless again," Doctor Baker reported.

"Never mind. I think we should push ahead with the treatment. I'm eager to see how she responds. Maybe it will help with these restless nights of hers."

Leah struggled and shouted as the orderlies led her back to the treatment room for the second time.

"Why do you do this?" she shouted. "It's not for my benefit. It doesn't benefit any patient. Why?"

"Have you got the gag?" Doctor North asked a nurse as Leah was strapped to the table.

"Close your eyes," the nurse advised Leah, but she was too scared, and her eyes remained wide open.

*

"Would you like a cup of tea, dear?" a nurse asked.

"Tea?"

Sunday, 7 December 1941 - Stalag XXA, Torun, Poland

The music, which had been coming out of the camp tannoy system, stopped, and the German announcer called for everyone's attention.

Fred stopped what he was doing to listen.

"Japanese aircraft have attacked and bombed American warships in Pearl Harbour and have destroyed the American Pacific Fleet." the voice said.

"They're getting good at this propaganda business," laughed Fusilier Jones.

"They've outdone themselves this time."

"Because of the pact between Germany and Japan," the announcer continued, "Germany has also declared war on America today."

"If that's true," said Fred, "and if America does enter the war, it might make a difference in how long we have to stay in this place."

"What do you mean?" asked Fusilier Jones.

"Well, if Germany is also at war with America, then the Americans might send their troops to Europe like they did in the last war."

"Or they might fight the Japanese first," said Jack.

The debate continued with enthusiasm as the German announcer continued to list the colossal losses the German military had inflicted on the Russians since their invasion of the Russian territory.

Friday, 12 December 1941 - Beverley, England.

"Right, here we are," said James, as he parked the van on Holme Church Lane. He saw the curtains twitch and then, as he was closing the driver's door, he saw Minnie Smith appear at a gate at the side of the house, followed by a man who James assumed must be her husband, Bill, and a girl who must be Shirley.

"Get yourself back inside the house, young lady," Minnie barked at the young girl, who turned on her heels and ran back inside. "You'll catch your death out here."

Minnie turned back to James and smiled as he helped young Jim out of the passenger side of the van, then reaching in and picking up Beattie, who was getting heavy at almost two years old. He closed the passenger door with a clunk behind him and led Jim up to the front gate.

"Here they are at last," said Minnie.

"Better late than never," said James.

"Did you have a good trip, Mr Stevenson?" asked Bill, offering his hand. "Bill Smith."

"Not bad. Please call me James. We met at Fred and Leah's wedding."

"Of course," said Bill, a bit embarrassed.

"Thank you so much for coming all the way down here," said Minnie, opening the gate.

"Don't mention it. I should be thanking you for agreeing to look after Jim and Beattie and getting them out of that terrible workhouse."

"We're all family," said Minnie. "Come in."

James left Jim and Beattie with Minnie while he popped back to the van for a case containing Jim's belongings, which he handed to Bill.

Minnie led them up the passage beside the house and through the kitchen to the back room where she offered them seats around the dinner table.

"You must be very tired after your trip. Supper is ready. Fish. Are you hungry, Jim?"

Jim was silent and just nodded.

"How about a drink?" Bill offered.

"Glass of sherry?" Minnie suggested.

"Or I think I've got a bottle of stout," said Bill.

"No, thank you," said James. "I have to get to your mother's with Beattie."

"And how about you, Jim," said Minnie. "Would you like some lemonade?"

Jim nodded.

"He doesn't say much," said James. "Not surprised, locked up in that place for four months."

"Well, you're here now," said Minnie, pouring the lemonade.

"What do you do, Bill?" James asked.

"I'm a baker."

"He's a confectioner."

"Ah, that's right. Leah did tell me. You're in a reserved occupation like me."

"That's right. You're a grocer, aren't you, James?"

"Well, I am now, yes. But I was a miner by trade. Hence the cough. I came into a bit of money and was able to buy the shop."

"Ah yes, Fred told me about that," said Minnie. "Very tragic, about your son. But I guess it's nice for there to be some kind of silver lining."

"I'd rather have my son."

"Of course."

"What do you think of Germany declaring war on the US?" asked Bill.

"I think it's a good thing," said James. "If the US comes and joins in, in Europe, that's got to shorten the war, hasn't it? Like it did last time."

"I just wish it hadn't taken the Americans so long to get involved," Minnie chipped in.

She noticed Shirley's head peeking around the doorpost.

"I suppose you'd like some lemonade too?"

Shirley nodded.

"Come on then."

"You'll have to excuse me," said James, getting to his feet. "It's already late, and I should get this little one to your mother's house."

"Of course," said Minnie. "Thanks again very much for bringing them down."

"Don't mention it."

"Will you have a chance to see Leah before you go back?"

"Yes, I'm going to try and see her tomorrow."

"Good, well please send her our best wishes. And bye bye for now, Beattie. I expect we'll see you tomorrow," Minnie waved at the confused little girl who looked like she just wanted to sleep.

*

Lizzie opened the door and saw James Stevenson standing on the path in the darkness with Lizzie's granddaughter, Beattie, starting to nod off in his arms.

"James, come in," she said. "Bring her into the front room. Where have you parked?"

"On the street. I think it'll be OK. By the way, you have a little bit of light poking out through your blackout blinds."

"Oh, thanks. Come in."

James managed to negotiate the front door without banging Beattie's head on the doorframe.

"Let me help you with that," said Fred Sr. Fred's father, as he entered the hall.

They negotiated the pram through the door, and Fred Sr. led James into the front room.

"How was your journey?" Lizzie said adjusting the blackout blinds. "Thank you ever so much for bringing her. I can't begin to tell you how grateful we are that you closed your shop to come down here."

James laid Beattie down to rest in one of the armchairs.

"Don't mention it," said James in between coughs. "I'm grateful to you for taking her in. I'm not sure what we would have done otherwise. She would still be stuck in that terrible place."

"I'll take her up to bed in a minute, but where are my manners," Lizzie remembered herself. "You must be parched after your journey. Here, let me take your coat. Sit down. The kettle has just boiled, I'll bring you some tea."

Lizzie hurried out of the room and returned a few moments later with a tray on which she had laid out the best tea set, reserved for guests.

"What time did you leave?" Lizzie asked as she poured James a cup of steaming tea. "Milk? Sugar?"

"Yes please, plenty of sugar. They didn't complete all the formalities until three o'clock. That's why we're so late. I thought about leaving it till tomorrow, but I need to get back to open the shop, and I'd like to see Leah before I go."

"How on earth did you manage to get hold of the petrol coupons?"

"We had a bit of a whip round."

"Well, I've made up the middle bedroom. Beatrice will sleep in a cot in our room. I've put Ron in with us tonight as well. He's already in bed. He wore himself out playing with his friends this afternoon and went straight to bed after his supper. Do you have any bags?"

"They're in the van. I brought everything there was of Beattie's in Cooper Street when we cleared it out, as well as what little the Institute gave me, which didn't amount to much. I dare say she'll grow out of it soon if she hasn't already."

"That's all right. We have all of Shirley's old clothes. We'd been saving them for Beattie anyway."

James looked confused.

"Shirley is my granddaughter, Bub's daughter. Bub is Fred's sister."

"Ah yes, Fred mentioned Bub. She works in Hodgson's house as a maid, doesn't she?"

"That's right. Shirley lives with my other daughter, Minnie. It's a team effort in our family."

James attempted a polite laugh, but it turned into a rasping cough.

"Yes, I saw Shirley at Minnie's just now," James said when he'd recovered enough to
speak.

"Goodness, was she not in bed yet? That's a nasty cough you have there." Lizzie commented.

"That's what comes from working down the mines. I'm going to try and see Leah at the hospital tomorrow. Is it close by?" asked James. "Broadgate?"

"Yes, it's up on the Westwood. It's easy to find. Well, I have some supper ready for you if you're hungry. Then I'll show you where to take the bags, and I'd better take little Beatrice up too."

"Fred said you had a soldier and his wife living with you."

"Yes, but when they wouldn't let Beattie stay at Minnie's, I told the Army what had happened and that I needed the room back."

Elizabeth got up, and James followed her through into the back room, where Elizabeth bid James sit at the table while she fetched his supper from the range, where it was warming.

Monday, 22 December 1941 - Broadgate Hospital, Walkington, England.

Leah woke up. It took her a few moments to realise where she was. She looked around at the other beds, which filled the room, and then it all started to come back to her how they had brought her here. How they had separated her from her children and all because she had discovered their scheme. Their scheme to steal her children. First, they had taken one of each of the twins, and now they had taken Jim and Beattie as well.

She sat up in bed. All was dark, but a little moonlight was seeping in through the windows illuminating the ward.

"Let me out of here," she shouted and started to get out of the bed. "Hello? Can anyone hear me? You need to let me out of here."

The ward door opened and the lights were switched on, causing a commotion amongst the other patients who had been sleeping.

"You need to let me out of here," she shouted at the figures walking across the ward towards her.

"Mrs Wooll, back into bed please," one of them replied.

"No, you need to let me out. I shouldn't be here. I need to speak with my father."

"Mrs Wooll, it is the middle of the night. Your father came to visit last week. He has gone back to Sunderland. Now please get back into bed. You are disturbing the others."

"Yeah, shut up," came a shout from one of the other beds.

"I will not shut up. Not until I'm let out."

"Now, now, Mrs Wooll."

One of the nurses had reached Leah and taken hold of her by the arms.

"Take your hands off me. Let go of me. I've done nothing wrong."

"Back into bed, Mrs Wooll."

"No, I will not."

Leah struggled to free herself from the grip of the nurse.

"It's no use," said the other nurse, trying to assist her colleague in manhandling Leah into bed. "We may as well put her in a side room."

"I don't want to go into a side room."

"Come on, then, Mrs Wooll, let's get you out of here."

Leah was surprised how easy that had been. They were going to let her out. She had expected more resistance to her demands. She allowed them to lead her from the ward and when the door to the main dormitory was shut behind her, she found herself being led into a side room, but no sooner was she in the room than the nurses had turned and locked the door behind them. Leah had assumed that this was where they were going to return her clothes so that she could get dressed while they called her father to come and get her. Then she remembered that her father was in Sunderland and they had moved her south to the East Riding, so maybe it was Fred's family who would come and collect her. She didn't like that idea, but in her predicament, she wasn't in a position to argue.

She looked around the room. There didn't seem to be anything that resembled her clothing. It was then that she realised she'd been tricked by the nurses, who did not intend to release her and had trapped her in this room as punishment. She looked around the room again. This time she was searching for something to break, but the nurses had been very clever and had nothing in the room for her to damage except a chamber pot, which was not made of clay and looked indestructible.

"What you need," the nurse shouted through the door, "is to be brought to your senses. What you need is a stay in Ward 5."

Tuesday, 23 December 1941 - Broadgate Hospital, Walkington, England.

"How many children do you have?" asked Doctor North, checking his watch.

"Four," said Leah.

"Do you know where your children are?"

"They are in Highfield Institution in Sunderland. I want so much to be with them."

Leah sobbed.

"Well you know, Mrs Wooll, I want to help you see your children, and the best way to do that is to continue your treatment. Do you understand?"

Leah nodded.

"Good," said the doctor and nodded to the attendants, who led Leah out of the ward to the treatment room without a struggle.

Dr North followed them out.

"It seems so barbaric," whispered one of the nurses to a colleague.

"Barbaric?" exclaimed Doctor North, who had overheard. "It is nothing of the sort, nurse. What you are witnessing is state of the art in treating this sort of disorder. There has been complete remittance in some cases."

"Forgive me, Doctor. I didn't mean to ..." the nurse was ashamed at having been caught questioning his choice of procedure.

The doctor's mood changed. He had a soft spot for Nurse Barton, and he realised she hadn't meant anything by her comment. It was just ignorance on her part.

"That's all right. I don't expect you to understand the intricacies of the science we practice here. The treatment involves administering electric shocks to the brain to induce a seizure. It's what we call the 'antagonism hypothesis' that schizophrenia and epilepsy are opposing disorders. I won't bore you with the details - it's all to do with differences in brain glial cell levels. The point is, there have been beneficial results using this method, and the work we are doing here is a very important part of helping us to understand conditions such as these."

"So the treatment is going to help her?" she asked.

"There have been very beneficial effects in other subjects," said Doctor North. "This is not like a general hospital where the wounds are visible and can be dressed with physical white bandages. We cannot see the wounds, but we still have to try to apply bandages. ECT is a tool in our armoury to help us do that."

Nurse Barton thought it strange how the doctors called the patients subjects as if they were mice in some kind of laboratory experiment. She assumed this was because she was new to nursing and that, as time went on, she would get used to terminology such as this.

Thursday, 25 December 1941 - Torun, Poland

For breakfast, Fred enjoyed tea with bread, jam, and some biscuits.

"Looks like Santa hasn't been to visit," said Jack. "Have you been a naughty boy?"

"Must have been," Fred laughed. "How about you? Anything in your stocking this morning?"

"My foot. And a few holes," said Jack.

"You must have been very naughty then."

"Rumour has it that it's roast pork for dinner."

Fred sat up straight.

*

Dinner was mashed potatoes, sauerkraut cabbage, roast pork, and beans. For dessert, there was Christmas pudding and Nestle's milk from the Red Cross parcels. For tea, they had tea, fruit cake, chocolate biscuits, bread, jam, and Canadian butter.

"You know what?" said Fred finishing off the last of his fruit cake. "I just realised that I've been full up all day."

"It's been a long time since I've been able to enjoy a full belly all day." Jack agreed.

"It's just a shame that there's no pint to finish it off with," Jones mused.

Fred looked at his blank Red Cross postcard and contemplated what he could write. He decided that he would ask his mother for books on psychology, not just to understand what was happening to Leah, but also to understand what was happening to his fellow POWs.

Thursday, 1 January 1942 - Broadgate Hospital, Walkington, England

Doctor North walked into Ward 5, where the attendant nurse greeted him. He looked annoyed at having to work on New Year's Day.

"Morning Doctor," she smiled. "I didn't expect to see you today."

"Quite. How is your newest arrival?"

"Mrs Wooll? She is in bed. Her noisy emotionalism continues. I'm afraid."

"Have you managed to talk with her at all?"

"Yes Doctor, in her quieter times she talks sensibly, but she has no understanding of her condition. She is often elated and jocular about the other patients."

"Hmm." The doctor rolled the information around in his mind. "And has she been weighed?"

"Yes, 8st 10lbs."

"Good. I think we should restart the treatment." He looked at his pocket diary. "Schedule it for the 13th."

"Yes, Doctor."

Tuesday, 13 January 1942 - Broadgate Hospital, Walkington, England.

When Leah awoke that morning, she felt agitated. She sensed what was coming and became restless. The nurses who had looked in on her worried and left. Then her door had opened, and four male attendants stood there. One for each arm and one for each foot.

Leah gritted her teeth. She wasn't going to give up without a fight. She kicked and punched and bit and screamed. Even if she couldn't win, she wasn't going to make it easy for them.

Doctor North observed the struggle.

"Perhaps we should suspend her treatments for a while," he mused.

Wednesday, 28 January 1942 - Broadgate Hospital, Walkington, England

When Leah awoke, it took her a few moments to realise that she was in an armchair in the Ward 5 day room. As her eyes came back into focus, she saw that someone sat in the armchair opposite. She rubbed her eyes and looked again. It was a woman, a woman who looked very much like Aida. Leah rubbed her eyes again. It *was* Aida.

"What are you doing here?" Leah asked.

"I guess I can't follow my own advice," said Aida. "Have they been giving you the treatment?"

Leah nodded.

"Me too. Still, it's better than the alternative." Aida nodded towards another patient who sat nearby. She had a shaved head and dark, hollow eyes.

"What happened to her?" Leah asked.

"Leucotomy."

"A what?"

"They push an ice pick into the eye socket, up into the brain and wiggle it about a bit. It makes people like that."

"Stop it." Leah looked at the woman sitting nearby, staring into the middle distance. Then she looked back at Aida, her eyes alert, darting backwards and forwards as usual. "How do you know all this?"

"I read an article in a magazine about a doctor in America who goes around sticking ice picks into patients' eyes."

"Stop it."

"Of course, they can remove part of the skull and go in that way."

"Stop it."

"Either way they're cutting up your brain."

Leah looked up and down the ward.

"Nurse! You!" Leah shouted at the nurse she spotted at the other end of the ward.

"Nurse! Nurse!"

The nurse sighed and began to make her way across the ward.

"What is it, Mrs Wooll," she shouted before she had even halved the distance between them.

"You have to move her," Leah shouted, pointing to Aida.

"Aida? Why?"

"She's too noisy."

The nurse laughed.

"Why? Mrs Wooll, the one making noise around here is you."

"You have to remove her."

"I have to do no such thing."

"But she's mad. Look at her. She's a gibbering idiot."

The nurse tried harder to suppress the next laugh.

"Do you have any idea why you are here?" the nurse asked Leah

"No, I have no idea why I am here," Leah mocked the tone of the nurse.

The nurse rolled her eyes and watched Leah, who appeared lost in her own thoughts for a moment.

"I know why I am here," said Leah at last.

"Why?"

"You are collecting blood from me."

"What?"

"You keep me here to collect my blood. That's why you put me to sleep."

"Put you to sleep?"

"Yes, you put those things on my head and put me to sleep, and while I am asleep you take my blood from me."

"Ah, the treatment."

Leah began to cry to herself, and the nurse moved closer, feeling sorry for her all of a sudden.

"The treatment is to make you better," said the nurse in a kinder tone.

Leah went silent and began to stare into the middle distance.

"What is it?" the nurse asked.

"I was thinking about my children," Leah wept.

The nurse didn't know what say, so just sat beside Leah and tried to offer a sympathetic smile.

"I cannot and will not stay here," Leah shouted, making Aida and the nurse jump.

Sunday, 8 February 1942 - Broadgate Hospital, Walkington, England

When the nurse asked Leah if she would be joining them at church that morning, Leah had to think about it for a moment before she said yes. She was attracted to any activity which involved her leaving the ward, with the obvious exception of her electroconvulsive shock treatments.

She wandered through the hospital's corridors following the last of the chronic patients, whom nurses were leading to the chapel like sheep. Leah had a plan, but she would have to be patient and put it into action at the right time.

She sat through the service, pretending to listen to the sermon and even pretending to sing at one point, but her mind was elsewhere - on her plan. She bided her time, and when the service was over, and patients began to be led back to the ward, Leah hung around at the back of the group. When she was confident she wouldn't be noticed, she slipped down a corridor which led off to the side and ran all the way to the door at the end, but it was locked.

She ran back to the main corridor and doubled back towards the chapel, turning down the next side corridor she came to. She ran to the door at the end, also locked. She tried all of the corridors she came to until she was back at the chapel, but someone had locked the door of the chapel as well. She must keep trying. She wouldn't let them cut her brain.

Undeterred, Leah ran all the way back to where she had split off from the rest of the group and continued until she found new corridors to try. She got as far as the locked door at the end of the first corridor when she discovered a group of male orderlies had cornered her. She knew her plan had failed.

Thursday, 19 February 1942 - Broadgate Hospital, Walkington, England

Leah was in a good mood and kept giggling to herself. She thought that if she was stuck in this place, then she might as well make the most of it.

"Did you hear about the time Hitler visited a lunatic asylum?" she shouted across the corridor to Aida, who sat in a chair opposite, as usual.

"What are you talking about?" the old woman shouted back.

"Hitler. He visited a lunatic asylum, and as he walked around the wards, the patients all gave him the salute. You know, the Nazi salute. You know, don't you?"

"I know what a Nazi salute looks like," said Aida. "What's your point?"

"As he passes down the line he comes across a man who isn't saluting. 'Why aren't you saluting like the others?' Hitler asks."

"Is this a joke?"

"'Mein Führer, I'm the nurse,' the man answers. 'I'm not crazy!'"

Leah laughed at her own joke. Aida stared at her.

"You're crazy," Aida said, and this made Leah laugh even more.

"You seem in a good mood," said Nurse Barton, taking a seat next to Leah.

"Yes," said Leah, still recovering from the effects of her joke. "Hey, I've got some gossip for you."

Nurse Barton looked interested.

"Did you know that Dr North is German?"

"Oh Leah, I thought you had some real gossip," said Nurse Barton, leaning back with disappointment.

"It's true. And he and the charge nurse spend their weekends together."

"Well, that might be true."

"You see her?" asked Leah, pointing to the old woman opposite.

"Aida? Yes, I see her."

"She's the father of my children."

Again, Nurse Barton had to stifle her urge to laugh.

"But Aida is a woman," Nurse Barton reasoned.

"No, she's not. They're all men in here. Why am I being kept with all the men?"

"They're all women."

"Look, she's coming now."

"Who?"

Nurse Barton turned to see the charge nurse coming down the corridor. Nurse Barton stood up in a hurry and so did Leah, running along the corridor, away from the Charge nurse towards the dormitory.

"What is Mrs Wooll doing?" the Charge Nurse asked.

"I don't know. She was in quite a good mood."

"Let's go and see," said the charge nurse, heading in the direction of the dormitory.

When she got there, she saw that Leah had climbed up onto her bed.

"What are you doing up there, Mrs Wooll? Come down at once."

As the charge nurse approached the bed, Leah leapt off it onto her shoulders, bringing her to the ground. A struggle ensued in which Leah tried to strangle the charge nurse and scratched her face.

It took four nurses to pull Leah off the charge nurse. They took her to the seclusion room.

The seclusion room had a thick door and walls to deaden sound. There was a peephole in one of the walls so that the staff could observe Leah at all times. There was a shutter covering the window, and the mattress cover and blanket were made of thick canvas. It smelt of stale urine, polish and straw.

Saturday, 14 March 1942 - Broadgate Hospital, Walkington, England

Leah sat in the seclusion room. They allowed her out for the nurses to bathe her while orderlies cleaned and made her bed.

The nurses gave her a bowl of porridge and two thick slices of bread and butter with an enamel mug of tea. Breakfast was her favourite meal of the day because it meant no treatment. Nevertheless, she still felt bitter at her incarceration.

She felt the sensation to go for a wee and contemplated calling for a nurse, but then thought it might be better to teach them a lesson and decided she would go on the floor.

"This'll show em," she said as she squatted, listening to the urine splash into the floor. "If they treat me like an animal, then I'll behave like one."

She heard a noise in the corridor and pressed her head against the door to listen. She could hear a nurse explaining to a doctor outside how someone had been 'wild' and 'unmanageable' that morning.

"She threatened to do in members of staff," said the nurse. "They are all afraid of her."

"We'll give her a shock treatment. A worse shock than she's ever had."

The door opened, and the doctor entered with two male attendants. Leah began screaming, and the attendants held her down while the doctor administered a sedative.

Her screaming diminished as the sedative began to work. The doctor examined her pupils.

"They are like points," he said, standing back to look at her. "She is very pale. Let's give her another treatment.

The attendants helped Leah into a wheelchair and pushed her to the treatment room where she lay quite limp and motionless during the preparation.

"Mrs Wooll, can you hear me?" asked the doctor as he placed the strap containing the electrodes in place. Leah did not answer. "Is there any discomfort, Mrs Wooll?"

No answer.

The doctor gave a signal, and the machine was switched on.

Sunday, 15 March 1942 - Broadgate Hospital, Walkington, England

Leah tore up her bedsheets and began stuffing them into her bedpan.

"Mrs Wooll, whatever are you doing?" asked a nurse, distressed to see Leah in such a mood.

"I'll do much worse than this if I'm ever interfered with again," Leah shouted.

She glared at the nurse and pointed.

"You! You are the father of my children!"

The nurse gave an involuntary squeal and left as quickly as she could to get help.

Leah could not now control her fear of the treatment. When she saw the nurses talking together, she knew they were talking about her. They were planning to murder her with electricity or send her to Hull Prison to be hanged. She would shout at the nurses to stop talking, or she would attack them because she knew they were hiding the truth from her and she had to know their plans. Otherwise, how was she supposed to defend herself?

Monday, 6th April 1942 - Broadgate Hospital, Walkington, England

From a distance, Doctor North and Doctor Baker observed Leah, who sat in one of the chairs in the corridor.

"Her convulsive treatment has been continued," said Doctor North. "She is, on the whole, manageable, but is quite deluded. For example, she is certain that the treatment is given to produce unconsciousness during which time blood is taken from her."

"She appears quieter," said Doctor Baker.

"Yes, she has been allowed up at her earnest request."

"And Mrs Benhope?"

"She's on her way to Sheffield. She should be back next week if all goes well."

"I hear Hartmann is going to start doing the operations at the infirmary."

"Let's hope so."

Monday, 1st June 1942 - Torun, Poland

"Oh, to be in England. Now that April's there. And whoever wakes in England. Sees, some morning, unaware. That the lowest boughs and the brushwood sheaf. Round the elm-tree bole are in tiny leaf. While the chaffinch sings on the orchard bough. In England - now!"

Jack looks at Fred, dumbstruck.

"You're not the only one who knows culture, you know," said Fred.

Fred had just received a parcel from home containing underclothes, socks, shirts, toiletries, and a toothbrush and toothpaste. All much-needed articles.

"Want to hear a joke one of the Poles told me?" asked Fred.

"Go on then."

"A Polish submarine captain is asked, 'You see in your periscope a German and a Soviet cruiser. Which one do you attack first?' 'Of course the German one' the Pole answers. Duty always comes before pleasure.'"

"Oh, I see," said Jack, not very amused. "Funnier if you're Polish. How about this?"

Fred waited for what he hoped would be a good one.

"How about some jokes about Italians?"

"Alright."

"What is the Italian battle flag?"

"Don't know."

"A white cross on a white background. What is the shortest book ever written?"

"Don't know."

"Italian War Heroes. What's got six reverse gears and one forward gear?"

"No, go on."

"An Italian tank. The forward gear is in case they get attacked from behind. What nation's soldiers have the most sunburnt armpits?"

"Italy's?"

"Correct."

Wednesday, 17 June 1942 - Broadgate Hospital, Walkington, England

Leah spotted Aida straight away when she entered the day room. The shaved head was what did it. Leah rushed over to her and crouched down in front of her, but the alert, darting eyes were gone, replaced with full staring spheres of nothingness.

"Aida. Aida! What happened?"

Leah tried shaking Aida, but still received no response, so she tried shaking her more.

"Mrs Wooll! Please leave Mrs Benhope alone," shouted the charge nurse as she headed towards Leah. "Stop interfering with the other patients."

"Stay where you are!" Leah shouted back. "Leave me alone."

"Mrs Wooll. You will have to be put into a side room if you cannot leave the other patients alone."

"What have you done?" Leah shouted back. "This man fathered my children."

"Right," said the charge nurse, turning on her heels to get help to have Leah taken to a side room.

*

Leah stared at the door as she squatted on her chamber pot. When she had finished, she carried the chamber pot over to the door and emptied the urine and faeces through the small crack between the door and the floor.

Leah laughed as she heard the disgusted commotion, which had ensued on the other side.

"Mrs Wooll? You will have to be taken for treatment," Leah heard the charge nurse shouting through the door.

When the charge nurse opened the door, Leah launched herself at the woman, punching her in the face.

Two male attendants pulled Leah off the nurse and pinned her to the bed. The nurse's lip was bleeding, and two small lumps were beginning to appear on her forehead.

"Are you not ashamed of yourself, Mrs Wooll?" said Doctor North, entering the room and observing the scene.

"I'll do much worse," shouted Leah. "But I'll be slyer about it next time."

Friday, 17 July 1942 - Broadgate Hospital, Walkington, England

"Here is your food," said the nurse, placing a tray in front of Leah who, despite her heavy sedation, was as truculent as ever.

"I won't eat it," said Leah.

"Why ever not?"

"It is all poisoned by the cook."

Leah sniffed the plate in front of her.

"I can smell the poison on it."

Leah shrieked, holding her nose in disgust at the food.

"It's not poisoned, Mrs Wooll."

"It is. Do you know they took my children away?"

"I believe your children are living here in Beverley, are they not?"

"I had two sets of twins and one of each was stolen from me."

Leah looked around the ward and pointed to Mary Hall, eating opposite.

"He is the father of my children," Leah pointed her finger in accusation.

"Mrs Hall?" exclaimed the nurse with surprise. "Why, Mrs Wooll, I thought you said that Aida had fathered your children."

"This food is poisoned," Leah pushed her plate away.

"It's not poisoned, Mrs Wooll. You must eat something. You've already lost a stone in weight."

Leah leaned towards the nurse as of about to tell her a big secret.

"In my sleep, I am overcome by fumes."

The nurse looked at Leah in a non-committal way.

"There is a plot to kill and eat me."

"Mrs Wooll!" the nurse was unable to disguise her amusement any longer.

"You think it's funny?" Leah shouted, "I'll show you what's funny."

Leah turned on the nurse, sending the plate flying, which shattered on the floor. She began attacking her, but the nurse was able to free herself and run down the ward to fetch help.

Tuesday, 1st September 1942 - Torun, Poland

Once the regular POWs had left on their various work parties, the guards kept Fred, Jack, and the rest of the NCOs in the compound for the commandant to address them.

The guards left them standing for some hours, and the weather was cold. The men were an odd assortment. Some had greatcoats, some not. Some wore boots. Others wore clogs. There was a smattering of military headgear but many wore balaclavas or scarves, and there was even the odd pair of earmuffs.

The camp commandant approached them.

"You can all go to the special camp for non-commissioned officers if you wish, but there are no lights, no games, and bad food with lots of barbed wire to look at."

"It'll be a change of scenery anyway. Let's go!" Jack shouted.

"You will not find them as forgiving as we are," warned the commandant, but it was too late. The NCOs were already committed to the idea.

After keeping the NCOs on parade for one more hour, the commandant realised he would not be able to change their minds and, turning to the German officer behind him, told him to dismiss the men.

The guards ordered them to gather their belongings and be prepared to move in two days' time.

Wednesday, 2nd September 1942 - Broadgate Hospital, Walkington, England

"No. It's poisoned," Leah shrieked as she held her nose while she pushed her plate away with the other.

"But Mrs Wooll, you must eat," pleaded the nurse. "You are losing so much weight missing all these meals."

"Pah," Leah scoffed.

"Now Mrs Wooll. There are others worse off on the other side of the world who would be grateful for this food."

"Give it to them then. Poison them. The poor buggers."

Monday, 21st September 1942 - Stalag 383, Hohenfels, Germany

Fred couldn't remember whether it had been three or four days they had spent in the cattle trucks on the railway. They had been only able to get a breath of fresh air each day when they made tea by getting hot water from the engine driver. Apart from a loaf of bread they had given him on leaving Torun, the tea had been the only other thing to pass his lips in that time.

The guards took them off the train at a station called Regensberg, where trucks were waiting to meet them. The trucks took them to a camp situated in a wooded valley high in the hills. As they pulled up to the gates, Fred noticed it was signposted as Oflag IIIC, and realised the Germans must have used it as an officers camp at some time.

The guards made the men line up outside the cookhouse, then the guards called their names and POW numbers, and they were told to which hut they had been allocated.

As Fred and Jack entered their allocated hut, they bumped into a POW leaving.

"George Millar," the POW said, stretching out his hand for Fred and Jack to shake.

"Frank Taylor at your service," said another POW who appeared in the doorway to the hut. He also held out his hand to the new arrivals. As he did, a cat brushed past him. "And that's Cat, the hut cat. God knows what he hangs around for. There's no food."

"Fred Wooll," said Fred, taking Frank's hand and shaking it. "This is Jack." Jack shook Frank's hand.

"Frank is the camp magician," said George. "He's been teaching us a bit of escapology."

"Escapology?" Fred wondered if he would be living with the camp's escape committee.

Jack perked up.

"They're coming," said Chuck rushing into the hut.

"Who's coming?" asked Fred.

"The goons," said George. "They're coming to put handcuffs on us."

"What?" said Jack.

"Don't worry," said George. "It's all Hitler's idea. It's his idea for revenge for the raid on Dieppe."

"What do you mean?" asked Fred.

"Well, the German prisoners were tied up on the beaches, so Hitler has sent us handcuffs so that we can be handcuffed for twelve hours a day."

George led him into the hut.

"Are you serious?" asked Fred, wondering why George had told him not to worry.

"They are not very good handcuffs. Frank was telling us how easy they are to pick."

"I hope you're right," said Fred.

Several German guards entered the hut, and the POWs greeted them with smiles.

The guards went around the men and, one by one, began attaching the handcuffs - first Joe, then Bob, then Chuck, then George, but before they reached Fred, Joe's handcuffs had fallen to the floor.

"Oh look, you haven't put them on properly," said Joe with mock sincerity.

The Germans returned to reattach Joe's handcuffs when Bob's fell to the floor.

"Look, mine weren't done up either," said Bob.

Then Chuck's and George's cuffs fell to the floor as well.

"Was geht hier vor sich?" demanded one of the guards.

They reattached Joe's cuffs, which fell to the floor before they had reattached Bob's.

"Was machst du gerade?" demanded the guard, but before the POWs had a chance to answer, another guard had entered the hut.

"Sie wissen, wie man aus ihnen herauskommt," the guard said in a panic.

"Was?" the senior guard didn't seem to believe what he was being told, but then looked at the handcuffs on the floor, then back at the prisoners. "We'll be back."

Once the guards were out of the hut, the POWs burst out laughing.

"Is it always like this?" asked Fred.

"No," said George. "You've caught us on a good day."

Fred looked around his new home. Although the hut was wooden, asbestos sheeting lined the walls. There were seven double-tiered beds, a stove, a table and two trestles. On the table stood a jug.

Monday, 28 December 1942 - Broadgate Hospital, Walkington, England

"Not again," Nurse Barton sighed on seeing that Leah had emptied the contents of her chamber pot on the floor.

Leah sat, twisting and rubbing her fingers as she watched the nurse.

"I don't know why I am here," said Leah. "Water poured out of the kettle would cure me."

Nurse Barton reminded herself that in mental health care, there were no obvious wounds, which could be dressed with clean white bandages. She had to bring the bandages herself to bind wounds that could not be seen or measured, but she got so tired, and there were so many patients and so much to do, and sometimes she felt the urge to shout at or push or hit them, and this made her feel guilty on top of everything else.

"You need to be taught a lesson. That's what you need." Nurse Barton was surprised at hearing her own words. Words which would have seemed much more at home in the mouth of the charge nurse.

Sunday, 3ʳᵈ January 1943 - Broadgate Hospital, Walkington, England

It was visiting day. The nurses told Leah to change out of the dirty torn dress she usually wore, and they gave her one of the nicer dresses, saved for visiting times. The nurses took out of storage a pair of socks, given by Leah's mother-in-law, and gave them to her to wear. The nurses took patients unlikely to receive visitors off to their rooms, out of the way.

"We keep these so you will be nice for your visitors," Nurse Barton explained. "You see, we look after you, don't we? Imagine if your visitors saw the mess you make of yourself the rest of the time."

Leah accepted all the procedures with passivity. She had developed fatigue because of her treatments, which left her indifferent and clouded all her activities. Perhaps in a day or a week or two, the fog would lift, but for the moment, she lived life with a dullness in which she accepted all that the nurses put in her path. Except for the food. The food was poisoned.

*

"This is a good day to see her," said the charge nurse to Fred's mother, Lizzie. "She seems to have recovered well from her treatment."

Lizzie followed the nurse, dragging a very nervous Beattie along behind her. With wide eyes, young Beattie observed her surroundings.

The nurse led Lizzie and Beattie to a room where Leah sat on a bed. Lizzie thanked the nurse and sat in a chair opposite the bed.

Leah smiled at Beattie and patted the mattress beside her. Lizzie urged Beattie to go and sit on the bed next to her mother, but Beattie did not want to leave the safety of her grandmother to sit next to this strange woman. Lizzie took Beattie over to sit on the bed next to her mother. Beattie looked very uncomfortable.

It shocked Lizzie how much weight her daughter-in-law had lost.

"Are they feeding you well?" Lizzie asked.

"The food is poison," said Leah.

Lizzie took this to mean that it did not taste very nice.

*

FRED & LEAH: A TRUE LIFE SECOND WORLD WAR DRAMA
OF LOVE, LOSS AND CAPTIVITY.

213

Before they left, Doctor North asked for a word with Lizzie. He described a new treatment, which might make a difference to Leah's disruptive behaviour.

"We call it a leucotomy," explained the doctor. "It can have very beneficial results. It works by separating the frontal lobe from the rest of the brain, thereby eliminating the disruptive emotions."

"I'm not sure," said Lizzie. "I don't like the idea of meddling with her brain. As you know, her husband, my son, is a POW."

The doctor gave a nod of understanding.

"I would have to seek his views on the matter," Lizzie continued. "Before making any rash decisions."

"I understand. Well, in the meantime we will continue her treatment, but I do feel a leucotomy could be the answer in this case."

Friday, 19 March 1943 - Broadgate Hospital, Walkington, England

Leah hid behind the door of the side room in which the nurses had confined her for what they had described as disruptive behaviour. She hated the nurses. Some had been kind, but most were mean. They had even ground down the kind ones with years of overwork and difficult conditions until they too were indistinguishable from the others. Leah couldn't tell the nurses apart. They were all the same as far as she was concerned. If a nurse slighted her, Leah would not think twice about exacting her revenge on another nurse. They all deserved it.

Leah bided her time, waiting for a nurse to open the door.

When a nurse did arrive, Leah leapt upon her tearing, scratching and scrapping.

The other nurses in the vicinity ran to pull Leah away from the nurse.

"I would have killed her," screamed Leah. "If there hadn't been so many people about."

"It's strange, she has been somewhat quieter," the charge nurse commented to Doctor North who had just arrived on the scene by pure chance. He was rarely in Ward 5, preferring to spend his time with patients who stood a greater chance of rehabilitation.

"Yes," said the Doctor. "You told me her impulsive violence has been in abeyance of late. Also, she seems to be continuing to lose weight. How much does she weigh now?"

"Six stone, Doctor. She's lost another stone. Although incidents have been less frequent, she can be violent and compulsive, and since she mistakes identities, no nurse or patient is safe alone with her. She is, apart from her weight loss, in good physical health."

"Sometimes it feels like we can do nothing for them. I do think leucotomy could be the answer," said Doctor North. "Let's continue the treatment anyway."

Friday, 14 May 1943 - Hohenfels, Germany

"You have to see this," said Fred, walking into the hut carrying a book about horse racing.

"I never was a racing man," said George.

"Oh no?" said Fred, approaching his bed. "Then how about now?"

Fred flicked open the book to reveal a miniature radio. George sat up.

"Jesus!" said George. "Don't let Jerry catch you with that."

"It has a small glass earpiece, which I can conceal, so I can listen to the radio and it looks like I'm reading a book."

George checked the door for the presence of any guards.

"Where did you get it?" he asked. "At one of the marts? What did it cost you?"

"Never mind where I got it," said Fred. "From now on, I am the news."

He climbed up into his bunk, arranged the wires so a casual observer would not spot them, and started listening to the radio as if he was reading the book. Cat jumped up to investigate.

"It's quiz time on Ack Ack Beer Beer," he informed his enrapt audience. "Oh no, it's just finished. Now it's the news."

The hut waited.

"It's the third anniversary of the home guard."

"How nice for them," said Bob. "Did they have a cake?"

"Churchill is making a speech about it," Fred prepared himself to imitate Churchill. "I have felt for some time that a tribute should be paid, through-out Great Britain and in Ulster..."

A German guard entering the hut interrupted Fred. It was a guard they called 'the snoop'. He spoke English and wandered the camp looking for plots and misdemeanours.

"But of course, Beverley racecourse is a right-handed flat racing course, over a mile," Fred continues without missing a beat.

"Ah, you English are always talking about betting on horses," commented the German in his usual slimy tone. "Now, for us Germans, we regard the horse as a mode of transportation. We breed horses so that they become the finest examples of their species. In the same way that humans can be bred to create the finest specimens of their kind."

The German moved closer to Fred's bunk. Fred had frozen stiff and was nodding at the Nazi.

"Well that may be true," said Bob as loudly as possible to try to distract the German from Fred. "But take Chuck as an example here. He is the product of years of the finest breeding in his community, and look at him."

"Eh?" said Chuck, slow to catch on. "Oh, yes. Look at me."

"My point," said the German turning towards them. "Here we have an excellent example ..."

Chuck fluffed up like a peacock.

"... which illustrates what happens when the wrong specimens are allowed to breed together."

Chuck was deflated.

The air raid siren sounded. The inhabitants of the hut, except the guard, breathed a collective sigh of relief.

"Excuse me," said the German as the guards extinguished the camp lights. "I must go and watch your friends planes being shot down over Munich."

Fred watched as the German left the hut.

"Thank God for the RAF," he said when the snoop had gone.

Monday, 9 August 1943 - Broadgate Hospital, Walkington, England

"What did you say?" Leah asked the voice. She looked around, trying to work out where the voice was coming from. "Where are you?"

"Up here," said the voice.

Leah looked up and spotted a small hole in the ceiling

"You think this is a ceiling, don't you?" said the voice. "It is not a ceiling but a cover which can be removed, so that we can spy on you."

"Who are you?"

"That's not important. What is important is the information I am about to give you."

"What information?"

"Aida is an old man."

"I knew that already," said Leah.

"He is part of the conspiracy to keep you here."

Leah mulled over this new insight.

"Your husband is dead, Leah."

"No, he's not. He's a prisoner of war."

"He is dead, Leah."

"How do you know?"

"We know."

"They would have told me."

The voice laughed.

"They are playing with you, Leah. They brought your sister here."

"My sister?"

"She had a child with her."

"A child? Yes, yes. I remember."

"That was your child, Leah."

Leah tried to picture the child.

"They are out to get you, Leah. You must defend yourself."

The door opened, and a nurse appeared with an orderly. Leah leapt from her bed and began attacking the surprised nurse.

"You were the one who tried to poison me yesterday," shouted Leah.

"I wasn't working yesterday," reasoned the nurse, as she tried to defend herself while the orderly struggled to pull Leah off her.

Thursday, 5th August 1943 - Stalag 383, Hohenfels, Germany

When they heard the first whistle, Fred and Jack grabbed their suitcases and marched through the camp. They passed Napoleon staring through the wire. A bit further on, they passed a cock-hatted Nelson peering through a telescope. A moment later, bands of painted Red Indians went whooping past. More whistles, a bit louder. Then a man riding an invisible bicycle and a man walking an invisible dog. Around the corner, they encountered a group of POWs playing marbles on the dry earth, and coming toward them, a group marching to a Chinese band. More whistles—they were getting close. After they had passed the band, they noticed a group staring up at a watchtower, viewed by two bemused sentries. On the sports ground, they could see a football game being played with no ball.

They were now approaching their destination, a row of huts near the fence. And just in time.

"Have your tickets ready," a voice warned them, as they got nearer. "The train is about to leave for England."

They handed their tickets over at the barrier and rushed into the hut where they got a seat by the window. They craned their necks out of the window as smoke billowed out the chimney.

"Goodbye," they shouted to those on the 'platform'. "See you in Blighty."

"Hurry, hurry, the train is leaving," the 'guards' and 'porters' shouted as late arrivals rushed through the barrier into the 'train'.

A POW dressed as a railway guard waved a red flag.

"The platform is closed," shouted the 'guard'.

"Bye, bye." Fred and Jack shouted at those left on the 'platform'. "We'll send you a postcard from England."

"The next train to England will leave at five o'clock." announced the 'guard' and everybody left the 'train' and dispersed around the camp leaving the sentries on the watchtowers and along the fence watching in bewilderment.

On their way back to the hut, Joe met Fred and Jack.

"The whole camp has gone bloody mad," said Joe. "What the hell is going on?"

"It's just to wind up the goons," said Fred.

"It's winding me up," said Joe. "Whose idea was this?"

Fred looked at Jack. Jack shrugged. Cat passed them, walking in the opposite direction, nonplussed by the shenanigans

"I know how it started," Fred remembered. "Some blokes were playing with a kite on the sports ground. And the sentry looks at them like they're a pair of bloody kids, so they start behaving like kids, and before you know it there's a whole bunch of them singing ring a ring a roses. It confused the guards so much they decided to make a week of it."

"Well it seems bloody daft to me," said Joe.

"Exactly," said Jack.

Thursday, 9th September 1943 - Stalag 383, Hohenfels, Germany

Fred, Jack, and George entered the hut to discover Chuck tearing up letters and stuffing them in the stove.

"What happened?" asked Fred.

"I don't know," said Bob, "He's been in a bad mood for a while, as you know."

"We were just sitting reading, he was on his bunk staring into space when he gets up shouting 'bitch bitch bitch' and tearing up the letters."

"What is it, Chuck?" asked George, convincing him to sit on one of the trestles, which Cat vacated sharpish to avoid this strange ranting and raving individual.

"It's Jean," he blubbed. "She met a Yank. She's having his baby."

The others exchanged sympathetic glances.

"Women are cunts, I hate them." he burst out.

"You and me both, pal," said Joe. "My wife said she 'could no longer be tied to a coward' so she`s found 'a real man'. Yeah, a real man with a reserved occupation. You know what I did?"

Chuck shrugged.

"I cut off her allowance. This so-called 'real man' left her, and I started getting these awkward apologies."

"I got a letter as well," admitted George. "She said she'd been to a dance. That it would never happen again."

George reached into his pocket and pulled out a photograph of his wife holding a newborn baby.

"We've called him Richard," George swelled with pride. "We could never have any of our own."

"Bloody hell, mate, you're more forgiving than I ever could be," marvelled Bob. "What about you, Fred?"

Fred thought about the letter that he had received suggesting that he allow the medics to slice into Leah's brain.

"I thought we were going to the Palais tonight for the dance?" said Fred, changing the subject.

"Sure," said Bob. "Come on, Chuck. It'll do you a bit of good. What do you say?"

FRED & LEAH: A TRUE LIFE SECOND WORLD WAR DRAMA OF LOVE, LOSS AND CAPTIVITY.

221

"Ah well, it's a grand life if you don't weaken," said Chuck, and he began to smarten himself up along with the others.

Once they were all ready, wearing their best, hair greased back, they made their way up to the big hut they called the Palais. At one end, on a platform, was Dennis Whiteley's dance band, wearing khaki trousers and blue shirts. POWs dancing the quickstep. In between the Air Force, the Navy, the kilted Scots, Aussies in their tunics, Kiwis, Canadians, Cypriots and Palestinians were the 'girls'. POWs wearing dazzling evening gowns, dainty shoes, and hairstyles tied up with headscarves.

The quickstep ended and the night's MC announced a tango. Dennis and his band slid into *Jealous* and most of the floor cleared except the most expert dancers and the 'girls'.

"Who's the piece in the blue satin," asked Bob.

"Dunno," said George. "Look at Ginger treading on the blonde's dress."

"Wig or not, it's pretty marvellous," said Bob.

"That Spanish turnout's wearing the pansy scarf my aunt gave me," said Joe. "Must have bought it on the Mart. Paint, powder, lipstick - beats me where they get it all."

"Wonder what real girls would think of this?" Fred mused.

Tuesday, 6th June 1944 - Hohenfels, Germany

"Listen to this," said Fred, sitting up on his bunk. "They're saying on the radio that British, Canadian, and American armies have invaded France."

"How much longer can the goons hold out?" asked Jack.

Within minutes, the Germans were announcing their own news over the tannoys.

"The Allied forces have invaded Northern France. The invasion has been contained. The Allied forces have suffered considerable losses."

"I don't believe it," said Chuck.

"Neither do I," said Jack. "The question now is how long?"

"And what will happen to us?" said Chuck. "What are they saying, Fred?"

"I don't know. It all sounds like gibberish to me. Crocodiles, boom tanks, bridge tanks, flail tank landing craft. I don't know what any of this stuff is."

"Did you hear the one about the man who walks into the records office and asks to change his name?" asked Jack.

"Is this one of Barnett's?" asked Fred.

"Who is Barnett?" asked George.

"A fusilier of ours," said Fred. "We lost him in France."

"Do you want to hear this joke or not?"

"Go on," said Fred.

"The clerk is not keen on helping the man, but asks the man's name, and the man replies 'My name is Adolf Stinkfoot.' The clerk is sympathetic and decides to allow the man to change his unfortunate name. 'What do you want to change it to?' asks the clerk. The man replies 'Maurice Stinkfoot.'"

Cat raised his head as if to indicate the laughter was disturbing him and then returned to his slumber.

Thursday, 31 August 1944 - Broadgate Hospital, Walkington, England

Leah sat in front of Doctor North. She hardly saw him at all these days and had to remind herself who he was at first. Doctor North spent less and less time in Ward 5 with the disturbed incurables. He decided instead to devote his time to those he felt stood more chance of reintegration into society.

"You look a little pale, Mrs Wooll, but otherwise you seem to be in good health. Seven stone four. I understand that you are still being kept in seclusion because of your ..." he consulted his notes. "... dirty and destructive behaviour. Is there anything you would like to say to me, Mrs Wooll?"

Leah stared at the doctor but remained silent.

"The doctor is a very busy man," warned the charge nurse. "He cannot have his time wasted by the likes of you."

"I'll leave you in peace," the doctor told Leah, thanking the nurse as he left the room and headed straight for the nurse's station where his colleague, Doctor Baker, had already finished his allocation of annual medical inspections and was waiting.

"Well, there are no signs of any disease or mental degeneration. She looks rested. On examination, she is clean. Otherwise, no change. Continue the treatment. I'll see whether I can get a positive answer from her family regarding the leucotomy. Otherwise, I fear she will be here among the chronics for the rest of her life."

"She's committed. Can you not just go ahead with the operation anyway?" said Dr Baker.

"I could. However, in my experience, it is always best if the family feels we have consulted them on such matters. Avoids any unnecessary unpleasantness later on."

Monday, 11th September 1944 - Hohenfels, Germany

"I heard that the goons are coming to search for unpierced tins," said Chuck bursting into the hut from the misty evening.

"I thought they were bluffing," said Fred.

"They're coming with sacks to put the tins in," said Chuck in a panic.

"Oh Jesus, we'd better be quick," said Joe stabbing a tin of margarine which sent Cat running out of the door.

"What are you doing?" asked Fred.

"Margarine will last for weeks," said Joe. "Come on, we've got to hide the rest."

Fred looked at his collection of tins. Meat, fish, and vegetables, all stored from Red Cross parcels.

"Mattresses are no good, they're ripping them open," said Jack, coming in the door.

Fred looked around the hut.

"Stovepipes are no good, they're pulling them down wholesale," Jack added.

Fred stuffed his tins into a small mailbag.

"Here you go, Fred," said Joe and George, adding theirs to the collection. "Go and find somewhere to hide them."

As he walked past the huts, Fred could see shadowy figures laden like Father Christmas, sneaking between huts. He could see the guards ahead shouting at prisoners dodging down alleys between huts. Fred ducked into a latrine, which was already full of other non-customers resting their well-filled sacks.

Fred headed for the hut of Frank Taylor, the camp magician, whom he happened to know was storing tins in a table with a false top.

"Frank, can you store our tins in your table? The Jerries are all over the camp looking for unpierced cans. They think we're going to store them up for an escape or something."

"Not today, Fred," said Frank. "We're not taking risks with the table. We've hidden ours elsewhere, but I can put yours with them if you want."

"Thanks, Frank," said Fred, and handed over the bag of tins.

Friday, 29th December 1944 - Hohenfels, Germany

Fred looked through the frost-smeared window at the snow-clad pines on the valley slopes, past the silhouettes of the watchtowers and the double barbed wire fence. He felt like he was living in a frozen swamp, miles from anywhere. Outside he could see one of the goons, 'Toadstool,' on guard. His sentry's topcoat, which went over his greatcoat, made him look like a tent. The outer pair of boots he wore over the first pair looked like barges. Fred watched him staring through the wire and imagined he must be frozen, bored, and maybe even a little envious of the POWs in the huts.

Fred wore a balaclava, mittens, and greatcoat. His legs in his old pants were stuck in his kit bag. He had two poor excuses for blankets wrapped around him and just removed his clogs before he went to bed. He suspected he was colder than 'Toadstool' and would have given anything for the sentry's topcoat.

Fred could see ice on the asbestos coating of the walls and on the roof. Icicles hung from the roof beams, and cakes of ice and snow littered the floor. Shirts and pants, frozen stiff, were suspended from lines across the hut. He could see the blue skullcap stitched from socks covering the head of George in the next bunk - his ears looked as blue as his cap. Cat had curled up at his feet.

The camp had reached a low ebb. There hadn't been any parcels, there was no fuel, the organised activities had ground to a halt. The school was a barrack room, the Palais a hospital, the sports ground was closed and the paths unwalkable. Fred just killed time waiting for the next bowl of soup. He felt as if he had been there all his life and the world outside was just a myth. There were even icicles on the stovepipe of the stove, which sat in the middle of the room next to the table and forms.

"Have you swept?" Fred asked Chuck Webb, whose turn it was to be the room orderly. He knew that there was nothing much Chuck could do to stop the inhabitants of the hut from treading the dirt in, but he had to complain about Chuck to ward off complaints about himself. Chuck was dressed head to toe in wolf skin and moaning about the habits of his thirteen roommates after whom he was attempting to clean up. He made the wolf skin for a production of Little Red Riding Hood and decided to wear it as a boudoir suit.

"Got a bit of toilet paper, Fred?" Chuck asked. "I found a couple of bumpers when I swept under my bed but I've no papers for a fag."

"Don't give us that about sweeping under the bed," said Fred, handing Chuck his tin.

"Just put a spot of mint tea in there, and I'll have a smoke myself."

Complaining, Chuck put into the tin some of the twigs and leaves the Germans doled out as tea, and Fred used a razor blade to cut the toilet paper and rolled a cigarette for himself.

"Got a light, Fred?" Chuck asked, knowing he hadn't. He looked at Bob, whom he knew did.

Bob sighed.

"One of these days," he said. "One of you jokers will get a lighter of your own, and then I will go nuts and scream. That's the fourteenth light I've handed out this morning. George has loads of fags. Why doesn't he swap them for a lighter?"

"Because I swapped my lighter for the fags," said George without moving an inch.

"This is terrible," said Chuck taking a drag on his homemade cigarette. "It tastes like fertiliser."

"Better than spud peelings, but not as good as tea leaves," said Fred, taking a drag.

"It's better as a smoke than a drink," admitted Chuck. "You don't have to get up ten times in the night if you've only smoked the stuff."

"Well?" A voice came from George's motionless body.

"Well what?" asked Fred.

"You know bloody well what," said George.

"But George, there's no water, and the tea leaves have been used three times. Anyway, they're frozen and..."

"There's plenty of snow out there, isn't there?" George interrupted. "Where do you think you are? The Ritz?"

Fred did not answer.

"OK," said George at last. "Muggins here will make it."

George dragged himself out of bed, slipped his feet into a pair of clogs made from Klim tins, picked up a jug also made from Klim tins, and stomped

out of the hut to scoop virgin snow from the piles by the wire, watched all
the while by 'Toadstool'.

"Ah well, it's a grand life if you don't weaken," said Chuck.

"I have to do all the bloody cooking around here," complained George
as he trudged back in, but Fred knew he would be upset if any of the others
tried to help.

Fred became aware of an annoying sound and then realised Chuck had
started practising Spanish again.

"Is that lingo hard to talk, Chuck?" asked Bob. "It's bloody hard to listen
to."

The door swung open, ruining any possibility of an argument. Joe
trudged in, bringing new drifts of snow.

"Another bloke's blacked out by the latrine," Joe announced. "They're
carrying him back to his hut. And there's two up, let's hope they don't bomb
our bloody parcels."

Fred looked out the windows and saw that Joe was right. Two sentries
atop every post, a sure sign an air raid was on its way.

"Well, what about it?" asked George.

"What about what?" said Fred.

"Fuel," said George. "It's going to take a helluva lot of something to make
a brew up."

"We've got a parcel lid left," said Fred. "Where the hell would I get fuel
from?"

"We need the parcel lid to collect the swede peelings," said George.
"Otherwise, we'll have damn all for grub tonight. I just need some of your
toilet paper and a bed board."

"Burn bed boards, my foot," said Joe settling on his bunk below Fred.
"One more board from that bed and it'll be me Fred is crashing through on."

"Well, there's nothing for it," said George. "We'll have to burn some more
of the hut and damn the consequences."

Fred knew they weren't as bad as some of the other huts, which had already burnt their forms and table legs, suspending their table from the ceiling with ropes. He watched as Bob and George unbolted a supporting beam,
leaving the roof sagging a little. Before long, they had sawed it into pieces
with a forbidden saw they had constructed from an old spring bed stay.

"Got a light?" George asked Bob, who sighed and produced his lighter together with a couple of pages of *Mein Kampf* saved for lighting fires.

"Take the perishing fire outside. I'm not handing out lights all day to be smoked and stunk to death in my own bed."

George followed Bob's advice and carried the portable stove out to the vestibule, complaining all the time about how Fred and Joe did nothing but recline in their bunks.

"I'll have you know I teach English down at the schoolroom," Fred shouted after George. "I've got a certificate for my long service."

"We could burn that," George shouted back.

"I hope it rots your guts," he said handing them their tea when it was ready.

"Good old George," said Joe. "Thank goodness we've got a cook in the family."

"Rations up, sixteen, get your Uncle Ned," a cockney voice was shouting from outside.

Chuck collected the bread and Bob collected the spuds. George, Joe, and Fred arranged the bowls made from biscuit tins on the table. Chuck cut the bread with remarkable precision, while Bob divided the spuds into fourteen lots, as even as he could make them. Chuck put a piece of bread with each of the spuds and Bob got his playing cards, two sets of fourteen. He placed one set face up, on each of the ration piles and shuffled and cut the other. Going around the room by the order of beds, Bob called out each man's name and turned up a card from the shuffled set for each name, thus allocating which ration that man should get.

"Joe, ace of spades. Fred, eight of spades."

Fred jumped down from his bunk.

"Well, would you Adam and Eve it," said George with sarcasm. "It can move."

Before the cookhouse called that the soup was ready, a siren wailed, meaning that a raid was on its way and curtailing all movement, delaying the arrival of the soup. While he waited, Fred looked at his ration. A slice of bread, about an inch thick. Five spuds, two the size of walnuts, one as big as an egg, and two of fairish size but foul appearance. One of the foul-looking potatoes was rotten to the core, but the other had edible portions. He sat and contemplated whether to eat his bread and spuds then or wait for the soup. If he ate it, then the sight of men who had waited eating theirs later would torture him. If he didn't eat it then, he would be able to think of nothing else until he did eat them.

"Will someone look after my bread till six so I don't eat it?" asked Chuck.

"Yes, I will," said almost the entire hut in unison.

"Don't bother," said Chuck, deciding to stuff his bread into his mouth as soon as possible.

They heard the flying fortresses pass overhead and not long after there was movement in the camp and George had fetched the soup.

"Well, what about it?" George asked Fred.

"What about what?" said Fred.

"What about grub, of course. What are you going to do?"

"I'm going to eat my spuds with my soup. George, and save my bread for tonight."

"No, you bloody well aren't," said George. "I've got swede peelings for supper. What did I tell you about that parcel lid?"

"George," said Fred. "You are a prince above all muckers. The chef above all chefs."

Tuesday, 2nd January 1945 - Hohenfels, Germany

"Listen to that," said Jack, as huge fleets of allied planes passed overhead.

"The tide of the war seemed to have turned," said Joe.

"Ah well, it's a grand life if you don't weaken," said Chuck.

"The trouble is that with every bomb the Allies drop, the chance of food reaching us gets smaller," said George.

"Where are those Red Cross parcels?" asked Bob.

"Stop talking about bloody parcels, will you? It's driving me mad," said Joe. "We haven't had any for six months. They're not coming."

"I won't have anyone bad mouthing the Red Cross," said Bob.

"No one's bad mouthing the Red Cross," Fred jumped in. "But the truth is that the allies are making it more and more difficult for anyone to get anything through to anywhere."

"Why don't we volunteer to work for the goons? They'd have to feed us then," said Chuck to general sounds of derision. "Why not? What's wrong with farm work? It won't save the Nazis now, but it might save some of us. There's no bigger fool than a needless martyr."

"I'd sooner starve to death than work for the enemy," said Bob.

"You'd sooner starve to death than work for anybody," said George.

Fred laughed along with the others, but it was a hollow laugh. The guards had cancelled roll call because too many men had been collapsing, making the counting all but impossible. He looked around the hut at the men, how skinny they looked in their ill-fitting clothing.

"We should all fight our way out of this bloody place," said Joe. "The allies could drop us supplies and arms by parachute. Look at the trenches they are building around the camp. We should go now before their defences get stronger and we get weaker."

The rest of the men ignored him.

"It's no good," said George. "We'll have to eat Cat."

Friday, 19 January 1945 - Stalag 383, Hohenfels, Germany

Fred listened to the men around him grumbling that the guards had called them for roll call. He looked at the six thousand prisoners gathered within the perimeter fence of the parade ground.

"Where are the bloody postern guards to count us?" complained Joe.

"Ah well, it's a grand life if you don't weaken," said Chuck.

"They're shutting us in," said Fred as he noticed the guards locking the gates behind the prisoners.

"I heard that the Jerry strong points around the perimeter have been completed and are manned," said Joe.

No sooner had he finished talking than a company of guards Fred and his fellow POWs had never seen before surrounded the parade ground. Fred also noticed that the sentries in the watchtowers were more evident than usual and the spouts of their Spandau machine guns prominent. The feeling among the men was that the metal-helmeted Germans did not look as though they were joking. The men were careful not to display any signs of fear, and after a while, the usual posterns arrived and carried out the count.

On the way back to the hut, Fred collapsed.

*

Fred awoke to find himself in a bed in the hospital hut. It was the same hut which they used to call the Palais, where they had enjoyed so many dances and Fred had participated in many theatrical productions.

"Well, you are malnourished, that goes without saying," said the medical officer. "You've also got a double hernia which needs to be treated, and we can't do that here. I'm going to put in a request to the Commandant to have you taken into Regensburg and have them operate on it at the hospital there."

Tuesday, 23rd January 1945 - Regensburg, Germany

There was no warning before the raid began. Fred and his guard had no time to get back to the hospital or to shelter before the bombs started to fall. One landed so close that it threw Fred face down onto the ground. Shrapnel was raining down around him.

When he gathered his wits, he looked around and saw the guard lying on the ground a few feet away, a shard of shrapnel protruding from the back of his neck. Fred went over and checked for signs of life, but the guard was dead. Fred could see the other end of the V-shaped piece of shrapnel sticking up into the air where the guard's Adam's Apple should be.

What few people there were on the street were running away in panic. No one was paying attention to Fred. He sat on the kerb. Bombs were still falling, but they were landing further and further away. Fred was alone, unguarded, outside the camp. He contemplated his options. He could try to escape, but he was wearing a British Army uniform, he was malnourished, and he found walking a struggle, let alone fleeing. He considered where he could go. If he changed out of his uniform and the Germans caught him, they would shoot him as a spy. If he went anywhere in his uniform, he would be spotted. With no papers, he could not get anywhere by train. In his present condition, he couldn't walk across the country to Switzerland. The Germans, miserable about the turn in the tide of the war, might enjoy shooting an escaped POW. The alternative was no better, to find some German soldiers, try to explain what had happened, and turn himself in. Even if they didn't shoot him on the spot in revenge for what the RAF and Americans had just done to their town, he would, at best, be taken back to the camp where he might well die of hunger or freeze to death before the allied forces arrived. Neither option seemed appealing. He also didn't want to be lynched by angry locals whose homes had just been destroyed, so he picked himself up from the kerb and wandered in the direction he had come, where he had seen German soldiers.

He turned the corner and saw a group of soldiers at the other end of the next street. Fred began walking towards them. Some of the younger soldiers trained their guns on him. He took a deep breath and continued walking.

"Halt!" one of them shouted.

Fred stopped. The young soldiers approached. Fred thought they might be more nervous than he was. He had learned some German over the years attempting to trade goods with the goons. Now was the time to discover how good he had become.

"*Was machst du gerade?*" one of the soldiers demanded.

"*Ich bin Kriegsgefangener auf dem Stalag 383 Hohenfels,*" Fred said.

"*Was machst du hier? Hast du versucht zu fliehen?*" the soldier shouted. They thought he was trying to escape.

"*Ein Wärter brachte mich zur Behandlung ins Krankenhaus. Er wurde von einer der Bomben getötet. Ich bin hier um mich zu übergeben. Ich möchte gerne nach Hohenfels zurückkehren,*" Fred tried to explain. The soldiers were looking at him with concern. Had he said something wrong?

"*Willst du aufgeben?*" one of the soldiers asked. "Give up?"

"*Ja, das ist richtig,*" said Fred, pleased he was being understood.

"*Wie lautet dein name?*" the soldier asked.

"*Sgt Frederick Wooll. 7th Royal Northumberland Fusiliers. 4262219. Häftlingsnummer 18590.*"

One of the soldiers went off to a little hut, inside which was a telephone. He picked up the receiver and dialled a number. Fred watched the soldier observing him as he talked.

A moment later, he returned and stared at Fred.

"Your story is true. You will wait here until someone arrives to bring you back to the camp," said the soldier. He had spoken English after all.

Wednesday, 14th February, 1945 - Stalag 383, Hohenfels, Germany

"With almost five years captivity behind me, it'd be a shame to pass out when the war is on its last legs," said Fred.

"Ah well, it's a grand life if you don't weaken," said Chuck.

Fred could sense the teeth grinding around the room of those fed up of hearing Chuck repeating that phrase.

"It's not on its last legs," said Joe. "Did you not hear about Rundstedt?"

"I've got a hunch that the parcels are on their way," said Bob.

A similar grinding of teeth followed.

"Will you lot just shut up," said George, who couldn't take any more.

"What's the matter, chum?" asked Bob. "Life getting you down?"

"Ah well, it's a grand life if you don't weaken," said Chuck.

"What about the toilet tin?" Fred asked with a smile, knowing this would stir things up.

"Yeah, some lazy swine didn't empty it," said George, whose turn it was to be orderly. "Perhaps he thinks I'm going to do it for him."

"Wouldn't do you any harm if you did it, chum," said Joe. "You're not too particular about whose tin you use at night and ..."

"Are you suggesting it was me who used your filthy tin the other night?" asked George. "I know my tin, and that's the one I use, but if you're too dopey to know which one is yours, then there's no need asking whose this is."

"Now, you two," said Fred, feeling guilty. "Let's not start all that again. It's easy to mix up tins in the dark. I dare say I've used someone else's before now and ..."

"Well, you can bloody well come and empty this one then," said George and Joe together.

George then tottered on his feet and blacked out.

The men rushed around him.

"Let's get him to the M.O.," said Fred. "Someone get a stretcher."

"He'll be sterile now," said Chuck.

"What?" Joe stared at him with incredulity.

"Have you not heard? Deficiency in the diet makes you sterile," said Chuck. "We're all sterile now."

The men looked at him.

"Get the stretcher," said Fred.

Thursday, 1 March 1945 - Broadgate Hospital, Walkington, England

"What's that?" Leah asked the nurse who was offering her a cup of tea.

"It's your tea, Mrs Wooll," said the nurse

"I know what you are doing," said Leah.

"I'm giving you your tea," the nurse insisted.

"Ha!" Leah laughed.

"You ought to be used to life in here by now, Mrs Wooll. You've been here long enough. Take it or leave it," said Nurse Barton, leaving the cup on the table and walking away.

She joined her colleagues at the nursing station at the other end of the ward.

"Do you think she'll drink it?" one of the nurses asked.

"Let's hope so. Then we might have a quiet night tonight."

The nurses watched as Leah picked up the cup and took a sip. She winced. The nurses looked worried, but then Leah downed the contents of the cup in one go, and the nurses breathed a collective sigh of relief.

Doctors North and Baker arrived on the ward.

"Doctor North," the charge nurse was almost excited. "Mrs Wooll drank her tea."

"With the paraldehyde?"

"Yes, Doctor."

"Good."

"How is she responding?" asked Doctor Baker.

"She is in good health, but there is no marked change in her condition since her last exam. Mentally, she's the same. We have been giving her paraldehyde and beronal for the night."

"And how is that going?"

"She seems easier to manage. Isn't that right, Nurse?"

"Yes, Doctor. Her door is kept open during the morning, but her destructive turns come on suddenly, and she has to be watched carefully."

"The problem is hiding the smell of the paraldehyde," said Doctor North.

"And how have you done that?" asked Doctor Baker

Doctor North looked at the charge nurse.

"We have managed to add it to her tea," she said.

"And was that successful?"

"It was today." The charge nurse looked down the ward towards Leah

Monday, 16th April 1945 - Stalag 383, Hohenfels, Germany

"They're marching us out of the camp," said Chuck, bursting into the hut in his usual way.

"But the commandant said we wouldn't be required to march," Fred complained.

"When did you ever trust the word of a goon, Fred?" said Joe.

Fred had to admit he had a point.

"The Commandant said that if we don't march voluntarily, they'll get the SS to come and move us," said Chuck. "They are allowing those in the hospital to stay, though."

"That's nice of 'em," said Fred.

"Well, I'm not going," said Joe.

"What are you going to do if the SS does come?" asked Fred

"I'll hide out here, under the floor."

"I think I'll join you," said Bob.

"We can't all hide here," said Fred. "Some of us are going to have to march out with the goons, otherwise they'll smell a rat."

"I'll come with you, Fred," said Jack.

"I think we'll all have to go. Apart from Bob and Joe," said Fred. "Unless the bulk of us go on the march, the camp will be cleared by force."

"What about George?" asked Chuck.

"We'll have to leave him in the hospital hut," said Fred. "He'll be all right."

Tuesday, 17th April 1945 - Stalag 383, Hohenfels, Germany

"Let us not end in bloodshed," the Commandant shouted at the POWs as they filed out of the camp.

However, no sooner had they left the camp than the goons did not seem to know what to do with them, so the POWs dumped their kit in a field and started a brew up.

The goons seemed even less keen on the march than the POWs and Fred watched the guards grin their indifference as some of the men tore down a sentry post for firewood, while others wandered off foraging. The guards just shrugged their shoulders as the men returned with wheelbarrows, handcarts, and bicycles. Fred could see men left behind in the camp guffawing behind the fence at the sight of the clowns on bikes and barrows. Then they started throwing bed boards over the fences to add to the fires and soup bowls, water jugs. and mattresses to help with the picnic but still the guards did nothing to intervene.

They seemed to be staring at the skies. The American Air Force was sweeping the sky and strafing the roads near the camp. A roar of Mustang engines came from behind the valley ridge, then the rattle of machine guns as they raked the nearby roads in a burst of flame and smoke. An American Thunderbolt had strafed the road and bombed a tractor.

One of the planes dropped a shower of leaflets, which came fluttering down all around.

Fred picked up one of them.

'*Warum verlierst du dein Leben in den letzten Tagen des Krieges?*' they read on one side, and on the other seemed to be instructions for surrender, so Fred took the leaflet and handed it to a Jerry, who seemed impressed. Fred imagined the guard felt that the sooner the allies took him prisoner, the better.

*

At six o'clock, the march began, and Fred and his friends joined it willingly.

"See you in Blighty," the men shouted at those left behind in the camp.

"We've been chucked out of better jails than this," they shouted at the Commandant.

By dusk, they had made it about two miles from the camp and settled down by a stream to cook some supper.

As they were doing this, some woman approached the group.

"We are refugees in Hungary," one of them said, but Fred knew what they meant and invited them to sit down.

"American gangsters?" the same woman asked. "Are blacks wild?"

Fred assumed she must have been asking about the black American troops and whether they would be savage.

"Will they harm our children?"

Fred looked at the little girls with pigtails clutching to their mother and guessed she must be worried about what the Americans might do with them.

"Don't worry," Fred told them. "The Americans are coming soon, we hope. They are very decent and will bring chocolate for the children."

Fred looked along the stream where many fires were burning, and POWs were chatting with other women, some bargaining for bread.

"*Raus!*"

Fred and the other men jumped in surprise when the guards started jumping on the fires and kicking over the cans of tea.

The reason for this sudden change in behaviour soon became clear. Another group of German guards were arriving to take over the POWs, and unless they began to toe the line, the first set of guards would find themselves in trouble. The panicking guards started firing shots overhead.

Fred and the men got their kits on in a hurry, and the march resumed. He now began to wonder why he had packed so much. In addition to what few clothes he owned, he had packed books, a blanket, a greatcoat, and a bottle. Between himself and Jack, they carried a pole on which he had strung a mailbag of potatoes and some boxes containing flour.

Around them, men were carrying packs as large as wardrobes and others were hauling baggage carts. Fred could tell the ones who were thinking of making a break for it. They were the ones who were travelling light. He didn't give them much of a chance. The moon ensured the night was light, the road on the right was steep and forested, and to the left it was open. Anyone trying to escape would be sure to make a noise if they chose the right and be spotted if they chose the left. The guards would investigate any suspicious movement with the kind of dogs that Fred did not fancy stroking.

As they walked, Fred heard the guards firing occasional shots into the woods. He wasn't sure whether these were aimed at anyone or just to act as a deterrent.

They passed some Russian prisoners being marched in the opposite direction. The Russians were wearing their blue and white striped prison uniforms. As they continued, Fred saw some dead Russians at the side of the road. Shot while trying to escape, he guessed.

After a while, Fred's feet felt like lead. He and Jack would take it in turns to ask a guard about a rest stop, but the response was always the same.

"Noch ein kilo."

This joke the goons had of telling the marchers one more kilometre reminded Fred of his march through France and did not fill him with optimism.

They started to pass dumped kit. Greatcoats, packs, blankets, even an accordion.

They passed a POW who had slumped to the ground. An angry guard was shouting at him. Two of his friends were pulling him to his feet and offering to help carry him, rather than leave him to the mercy of the guards whose job it was to clean up the stragglers at the end of the column. Fred had learned from bitter experience that they might not see those left behind again.

Wednesday, 18th April 1945 - Somewhere in Bavaria, Germany

At three o'clock, they reached a large field, which the guards had cordoned off. The guards called them to a halt. The ground was waterlogged, and there were bulrushes, but Fred was so tired, he lay down his blanket, put his greatcoat on, and went straight to sleep.

After half an hour, Fred woke. Shouts of '*Raus!*' were filling his ears, and he and Jack had to gather their belongings and move off once more.

As the dawn began to break, a message was being passed along the column from man to man, so that when they reached the first big village of the morning's march, they all dumped their kit bags on the ground and settled down to prepare breakfast.

The whole procedure appeared so organised that the German guards assumed it must have been authorised and just stared at each other. Once they realised what had happened, they started raving at the prisoners, drawing back their rifle bolts and firing into the air.

Fred laughed at the stubborn refusal of the men to move. They were going to have breakfast, and that was that.

A guard near Fred raised his rifle, ready to bring it crashing down on Fred's head. Fred looked down at his breakfast and waited for the inevitable, but the inevitable didn't come. He looked up to see another guard ushering the rifle brandisher away.

"Der Americans kom...nix fergessen," Fred could hear the intervener warning his colleague.

A moment later, some guards marched up and down the column announcing that there would be a general halt and berating any guards who were still shouting '*Raus!*' The POWs cheered, and Fred sensed the atmosphere ease.

Jack had been moving around, chatting to some of the other POWs, and returned to share the gossip with Fred.

"They think Frank has been shot," he said. "He's missing anyway."

Fred was taken aback.

"Are you sure?" he asked.

"No, but what I'm sure about is that we are heading for Regensburg on the Danube. They're taking us to Salzburg. They're planning to use us as a human shield for their last stand."

"Rubbish," said Fred. "It must be 200 kilometres to Salzburg."

"Well, I wouldn't dismiss it out of hand."

"No, perhaps you're right. We might have to make a break for it after all. Let's just wait and see how things develop for now. No point taking unnecessary risks. The place is thick with Nazis and we have no idea where the Americans are. Why risk our lives in the last days of the war?"

Jack agreed.

*

After the march restarted, Fred watched as one POW made a suicidal attempt to escape by running across an open field. The Germans could have shot him, but viewing him as mad, decided instead to chase him into the corner of the field and beat him up.

Fred watched as the guards picked the man up and led him back to the column. Fred could see him ahead of them, and as they marched he realised they were catching up with him. He seemed to be smoking a cigarette.

"Got a light?" Fred asked as they drew alongside and then realised he wasn't smoking a cigarette, his mouth had just been bashed in so much that it looked as though he was. "Oh, sorry."

"Don't worry, Sarge," said one of his friends. "He's bloody lucky to get away with just a beating."

Instead of escaping, most POWs contented themselves with walking as slowly as possible. Some would get near the front of the column and then sit down for a rest until the guards at the back shouted for them to move on.

*

By the time the sun had disappeared and dusk was falling, the march had come to a halt in the village of Pielenhofen, dominated by a huge convent.

Thunderbolts flew overhead, strafing neighbouring roads. Fred marvelled at how his fellow soldiers had settled in. Many, like himself, had made themselves comfortable in a meadow, but many others like Chuck had gone into the village to bargain for bread, and there were even some who had found themselves a local woman and had taken them rowing on the Regan. Jack soon came back.

"The SS are in the woods, Sarge," he said, handing Fred half of his gains for looking after his belongings while he was away.

"How do you know?" asked Fred.

"The villagers told me, but some of our own men went for a scout and backed up the story."

"I doubt we'll get a better chance to make a break for it once we're the other side of the Danube."

"How about we find a place here to hole up for a couple of weeks? Then we can double back, hiding in the day and travelling at night."

Fred and Jack had no chance to develop the plan further before the Germans rounded up all the POWs and locked them in the grounds of the convent.

They made themselves comfortable under one of the trees, lit a fire, and made flapjacks while watching the planes overhead. It wasn't long before they both fell into a restful sleep.

Thursday, 19th April 1945 - Pielenhofen, Germany

When Fred awoke, he felt refreshed and optimistic until the SS arrived, sending their German escort into a panic.

One of the Germans begged Fred and Jack to get moving.

"The SS are a bad lot, and their commander is in a bad mood after seeing the prisoners fraternising with the villagers," he said in earnest. "He is capable of anything."

Fred looked at the SS Commander and believed that was true.

The SS followed them for several kilometres, walking on banks on either side of the road, holding their rifles at the ready and staring at the column with a malevolent gaze. Some of them looked doped, all of them looked fanatical, and there was an 'aura of death' coldness about them, which chilled their vicinity.

The column joined the main road to Regensburg, where groups of Russians, Italians, Jews, political prisoners, and pram-pushing refugees were also moving. The SS left Fred's column and turned back. The only other traffic coming the other way was the occasional German staff car and weighty girls on bicycles wearing what looked like several pairs of Luftwaffe slacks and carrying revolvers at the hip.

*

Regensburg, where they crossed the Danube, had taken a hell of a battering, and the column halted on some waste ground.

A couple of German guards approached Fred and Jack and sat on the bank next to them.

"The march is over, we have crossed the Danube," one of them told Fred. "They should follow the general south."

Fred took this to mean that they should follow the groups of others ambling southward.

"You should move very slowly. You should mark time for Americans," he continued. "When they arrive, no one will be more pleased than we are."

"What about Salzburg?" Fred asked.

The German laughed.

"The SS are fighting. We have enough," he said.

A German sergeant approached and shouted at the guards.

"Du darfst dich nicht mit Gefangenen mischen," he shouted.

Nevertheless, the guards just kept lolling on the bank with Fred and Jack.

"Wir werden bald selbst Gefangene sein. Du auch, mein Freund," one of them shouted back at the sergeant.

The sergeant shouted something Fred couldn't understand and grabbed a rifle from a nearby guard and held it at his hip as if he was about to go berserk.

Fred and Jack scrambled over the bank and, once on the other side, they heard an explosion.

"Bloody hell, he's lobbed a hand grenade," said Jack.

They waited for a moment and then raised their heads over the bank. The German sergeant had gone, and so had the guards.

There was a commotion among both POWs and guards, and they had all gathered around something.

When Fred and Chuck got closer, they realised what had happened. The POWs had lit a fire on the waste ground, which had exploded a small bomb buried in their midst.

Friday, 20th April 1945 - Regensburg, Germany

Fred woke up in a wood. It took him a few moments to remember where he was and then it all came back to him. The Germans had marched them into the wood and surrounded it by guards. Fred could hear the guards now, shouting at the prisoners to get up.

They grabbed their belongings once more and rejoined the march. They hadn't been marching long when Fred realised that he was unsteady on his feet.

"You all right?" Jack asked him, but before he could finish getting the words out, Fred had pitched forward and fallen flat on his face.

Captain France, the medical officer, who by good luck just happened to be nearby, rushed over and examined Fred, who was just coming to.

"He blacked out," said the M.O. "Try to get him back to the hospital in Regensburg."

Fred knew very well the hospital in Regensburg. He had been on his way to the very same hospital when the raid killed his envoy. He waited by the roadside with Jack, watching the POWs disappear and waiting to recover himself to begin the journey back to Regensburg.

As soon as he felt well enough to walk, they turned back, but found that German guards were stopping them every few minutes to question them. Frustrated, they decided to get off the road and slipped into the yard of an inn to make a brew.

The water hadn't boiled when a woman carrying a baby entered the yard.

"The baby is a seven-month child because of an air attack," the woman told them. "I am expecting another child soon. Some wounded prisoners seek refuge in my house."

They followed the woman into her house and found two soldiers there, along with an old woman whom they assumed to be the pregnant woman's mother, and some children who may have been hers also.

"Sergeant Fred Wooll, 7th Northumberland Fusiliers," Fred announced himself as he approached the men.

"Corporal Jack Cooper," said Jack.

"Sergeant," Fred corrected him.

"Sergeant Honeyset," said the first man. Bandages covered his whole face, apart from his lips and nostrils, which appeared to be burnt.

"I'm Cracker King," said the other with a cockney accent. He also had a pitted and burned face.

"What happened to you two?" asked Fred.

"We were making a brew yesterday in the waste ground in Regensburg when the heat from our fire detonated an unexploded bomb," said Cracker.

"We saw that," said Jack.

"Is he OK?" asked Fred nodding to Sgt Honeyset.

"He was blinded by the explosion," said Cracker. "But the MO said there is hope that his sight might be saved in one eye. He is bearing up well ... considering ... it must be bloody painful. We are trying to get back to the hospital."

"So you caught it too, Cracker?" said Jack.

"Course I did," said Cracker. "I'm his mucker see. Anything coming to him, I gets 'arf."

When the tea they had brewed had cooled, they tried to pour some between Honeyset's swollen lips. As they were doing so, the air raid siren sounded, the ack-ack guns started up, and bombs started falling almost at the same time. The old woman and her daughter fell to their knees, and the children started screaming.

A few minutes later, the bombing stopped, and the children stopped screaming and ran outside to inspect the damage.

"Setzen Sie ein Schild auf das Dach, damit die Amerikaner unser Haus nicht bombardieren," pleaded the old woman.

Fred, Jack, and Cracker went outside to examine the damage for themselves and saw British POWs pushing a handcart up the road towards them.

Cracker knew the men, who had gone to get the cart from a nearby working camp. They placed Honeyset on the cart, Fred and Jack followed as the POWs pushed it along the road.

When they arrived at the camp, the POWs treated them well, and the goons treated them with suspicion.

"When the unwounded unofficial officers leave their bunk in the barn, they are shot," one of the Germans tried to explain.

Fred believed the threat, and when he felt the call of nature in the middle of the night, he was happy to find a tin in the barn so that he could relieve himself without fear of a guard shooting him.

Saturday, 21st April 1945 - Neutraubling, Germany

A volley of rifle shots woke Fred. He looked out of the barn to see that a political prisoner the guards were holding with a group in a nearby field had tried to make a run for it, but had been picked off by the guards just a few yards up the road. A barefooted German woman in the yard who was forking hay paid no attention to the shooting, as if it were just a rabbit that had been shot.

The sirens sounded again, and the ack-ack guns started firing at an American bomber, which they hit. Fred watched as three of the crew bailed out of the falling wreckage. One of the airmen seemed to be steering towards them.

"Why is he coming this way?" asked Fred.

"The men have painted POW on the roof of the barn," said Cracker. "He must have seen it."

The airman didn't quite make it to the barn and landed on the road outside. The Germans ran at him from all directions but did not molest him.

"How is it going?" Fred shouted as the Germans were taking him away.

"Patten is in Nuremberg," he shouted back.

The hospital wagon arrived, and Honeyset, Fred, and Cracker King were loaded on board.

"There's still room," Cracker shouted down to Jack.

"Well, I haven't got any other plans," said Jack, climbing into the wagon.

Thursday, 26th April 1945 - Stalag VIIA, Moosburg, Germany

As he ate his two slices of black bread, which tasted like a mix of flour and sawdust, Fred looked at the sprawling set of tightly spaced rows of drab, rundown, one-story military barracks and collection of muddy tents that comprised the Stalag, which had become his home for the last few days. The Germans had designed the camp to accommodate around 10,000 personnel, and now the Germans had packed in over 100,000. Each building designed to hold 180 contained 400. Fred watched the clusters of gaunt, emaciated men in shoddy, worn out clothing occupying every inch of unused space they could find. He tried to keep upwind of the foul-smelling latrines, outside of which was a long line of men waiting their turn.

As a late arrival, Fred's bunk was on the floor of one of the huts. He considered himself lucky he wasn't outside in one of the muddy tents. He scratched one of the insect bites which now covered his body. He was staring at the hills to the north, beyond which Fred swore he could hear the distant thumping of artillery.

He ducked as he heard a shell going overhead. Jack laughed.

"If you can hear the shell, then you are all right, because it means it's missed you," he joked.

Saturday, 28th April 1945 - Stalag VIIA, Moosburg, Germany

Fred lay awake on the floor of his hut. He had been listening to the sound of German trucks leaving all night.

Sunday, 29th April 1945 - Stalag VIIA, Moosburg, Germany

"There's a Yank jeep in the camp." Fred heard some of the POWs shouting.

Fred didn't pay much attention at first. He was too busy gathering fuel. He relished the thought of liberation as much as any of them, but he also relished the thought of not being cold that night, so he finished gathering his fuel before going to investigate.

Once the fuel was stored in the hut, he wandered down to the gates where he discovered a group of American POWs gathered. As Fred walked down to see what was happening, he saw two German staff cars with red crosses painted on the side pull up. Out of one of the cars stepped a US Colonel and an RAF Group Captain. The Colonel appeared to address the POWs, who started running back into the camp. Among them, Fred saw Jack coming towards him.

"What was it?" asked Fred as Jack approached.

"The yank colonel said we'd better find a hole, the war's about to start."

They watched as some of the remaining skeleton crew of guards handed over their weapons to POWs and deserted.

"German troops have been seen taking up defensive positions outside the wire," said Jack.

At around 9:00 am they heard the first shots. Small arms fire coming from somewhere in the woods just outside the fence. Within minutes, the noise from the incessant firing of hundreds of small arms and heavy automatic weapons was deafening.

POWs were everywhere scrambling for cover. Some were trying to burrow into the ground like moles, while others were climbing on top of guard towers and buildings to watch the excitement. Fred and Jack flattened themselves as best they could beside their hut. Bullets were ricocheting all over the compound and from the shouts, it was clear that several POWs had been hit though, from the levels of cursing, not seriously.

*

About an hour after the shooting started, it stopped. The silence was almost deathly quiet, too quiet, strange and unnatural.

Fred and Jack sat up and looked about. They sat motionless for minutes before they were shaken back to reality by the rumble and clanking of heavy armour approaching the camp from somewhere outside the perimeter fences.

Three Sherman tanks of the American 14th Armored Infantry Division crashed through the fence near the main gate.

They followed the crowds down towards the gate to get a better view of the tanks. Poking out of the top of one of them was an important looking American.

"That's General Patton," shouted an American POW in excitement.

"Has he got any food?" Jack shouted back. However, the rest of the POWs drowned out his comment, shouting, screaming, and cheering as they surrounded the tanks, which drove a short distance down the main street of Stalag VIIA before halting and becoming swarmed by the POWs.

"I've never seen such a crazy bunch of ragged ass people," shouted an American Sergeant driving one of the tanks.

Fred burst into tears and turned to look at Jack who was already crying. The two slumped to the ground and spent a few minutes sobbing with joy.

They got to their feet and watched as, in the distance, the stars and stripes were being raised on top of the steeple of the church in Moosburg a short distance away. Even more incredible was the sight of 8,000 American POWs turning and saluting almost in unison.

Sunday, 6th May 1945 - Landshut, Germany

The American soldiers showed Fred and Jack a block of flats and told them that they and their fellow liberated compatriots would be spending the night there.

"If there's anyone is in there just kick them out," said one of the Americans who had escorted them.

Fred and the rest of the men found that the apartments were deserted. They began burning furniture to keep warm, but the basic apartments were so sparsely furnished that they soon began to run out of furniture to burn.

"Let's go for a walk," said Fred, eager to experiment with his new freedom and look at the river.

They walked through the town and soon arrived at the gates of what looked like a brewery. A group of soldiers from Britain, Australia, New Zealand and a smattering of other nations had already gathered and were worrying a nervous looking American soldier whose job it was to guard the gates.

An American officer arrived to find out what the fuss was.

"What do these men want?" he asked the soldier.

"They want to get into the brewery, sir."

"Let me get as far as that building," said the officer, pointing to the next corner. "Then let them in."

The officer walked away and, once he had reached the designated point, the soldier opened the gates to the delight of the men, including Fred, who poured through the gates and into the buildings.

Fred found a vat of beer and filled a bucket. It tasted terrible, but he decided to take a bucket of it back to the flat all the same.

He wandered around the brewery with his bucket, exploring all the side rooms. In one room he stopped. The room was almost bare except for two pianos against one of which rested an axe. The combination of these two objects was too much for Fred to bear. He put down his bucket and considered the strangeness of the contents of the room. He picked up the axe and contemplated its weight, and then he looked at the two pianos. It seemed the right thing to do, he began swinging the axe into the first piano. He felt a twinge in his hernia, but he seemed unable to stop himself and continued swinging the axe into the pianos until they both lay in pieces on the floor.

Jack came in to see what all the noise was.

"Great. You found some firewood," he said as he gathered up some of the wooden splinters.

Fred just felt that he had done what he felt had to be done and gathered up as much wood as he could carry under one arm and picked up the bucket of terrible beer with the other.

They left the brewery and, trying to find their way back to the flat, wandered the streets, which were awash with soldiers of all nationalities except German.

Fred approached one of the Americans.

"Hello buddy, what can I do you for?"

"Any idea where we might find a candle?" asked Fred.

"As a matter of fact, I do. You are in luck chum. Follow me."

Fred and Jack followed the American through the town until they arrived at a row of American military trucks, which some of the largest soldiers Fred had ever seen, were guarding. A short while later the American returned with the biggest candle Fred had ever seen.

"Thanks," said Fred.

"Don't mention it. Where are you guys off to now?"

"Back to our repose to drink some of this terrible beer," said Fred, nodding towards the bucket. "Would you like to join us?"

"Don't mind if I do. Here, let me give you a hand with some of that wood," he took the pile from under Fred's arm.

"Hmm, Steinway. Looks like you guys are going to have an expensive fire."

"Do they make good pianos?" asked Jack.

"I don't know about that," said Fred. "But they make excellent firewood."

In the flat, they broke the candle in two and added some piano to rekindle the dying embers in the fireplace. Each of them filled a cup with beer from the bucket. Fred and Jack winced at the taste, but the American seemed to enjoy it and refilled his cup several times throughout the evening.

Tuesday, 8th May 1945 - Landshut Airfield, Germany

With a stinking hangover, Fred sat in the back of an American military truck. It was the fastest, wildest drive he'd ever experienced and it didn't help that he was sitting on the tailboard surrounded by dust and fumes.

Fred was glad when the truck arrived at an abandoned German airfield. The Americans told them they would have to wait a while, so they filled their time wandering around the buildings, damaged by Allied bombing.

Fred watched as the other men went around smashing up anything they could get their hands on, typewriters, desks, office equipment, anything they could get their hands on that seemed to be associated with the Nazi regime. The destruction all seemed so pointless, but Fred was not about to argue with anyone. He had already had his moment in the brewery with the piano. He knew how they felt and he knew they had to get it out of their systems. He had already had his therapy, and he realised now how pointless it all was. Not just the destruction of property in the airfield but also the destruction of property of art of people's belongings in all the homes and buildings that the war had destroyed or damaged. Of all the senseless deaths of the countless people. The soldiers. Fred's friends and colleagues. The friends, colleagues, and families of all the other soldiers and civilians who had died and for what? For greed and hatred. It made Fred feel sick when he contemplated the scale of the senseless waste.

Planes came and went but no one called Fred's name. It was very frustrating because for all his freedom he was not able to get out of Germany until some-one called his name. On top of that, no one seemed to know where he could find any food or drink.

"Hey you there." an American voice shouted.

Fred turned to see a GI beckoning Fred over to his guard post. For a moment, Fred's heart raced, and he wondered whether this was his opportunity to leave.

As he drew closer, Fred noticed that the GI was listening to a radio at his post.

"Hey, limey. Your King is about to speak on the radio. You wanna listen?"

The novelty of listening to the radio again soon replaced Fred's initial disappointment that the American was not calling him for an aircraft and he smiled at the American.

"Today we give thanks to Almighty God for a great deliverance. Speaking from our Empire's oldest capital city, war-battered but never for on moment daunted or dismayed - speaking from London, I ask you to join with me in that act of thanksgiving." Fred heard the unmistakable sound of the King's voice. He wondered whether it was all over. Not just the war in his part of Germany but everywhere. Perhaps the war was over. "Germany, the enemy who drove all Europe into war, has been overcome."

So it was true. Germany had surrendered. It was over.

"In the Far East we have yet to deal with the Japanese, a determined and cruel foe," the King continued.

It wasn't quite over.

"To this, we shall turn with the utmost resolve and with all our resources. But at this hour, when the dreadful shadow of war has passed far from our hearths and homes in these islands, we may, at last, make one pause for thanksgiving and then turn our thoughts to the tasks all over the world which peace in Europe brings with it."

Fred listened to the rest of the speech, thanked the GI and then went to find the others to share the news.

As night fell, Fred and the others found what space they could, to sleep. Fred settled down under a steel bomb rack.

Wednesday, 9th May 1945 - Landshut Airfield, Germany.

On the grass next to the runway, the Americans had lined up two rows of Dakota C-47s, nose to tail. Fred estimated there must have been at least a couple of dozen, maybe more. They stretched out into the distance.

They called Jack's name before Fred's, and they lost contact with each other. Fred thought it odd they should not be on the same plane, given that they were in the same platoon, but he imagined it had something to do with the fact that Fred would be going back to East Yorkshire and Jack to Scotland.

Not long afterwards, around noon, an American called Fred's name, and they led him over to a queue, which was forming near a Dakota standing on the grass. He looked at its huge grey nose pointing into the air like an obedient hound waiting for instructions.

As he waited, the Dakota in front of Fred's finished loading, closed the doors and began to taxi to the runway. Fred watched it line up, about to take off, and he wondered whether Jack was on board. The sound of the engines, as it picked up speed, was impressive but, as he watched, he noticed that the plane didn't seem to be gaining any height. It was too near the end of the runway to stop but looked like it would be unlikely to clear the trees in the field adjacent to the runway. Fred was willing the plane to climb and just when he thought it might make it, one of the wings clipped a tree, spinning the plane around 90 degrees and it crashed into the field.

"Hurry up, get on board," the Americans were saying, pushing Fred and the others onto their plane as quick as possible.

"Wait a minute...didn't that..." Fred tried to protest as a large GI pushed him up the stairs, at the top of which another was waiting to drag him inside to his seat.

Fred couldn't believe what was happening. Were they trying to get them on board before they had time to think about they had just witnessed? He was one of the first on board and had to climb the steep hill inside to sit near the cockpit where he strapped himself in. The plane smelled of oil. He hoped it wasn't leaking. He kept thinking about whether Jack had been on board the plane in front.

It was the first time he had flown, and he was feeling more than a little nervous given that he had just witnessed the plane in front of his crash. He had travelled with the army to India and Shanghai, but that had always been by boat. He wasn't sure what to think about being up in the air. Men weren't designed to fly. They had no wings.

The engines started, and a moment later, he heard a large metallic crash.

"What was that?" he said. "It sounds like something just fell off the plane. Do you think everything's all right?"

An American GI sat opposite laughed.

"It's just the chocks being pulled away."

""Chocks?"

"Sure. They put these big metal chocks under the wheels to stop the plane rolling away. They were just taking them out so we could go."

"Oh," Fred felt embarrassed.

The plane began to move. The sound of the engines was deafening.

The GI leaned over and offered Fred some chewing gum.

"No thanks," said Fred

"Trust me you're going to need it. It helps equalise the ears."

Fred smiled and took the chewing gum. The GI seemed to have several pieces on the go, which he masticated with his mouth wide open. Fred felt very British, politely chewing on his gum.

Fred held on tight as the Dakota picked up speed. He closed his eyes, waiting for the impact as they collided with the trees.

Then he felt the plane lift further and further into the air and breathed a sigh of relief.

After about an hour, the GI unstrapped himself and went into the cockpit. A few moments later he poked his head around the corner and stared at Fred

"Hey buddy, this is your first time in a plane right?

"Right."

"Wanna come in here and have a look?

"Er...Alright."

Fred was uncertain but also wasn't sure whether he'd ever get the opportunity to enter a C-47 cockpit again. He unstrapped himself and followed the GI.

"What's your name buddy?" the pilot asked when he entered.

"Sergeant Frederick Wooll."

FRED & LEAH: A TRUE LIFE SECOND WORLD WAR DRAMA
OF LOVE, LOSS AND CAPTIVITY.

259

"Well Sergeant Frederick Wooll," said the pilot. "Tell me. For how long were you a POW?"

"Five years."

The pilot gives a long whistle.

"Have a look down there," he says pointing outside past the nose cone. "See what we did to Nuremberg."

Fred looked out of the window and saw that the Allied bombing almost flattened the town. Complete devastation. Homes, churches, factories. Everything destroyed. Fred had never seen anything like it on such a scale. Every kind of building demolished.

"May I ask you a question?" Fred asked the pilot.

"Sure. Shoot."

"The plane in front of us…"

"You're worried about your pals," the pilot interrupted. "Don't worry, the crate didn't catch fire, and it looked like they were getting the passengers and crew out when I flew over.

Thursday, 10th May - Brussels, Belgium

Fred wandered around the centre of Brussels, which the Army had allowed him and the others to visit while they waited their turn for the next flight back to England. Fred was very anxious to get back and see Leah, his children and the rest of his family. He was sure that once Leah saw him, she would become her old self once more. Beattie, who he last saw as a baby was now 5 years old. Perhaps Jim wouldn't recognise him either. He decided to try to buy some gifts to take home and was looking in a shop window at an oriental looking plate with a wickerwork cage of thin reed around it when along the street came walking Fusilier Bobby Jones.

"Sarge!" Bobby said with delight on seeing Fred. "Is the Corp here?"

"I don't know," said Fred. "We were separated when we were getting our flights out of Germany."

Bobby looked very thin. Fred had heard stories of the long march the Germans had forced the prisoners to make. One in three had perished on the way, and Fred thought better than to mention what must have been a very traumatic experience for the fusilier.

"I've got some photos to show you, Sarge," Bobby said taking some pictures from a wallet.

"I'd love to see them. I've got some here you might be interested in too," said Fred, putting his wallet on the windowsill behind him so that could get his pictures out.

It only took a couple of minutes to look at Bobby's pictures. He said goodbye to the fusilier, and when he turned back to retrieve his wallet, it had already gone.

"Damn it!" he said.

The wallet had contained his money, letters, St Valery mementoes, and saved Camp Money, from a one-pfennig piece up to a twenty-mark note. He had become so used to the camp that he almost forgot he was back in the real world. Now he would be unable to buy anything for his family.

"Oh well, no point crying over spilt milk," he said to himself and went off to see if he could find Jack wandering around.

*

At the airfield, they were led to a Lancaster bomber which had had the inside 'ammo' taken out so that twenty men could sit in the floor. Fred wasn't comfortable, but he didn't care, he was on his way home. He couldn't see outside either, but it didn't matter. This was the last lap. The navigator invited them into the cockpit so that they could see as they passed over the white cliffs of Dover. Fred felt tears welling up in his eyes. After five years. He felt it was a beautiful sight.

The Lancaster landed in Surrey and soldiers led Fred to a building and into a room where a chaplain was waiting to debrief him. As Fred recounted his story to the chaplain, he found himself becoming angrier and angrier until he burst into tears at the injustice of it all.

After the debriefing, they gave Fred a pass and some money and loaded him into the back of a three-ton Bedford lorry. Fred marvelled as the truck passed through lanes and country roads. The hedgerows were bursting into leaf from new buds, beautiful greens of many hues. He was back in England.

The trucks drove them to a reception camp where Fred was able to pick up the necessary paperwork and was able to get a train to Waterloo Station in London. At the station, Fred saw a kiosk selling cigarettes and chocolate and thought he might buy a gift for his children.

"A packet of Woodbines and some of that chocolate please."

"Do you have your coupons?"

"Coupons?"

"You can't buy chocolate without coupons, sir." The owner of the kiosk felt he was stating the obvious. "Where have you been living? The moon?"

"Something like that," said Fred. He realised he had much to learn about this new England. When he left, the Government had rationed petrol, but it made sense that they would have to ration so much more as the war progressed.

Friday, 11th May 1945 - Beverley, England

When the train slowed to pass through Hull, Cottingham and now Beverley, Fred saw the Union Jacks everywhere. Hanging from almost all of the houses.

As the men alighted from the train in Beverley station, the officers asked Fred to order them to line up on parade while local press photographers took their photos. Then Fred dismissed them, and they dispersed in search of their families. Fred struggled to find anyone he recognised, and then he saw his mother and Minnie with four children. At first, he thought that maybe Leah had been right and that somehow they had found the missing children, and then it dawned on him that the two other children were his nephew Ron and his niece, Shirley.

He rushed over as fast as he could and said hello to them all

"I've got six weeks leave," Fred told them. "On double rations."

"Good job too," said his mother. "You're wasting away.

Saturday, 12th May 1945 - Beverley, England

Fred sat in the living room, listening to the wireless. His mother and visitors had been encouraging him to go out but the thought of all those people, all those things out there, rushing about. It was too much for Fred to cope with all at once. He had become used to his routines in the camp, and his new freedom was overwhelming.

On the one hand, he welcomed the thought of getting back to his army duties and the order that would reintroduce to his life. On the other, he had heard rumours that those found fit for service were being sent off to fight in the far east. The thought of repeating his experience of the last five years but in the tropics was not one that appealed to him.

He knew he couldn't sit in the front room for long. Apart from the fact that he had been ordered to report to the military hospital in York, there was one task, which needed to be undertaken first. He must visit his wife. He had listened to many stories from his mother and sister about Leah's condition, the previous evening, but he still hoped that seeing him might do some good and that there might be hope of recovery.

Beattie came into the room. She had been very shy and still seemed to view him with suspicion. Minnie had brought Jim to see him, and he was the same, unsure what to think about the strange thin man who had appeared in his life.

Fred felt it difficult to unwind. He felt it difficult to speak with anyone without fear that someone would report his words, as might have been the case in the camp

*

Fred got off the bus at the entrance to the grounds of the large red brick building. Standing next to the small cottage, which looked like the gatehouse, Fred, looked along the long drive, took a deep breath and started to make his way towards the imposing building. His civilian clothes felt about three sizes too big, which of course they now were.

"Ward 5?" he asked at the reception.

"And who might you be?" asked the security guard of this strangely dressed individual.

"Sgt Frederick Wooll, 7th Royal Northumberland Fusiliers," said Fred, hoping that his rank might shame the man whom Fred guessed might have spent the duration of the war in England. "I'm here to visit my wife, Leah Wooll."

"Wait here," said the security guard and picked up a telephone, dialling a few numbers. "I've got a Sergeant Wooll here. He says he's the husband of a Leah Wooll. You got a Leah Wooll there? Right."

The security guard hung up the phone and proceeded to ignore Fred.

Fred waited.

After a while, one of the doors was unlocked, and Nurse Barton walked through.

"Mr Wooll. At last. Come with me."

She led him through the door then locked it behind her before leading him up the corridor.

Every so often, a strange shout of indeterminate origin would echo along the corridor, but Fred kept following the nurse until they reached a large lift with a metal shutter door. The nurse pressed the call button and waited for the lift to descend. When it arrived, she slid the shutter door open to reveal a second door, more of a gate, made from strips of metal fastened together to allow it to concertina open. Once they had entered, she closed the two doors, pressed another button, and they ascended.

At the entrance to the ward, the nurse unlocked another door and let them both in before locking it behind her.

"She's in the day room," Nurse Barton said.

Fred followed her into the ward and realised the odd smell permeating the hospital, much stronger in the ward, was stale urine. The nurse led him into a large room filled with armchairs many of which were occupied by inanimate women. He scanned the room, searching for his wife, wondering whether he would still recognise her. Then he saw her. She looked older and thinner, but it was her, without a doubt. She seemed to be rocking, forwards and backwards.

"Mrs Wooll. Your husband is here," Nurse Barton told Leah with a raised voice as if Leah was deaf, stupid, or both. Leah seemed oblivious to the fact that the nurse was addressing her.

"Call me if you need anything," said Nurse Barton to Fred, before turning on her heels and heading back to the nurse's station.

Fred offered her a smile of thanks and sat down next to his wife.

"Hello Leah," he said. "It's me, Fred."

Leah seemed to be in a world of her own.

"Leah," he said, a little louder.

She looked at him as if noticing him for the first time but there were no signs of recognition. Then she let out a random, but loud, burst of laughter as if she had remembered some private joke.

"It's me. Fred. Your husband."

"Who?"

"Fred. Your husband."

"Oh, yes?" she said as if someone had just told her an interesting fact.

"How are you?"

"Mmm?"

She didn't seem to be listening.

"How are you feeling?"

Leah just stared ahead. She seemed to be chewing on something.

"I'm back now Leah. I'm back for good."

Leah nodded.

"Who are you?" she asked.

"I'm your husband," he persisted. "Fred."

"My husband was called Fred," she laughed again.

"That's right. It's me."

"He's dead now."

"No Leah."

"They told me he's a prisoner of war," she nods towards the nurses. "But I know he is dead."

"I'm not dead Leah. I'm here."

"The voices told me."

"The voices?"

"They talk to me through the ceiling. It's not a ceiling. They can remove it to spy on me."

"She's quite talkative today," Nurse Barton commented as she passed by.

"Yes," Fred forced a smile, wishing Leah were less talkative and more coherent.

He sat and looked at her. He was struggling to believe that she was the same woman he had married. He tried to understand what could have happened to change her so much but he could see no reason in it.

"Leah, I have to go away for a while. I've been ordered to report to Fulford Hospital in York. I'm not well, Leah. I need time to get better. But I'll be back. I promise. I'll help you get better too."

Leah didn't seem to be paying attention to him.

"Jim and Beattie are doing fine. Minnie and Mum are doing a grand job looking after them. Mum told me she brought Beattie to see you."

"Did she?" Leah asked.

Fred was emboldened by receiving a response.

"Yes, do you remember, Leah? Do you remember Mum bringing Beattie to see you?"

Leah shook her head and continued chewing on something invisible in her mouth.

"I have children," she laughed again.

"Yes, you do."

"I have four children."

"No, Leah."

"Two of them were taken away. Twins."

Fred sighed. He realised now that what his family had been telling him was true, but five years of treatment seemed to have done little to make her better. She was thin, and she didn't recognise him. He thought if she saw him, it might take her back to the time before the war. He had been wrong.

Monday, 14th May 1945 - Military Hospital, York

"You're suffering from malnutrition and a double hernia," the doctor told Fred. "Both are treatable, but you'll need to spend a bit of time convalescing."

"Thanks," said Fred. "I'm eager to get away."

"These things can't be rushed. You'll have to stay here, I'm afraid."

"But I'm meant to be on leave."

"Can't be helped."

"Doctor, I've been trying to find a member of my platoon, Corporal Cooper."

"Sorry, can't help you there. Have you tried Regimental HQ?"

"I did but got nowhere."

"Sorry."

Fred left the doctor's office disconsolate. His desire to get back to Leah was not Fred's only reason to get away from the Hospital. The huts they had constructed in the grounds to accommodate the influx of soldiers from the liberated prisoner of war camps reminded Fred too much of the Stalag from which the Americans had just liberated him. Nightmares haunted his sleep.

Sunday, 29 July 1945 - Broadgate Hospital, Walkington, England

Leah sat rocking forwards and backwards in the day room, staring at the fireplace. She felt fearful all of a sudden and, looking around, realised she had no idea where she was.

She got up out of her chair to go to the bathroom. As she was passing the fireplace, her legs gave way, and she fell, face first into the fireguard. She lay on the floor, her limbs twitching, droplets of blood beginning to swell on her forehead and the bridge of her nose.

"What happened?" asked one of the nurses as she arrived to help.

"Epilepsy?" asked another.

"She's never fitted before," said the first.

*

Leah appeared pale and unwell as the doctor examined her.

"Do you remember what happened, Mrs Wooll?" he asked.

"No," said Leah at once and then thought about it for a moment. "It was the nurses. They did it. They injured me."

The doctor reached to open her blouse and Leah batted his hand away.

"Now, now, Mrs Wooll. I am going to need to examine your chest."

"No."

"Nurse?"

The nurses held Leah so that the doctor could examine her.

"You just want to see my breasts you pervert," she shouted. "It was her. This one holding me. She's the one who pushed me into the fire."

FRED & LEAH: A TRUE LIFE SECOND WORLD WAR DRAMA
OF LOVE, LOSS AND CAPTIVITY.

269

Friday, 3 August 1945 - Broadgate Hospital, Walkington, England

"Father? Is that you?"

Leah could have sworn she heard her father's voice but this time the voice was not coming from the ceiling, it was coming from the other side of the wall.

"Dad! Dad! In here!" Leah shouted but her father didn't seem to be able to hear her, and she knew from experience that the nurses would just ignore her. That's what mad people did after all was shout.

Sunday, 12th August 1945 - Broadgate Hospital, Walkington, England

"You used to live in Sunderland?" asked Jane, as she helped Leah to weed the flowerbeds of the ward garden.

"That's right. I lived in Monkwearmouth and then Roker, but I'm from Horden. My family were all miners."

"So how did you end up in here?"

Leah thought about it for a moment.

"No idea," she said at last and then carried on weeding. Doctor North had just transferred Jane to Ward 5. Leah couldn't imagine why. She didn't seem at all incurable like the rest of the patients in the ward. It reminded Leah, and she turned to look back through the window where Aida was slumped in the armchair in which she now spent all of her days. When the first leucotomy hadn't done the trick, Aida had been taken back for a second which had fixed her for good without a doubt. Now she spent all her time in the same old armchair staring into the middle distance, all sparks of vitality extinguished for good. Leah wondered when it would be her turn to have her brain sliced. She looked at Jane and wondered how long it would be before they turned Jane into a lump like Aida.

"I've never been to Sunderland," said Jane. "Is it nice?"

Leah didn't answer but just stared straight ahead. Jane looked to see whether she could see what Leah was looking at, but Leah seemed to be just staring at some invisible object a few feet in front of her.

"Are you OK?" asked Jane before thinking how silly she sounded, asking a mental patient if they are OK. "I mean, you're not okay. Otherwise you wouldn't be here. Leah?"

Leah turned to face Jane.

"Who are you?" she asked. There was a look of panic in her face. "What is this place? What am I doing here?"

Leah stood up to run away but managed two steps through the flowerbed before she collapsed on the lawn on the other side, her arms and legs jerking.

"Nurse! Nurse!" Jane shouted. "Something is wrong with Leah."

After a few moments, the fitting stopped, and Leah lay unconscious.

Friday, 28th September 1945 - Broadgate Hospital, Walkington, England

"Physical condition for Leah Wooll. General body condition is well nourished. Skin healthy. The respiratory configuration of chest symmetrical."

Leah had her annual examination, and Doctor North was dictating notes to Nurse Barton who was scribbling as quick as she could manage.

"The cardiac area is normal, pulse regular, urine analysis strong acid, pupils equal reacting to light. Reflexes deep and superficial and very active, except her abdominals which acted sluggishly. There is a slight increase in thyroid glands no increase in pulse rate."

When the medical examination was over, Doctor North allowed Leah back into the day room where she slumped into one of the armchairs.

"Jane!" she shouted across the ward at the young girl who jumped with fright and then plodded over to sit near Leah.

"Now a young girl like you," Leah continued. "A girl like you. I can understand someone like me but someone like you. What are you doing in this ward?"

Jane shook her head.

Leah was bored.

"Go and see Aida," Leah waved her hand towards where the old woman sat dribbling in her usual chair.

Leah got up and walked through the passages, all the time looking for a chance to get away. She walked through the ward and out onto the garden. Maybe there she would find a way out. After a while, she gave up and went back into the day room where she slumped into an armchair.

A new nurse was doing the rounds with a trolley, and she placed a cup of tea in the small table next to Leah.

"There you go Mrs Wooll. That'll make you feel better," said the nurse already on her way.

"I know what you are doing," Leah shouted after her.

The nurse ignored her.

"You are trying to poison me."

The nurse continued without looking around.

Leah, filled with rage, picked up the cup and launched it at the nurse. It fell short of its target by a few feet and shattered on the floor.

"Alright Mrs Wooll. That's seclusion for you," the voice of the charge nurse came from the other end of the ward.

Saturday, 30 March 1946 - Broadgate Hospital, Walkington, England

"Leah? Do you know how much weight you've lost? You have to eat something," said Fred.

"Then tell them to stop poisoning my food," Leah shrugged and then went back to rocking forwards and backwards.

Fred sighed.

"You're five stone. You've lost two stone. The doctor says that you are malnourished. He says it is very difficult to get you to take sufficient food."

"Well, then he shouldn't keep me locked up in that room all the time."

"But the doctor told me that whenever it is possible, you are given fresh air and exercise. But he says that you are undependable and often dangerous."

Thursday, 20th June 1946 – Fulford Barracks, York

Fred looked at his discharge papers. He couldn't believe it. So this was it then. All those years in the Army reduced to this piece of paper. India, Shanghai, France, the camps. He waited for the young officer to come and tell him what they had planned for him but he knew what was coming.

"You've heard of the Commissioner Corps?"

Of course, he had. Everyone knew that was where they put old soldiers out to pasture.

He nodded.

"They've come up with something which I think is the perfect opportunity for you."

Fred marvelled at the young officer's ability to deliver bad news as if it was the best thing in the world.

"It's at the Meredith and Drew biscuit factory in Brighouse. Here is the Corps address. You'll need to report there first."

He handed Fred a piece of paper on which was written an address.

"Brighouse?" Fred thought aloud. "Is there nothing closer to Beverley? You see my wife and..."

"Sergeant. Do you know how lucky you are to get this? Do you know how many faces I have coming through this office and how limited the opportunities are? I wouldn't look a gift horse in the mouth if I were you."

Fred knew he was right and turned to leave.

"I don't suppose you could help me with one more thing."

"What is it?" the young officer was disinterested.

"I'm trying to track down a Corporal Jack Cooper. I don't suppose you've come across him have you?"

"Sergeant, have you any idea how many soldiers I demobilise every day?"

"Thanks, anyway," Fred turned and left.

Friday, 28 June 1946 - Broadgate Hospital, Walkington, England

"The ECT seems to be showing some benefits," says Doctor North, observing Leah at a distance from the nurses' station.

"She is already cleaner in habit and has been able to be out of doors more often," agreed the Charge Nurse. "The thing is her menstruation."

"Oh yes?"

"It has been very irregular, and her present flow has lasted over two weeks."

"I see. We will examine her as soon as her mental state permits."

Friday, 26th July 1946 – Meredith and Drew Biscuit Factory, Brig-house, England

"Come on Fred, let's go get some grub. I'm starving," said Albert as he locked up. Albert was a janitor and handyman who had become good friends with Fred.

Albert headed off down the street but then paused when he realised that Fred was not following.

"What's the matter?" he asked.

"Don't say that," said Fred.

"Don't say what?"

"Don't say you're starving."

"Why not?"

"Because you've no idea what it feels like to be starving."

"What do you mean? I just said we should get some grub."

"Yes, but don't say you're starving because you've no idea what it feels like."

"Whatever you say. Let's not get ourselves in a twist about it. How about I buy you a pint down at the Railway."

"All right," Fred began to soften. "But just a quick one. I have to catch the train to Beverley."

"Is there anything else you don't like? So I can avoid upsetting you again," Albert asked.

"Yes, I don't like going to zoos."

"Well, that's just as well because I wasn't going to take you to one."

Friday, 8th August 1947 – Broadgate Hospital, Walkington, England

Leah sat in front of Dr North for her yearly physical examination. She reflected on the fact that her annual examination was the only time she saw the doctor these days.

"Well, Leah, you seem in better health," the doctor said.

Leah couldn't believe it. In all the years, she had been in the hospital it was the first time the doctor had called her by her first name.

"The APO examiner was negative for any gross pathology," he continued, reading his notes to himself. "No sign of active disease or degeneration found in any system."

He looked up at her.

"There is no mental or behavioural change, Leah. After six years in this hospital, you are still hallucinating. However, more worrying, Leah is your violent and impulsive behaviour."

Leah began to cry. She felt like a naughty child being told off by the headmaster.

"We don't like to see that behaviour from you," the doctor continued. "There is an operation which changes the personality and will reduce the tension you feel. We've decided it would be best for you to have the operation. Your husband will sign the paper. I've asked him to come here for an interview."

Leah's heart began to pound.

"You will be changed," said the Doctor. "The tension will be reduced."

"What will they do?" Leah managed to force out the words.

"It's an operation on the brain of course."

"I want to go home," said Leah, thinking about the pictures of brains she had once seen in a magazine and thinking about how much it looked like a soft pink walnut. She had said the word home, but she then realised that she had no idea where the home was anymore.

"It'll cure your violent behaviour," Dr North said, but then mumbled to himself. "But it can hardly be expected to cure your malady."

Thursday, 22 July 1948 – Broadgate Hospital, Walkington, England

"She is still suffering from paraphrenia, Mr Wooll," Doctor North addressed Fred who sat in his office. "There has been no change since I last made this request to you a year ago. She is still hallucinating, still hearing the voices of her relatives and acquaintances in Sunderland, shouting abuse to her through the walls. In consequence, she becomes noisy and overactive and will strike out at her nurses and the patients."

"But you've been treating her for seven years," Fred complained. "And all she's gained are a couple of episodes of epilepsy."

"In her quieter moments, she talks sensibly, when her memory is good."

"I know. I visit her every weekend."

She is in good physical health. Nevertheless, as I told you before, we have reached the end of what ECT is able to offer us. The operation is our best chance for her recovery."

"Alright. I'll think about it."

Fred had thought about it a good deal, and the decision to perform an irreversible operation on Leah's brain was not one he was going to take lightly. At the same time, it pained him to see her in this place. He longed for the woman he had married and perhaps the operation was the way to achieve this, even if it changed her personality, at least they would have a chance of a life together.

FRED & LEAH: A TRUE LIFE SECOND WORLD WAR DRAMA
OF LOVE, LOSS AND CAPTIVITY.

279

Sunday, 26th December 1948 – Beverley, England

Fred sat up with a start. He had had another nightmare.

He looked at the bed next to him where 8-year-old Beattie was still sleeping, at least she appeared to be sleeping.

Fred sank back into his pillow and sighed. If only he could rid himself of these infernal nightmares.

It had been a good Christmas. He had gone down the pub with his dad, Harry and Bill and, as usual, his mum had told them all off when they arrived late for Christmas dinner. Bill was always very worried about getting into trouble with Minnie, but it didn't bother Fred and his dad. Every year they would arrive late, and every year his mum would insist on getting dinner ready at the same time so whose fault was that?

It was just a shame Leah couldn't be there to enjoy it with them. Fred longed for the day when he would get in trouble with Leah for getting back late from the pub. It was an argument he would dream of if he weren't so busy having nightmares.

Wednesday, 5th January 1949 – Broadgate Hospital, Walkington, England

Leah sat in her room, rocking forwards and backwards and smiling at the nurse who took in her dinner. The nurse was new, a part-timer. She smiled at Leah. Although new to the ward, the nurse had heard stories of Leah's attacks. Some of the other nurses had told her how they were loath to sleep, as her attacks were always surprising to them. The nurse was nervous about being alone with Leah, as this seemed to be when she was most likely to strike, like a wildcat picking off its victim when it strayed too far from the herd. The nurse was relieved that Leah seemed to be in a good mood, smiling. The nurse returned the smile and told Leah she would be back later to collect her empty dishes.

*

When the nurse returned to collect the dishes, she was puzzled when she could not see Leah. Just then, Leah emerged from behind the door and leapt on the nurse, scratching and beating her with a ferocity, which made the nurse scream.

*

"I don't know what comes over me," said Leah, once she had had time to calm down.

"Doctor North has spoken to your husband," said the charge nurse. "He is going to come in and sign the papers. With your personality changed, no one will recognise you. So many patients have already had the operation, and many more are going to have it. I know one woman who was here for twenty years, and now she is working in town. She used to be in seclusion, like you."

"Do you think it would help me?" Leah asked.

"You'd be out of here in no time, instead of spending your entire life in here, which is what you'll have to do otherwise. I'm sure you'll get a good job, and you'll never regret having your leucotomy. "

Wednesday, 12th January 1949 – Broadgate Hospital, Walkington, England

"Do you know, Mr Wooll, there are rumours that Egas Moniz will get the Nobel prize this year?" Doctor North said, handing over the paperwork.

"I don't know who he is," said Fred.

"A brilliant man. He hypothesised that patients with obsessive behaviour were suffering from fixed circuits in the brain. Patients who had been horrific burdens on their families, violent or suicidal, were calmed down by the surgery, which your wife is about to have."

"I very much hope you are right."

*

Leah was barely aware of what was happening as she lay on the stretcher, which an orderly was wheeling through the hospital corridors towards the entrance, where an ambulance was waiting. They had given her something that morning to make her sleep, and she was fighting against the drowsiness. Leah had managed to stay conscious for long enough to know that they had shaved her head. She managed until the orderly pushed the stretcher into the back of the ambulance and then she lost the battle and slipped into unconsciousness.

Thursday, 13 January 1949 – Hull Royal Infirmary, Kingston-upon-Hull, England

When she awoke, Leah examined her surroundings. Wherever she was, it wasn't Broadgate. Events of the night started to return to her. She remembered vomiting, and she remembered nurses cleaning her and changing the sheets because she had peed in the bed.

Monday, 17 January 1949 – Broadgate Hospital, Walkington, England

Leah was looking in the mirror when Doctor North arrived to examine her. She stared at her shaved head, a stubble already covering her scalp.

"How do you feel, Mrs Wooll?" asked the doctor.

"I like the shape of my head. It looks clean."

"Yes, the lateral burr holes seem all right."

Leah lifted her hand to touch her left cheek, where a large patch of herpes had taken hold.

"Hmm. We'll have to get that treated," said the doctor, examining the sore. "Best not to touch it though, eh?"

Thursday, 27 January 1949 – Broadgate Hospital, Walkington, England

Leah touched her face. Her herpes had cleared up. She touched the scarf, which was covering her head.

"People will assume you are just covering curlers," Nurse Barton had told her, but everyone knew it was a leucotomy scarf.

One of the nurses took her for a walk in the grounds. Leah felt they were retraining her, rehabilitating her. Leah was enjoying the newfound patience that the staff had for her, as if they saw Leah as a blank slate on which they could doodle the designs of their fancy.

As they returned towards the main hospital building, Leah could see Doctor North standing on the steps, watching them approach. He was taking an interest in them.

"No violent outbursts as yet," she overheard the nurse whisper to him as they passed.

Leah had to admit that she did feel cleaner and tidier and was able to sleep well at night without the medication they used to hide in her tea. She knew they had stopped because the tea tasted and smelt like tea again. She was worried at first that without her medication her nights would be restless and troubled, but her worry was soon proved unfounded when she awoke feeling well rested. She also resented the nurses because it seemed as though they were waiting for the rage to rise within her again, and with that careless remark from a nurse to a doctor, Leah began to simmer once more. No amount of rest would change the fact that they had taken her children from her. All four of them.

FRED & LEAH: A TRUE LIFE SECOND WORLD WAR DRAMA OF LOVE, LOSS AND CAPTIVITY.

285

Saturday, 19 February 1949 – Broadgate Hospital, Walkington, England

"I'm worried about Leah," Nurse Barton confided to the charge nurse as they watched Leah returning to her room after her morning bath.

"Mrs Wooll? What of her?"

"Yesterday evening, she was noisy."

"And?"

"Well, it's unlike her. Now I mean. Since her operation."

"Sometimes you can't teach an old dog new tricks," said the charge nurse.

"Shh, she'll hear you," whispered Nurse Barton.

"And what if she does? I'm not afraid of her."

As Leah entered her room, she slammed the door behind her. The two nurses arrived at the closed door just in time to hear the chamber pot crash against it.

"Why can't you just leave me alone," Leah shouted. "I hate you. I hate all of you."

Thursday, 17th February 1949 – The Railway Inn, Brighouse, England

Fred and Albert sat in the corner of the Railway Arms, nursing their pints of mild around a small table.

The door opened, and a man about Fred's age came in, and Fred had the strange sensation that he knew him from somewhere.

"They told me I would find you in here. you bloody alcoholic," the man said, and Fred was about to feel affronted when he realised who it was.

"Bloody Hell. Corporal Jack Cooper," he said getting to his feet. "Don't you stand to attention when addressing a superior anymore?"

"Not since they threw me out, no," said Jack.

Fred shook Jack's hand, and then the two men hugged.

"Sit down. Let me get you a pint," said Fred, still taken aback and unsure of where to start. "I thought you were dead."

"Me? Never."

"I've been trying to find you."

"And doing a bloody awful job of it, by all accounts. I've been trying to track you down as well. I guess I make the better detective."

"What'll it be, mild?" asked Fred. "Three pints of mild, please."

"Well, aren't you going to introduce me to your friend?"

"Yes, sorry. Jack, this is Albert. We work together at Meredith's."

"Don't get me another," said Albert. "If I don't get back soon, the wife'll kill me. Anyway, it seems like you two have a lot to catch up on. Nice to meet you Jack, enjoy your stay in sunny Brighouse."

"Thanks. Good to meet you, too, Albert."

"How did you find me?" Fred asked. "Oh, just two pints please."

"Your landlady said I might find you in here. Nice piece of skirt that one."

"Give over. No, I mean how did you know I was in Brighouse?"

"I thought to check out the Corps and tracked you down here. A bloke at the factory told me where you lived."

"And what about you. What have you been doing?"

"I hid in Scotland for a while, but then me and the wife decided to move to Canada. I got a job as a policeman."

"You? A policeman?"

FRED & LEAH: A TRUE LIFE SECOND WORLD WAR DRAMA
OF LOVE, LOSS AND CAPTIVITY.

287

"Why? What's wrong with that?"

"No, nothing, sorry."

Fred handed Jack his drink.

"So tell me," said Jack. "How's your missus?"

Fred told Jack the whole story.

"Bloody hell," said Jack. "So she's still in the asylum then?"

Fred nodded.

"You know, Fred, because she was committed, that's grounds for divorce, that is. You could find yourself a new wife. That landlady of yours is not half bad."

"I can't, Jack. Leah is my wife. When we got married, we took our vows. We said that we would be there for each other, for richer, for poorer, in sickness and in health ..."

"Till death do us part, yeah I know. But they are vows, Fred. No one is going to hold you to those under the circumstances."

"I know, Jack, but it doesn't change the fact that she's my wife and I have to be there for her, no matter what."

Saturday, 5th March 1949 – Broadgate Hospital, Walkington, England

"It's Beattie's birthday on Tuesday," Fred told Leah, trying to make conversation. "She'll be nine."

"Is she here?" Leah asked as she rocked forwards and backwards.

"No, children are not allowed to visit between 5 and 16."

"Five? Is it tea time?"

"No, Leah, between the ages of 5 and 16 they don't allow children in the hospital."

"I have children."

"Yes, I know."

"I have seven."

"No, Leah. Two. Jim and Beattie."

"I left them in a nursing home, but now they are in the children's part of this hospital."

Fred sighed.

"I'm pregnant again," she giggled. "I think the cat must be the mother."

Leah found this very funny and chuckled away to herself. Fred forced a smile. He watched a man enter the ward dragging a small boy, no more than four, behind him. The boy observed his surroundings with uncertainty, and with reluctance allowed the man to drag him along. Fred could tell the man was also nervous, not yet accustomed to the surroundings and perhaps bringing the boy for the first time. He was walking with a bravado, which he'd convinced himself was to set an example to the boy, but was to set an example to himself.

As they passed Leah's chair, she grabbed the boy by the arm.

"This is Jim, look, this is my son."

"Leah, stop it," Fred shouted.

"Let go," the man said in a panic. The boy, startled, looked from his father to Leah and back again with a questioning look.

"Leah, let go," Fred repeated, getting up.

She wouldn't let go, so Fred had to pry her grip from the arm of the boy who rubbed at his liberated arm as he sheltered behind his angry father.

Fred offered an apologetic smile, and the man realised that where he was, this kind of thing was to be expected, and it was his own stupid fault that he insisted his four-year-old son come with him to visit the boy's mother. He looked at Fred and Leah one last time and led the boy away.

Fred looked at Leah, and he realised there was nothing to be done.

*

Did you enjoy this book? You can make a big difference.

Reviews are the most powerful tools in my arsenal when it comes to getting attention for my books. Much as I'd like to, I don't have the financial muscle of a large publisher. I can't take out take out full-page ads in the newspaper or put posters on the subway.

(Not yet anyway.)

However, I do have something much more powerful and effective than that, and it's something those publishers would kill to get their hands on.

A committed and loyal bunch of readers.

Honest reviews of my books help bring them to the attention of other readers.

If you've enjoyed this book, I would be very grateful if you could spend just five minutes leaving a review[1] (it can be as short as you like).

Thank you very much.

---

1.   https://www.goodreads.com/book/show/42774811-fred-leah?from_search=true

Endnotes

My grandfather died before I was born of a heart attack. I did see my grandmother, Leah, every fortnight as I was growing up, when my mother took me to see her in Broadgates Hospital. She was not very talkative, but had a good sense of humour and once mistook me for her nephew, Ron. She never knew that my mother was her daughter and used to call her 'the visitor'. Much of the details for the Broadgate Hospital sections were taken from Leah's medical notes, which my mother read and recorded onto audiocassette after Leah's death in 1997 of cancer. There is a book about Broadgate called *Across the Westwood: The Life and Times of Broadgate Hospital, Beverley*.

Most of the rest of the background to the story was pieced together from information from my mother. She saw her father often until his death, and they would watch cricket together at The Circle in Hull's West Park. However, he spoke little of his experiences between 1939 and 1945, and therefore, most of the details included in this novel are sourced from his contemporaries, who must have had very similar experiences.

A great help in finding these sources was Major Chester Potts. His grandfather was my grandfather's commanding officer and Chester now runs the 7th Battalion Royal Northumberland Fusiliers St Valery 1940[2] page on Facebook. There is only one surviving member of the 7th Battalion, Jimmy Charters. At the time of writing, Jimmy Charters has just turned 100 years old. I didn't interview Jimmy, partly because he was in B Company and therefore wouldn't have known my grandfather, who was in D Company, but also because Jimmy's story is well documented elsewhere.

What follows is a resume of the sources which I used to help piece together what I hope is a novel which gives a flavour for what tens of thousands of soldiers and hundreds of thousands left at home must have experienced during the period.

No Cheese After Dinner by Fred Kennington is an account of the 51st Highland Division and their journey to 'Poland and back via Hell'. Fred interviewed Jimmy Charters and Dick Taylor for the book. Dick was in the

---

2.   https://www.facebook.com/7th-Battalion-Royal-Northumberland-Fusiliers-St-Valery-1940-320371207807/

same Company as my grandfather, D Company, so I was able to read about experiences which would have been very similar to those of Fred.

Stanley Rayner was a dispatch rider, captured at St Valery em Caux, his autobiography, *I Remember*, was another good source of information.

There are many photos of Stalag 383[3] on the Pegasus Archive site, which also has many POW stories. Most useful is the site's archive of *Barbed Wire: Memories of Stalag 383*[4] by M. N. McKibbin, which contains the most detailed account of life in Stalag 383 and formed the basis of my account of Fred's liberation. I have no way of knowing Fred's exact journey when he left Stalag 383 but I do know that he was flown from Landshut airfield. The story about the Dakota crash was Fred's own, although I had to invent the details.

For general background information about the period, I turned to *The Highland Division: The Army at War* by Eric Linklater, *Dunkirk: The Men They Left Behind* by Sean Longden and, *After Dunkirk: Churchill's Sacrifice of The Highland Division* by Saul David. *Panzer Commander: The Memoirs of Colonel Hans von Luck* is an honest account of the same period from a different perspective.

YouTube has a video of the memories of Private Harold Pitt[5], a transport driver in the 7th Battalion, The Worcestershire Regiment, which helped me with some details. There is also an interview with C Denys Cook[6] who was imprisoned in Stalag 383 in Hohenfels.

The jokes come from jokesoftheday.net[7] and Some old jokes[8] on the Internet and David Crossland's article[9] on Speigel Online. Forces.net has their 9 favourite WW2 jokes of all time[10]. My extract of King George IV's speech on VE day was taken from the BBC News site[11]. The BBC also has a WW2

3.   http://www.pegasusarchive.org/pow/pSt_383.htm

4.   *http://www.pegasusarchive.org/pow/cSt_383.htm*

5.   https://www.youtube.com/watch?v=sEtgKZdY7-E

6.   https://www.youtube.com/watch?v=VFkRYc1pBEM

7.   http://www.jokesoftheday.net/the-best-jokes/

8.   http://someoldjokes.tumblr.com/

9.   http://www.spiegel.de/international/new-book-on-nazi-era-humor-did-you-hear-the-one-about-hitler-a-434399.html

10.   https://www.forces.net/news/our-9-favourite-wwii-jokes-all-time

11.   http://news.bbc.co.uk/1/hi/uk/4515885.stm

People's War site which is a collection of memories of the war. Most helpful to me were the stories of Fred Hirst[12], Joan Quinn[13], and George and Mary Smith[14]. Other good sources on the Internet included the 1st Lothian and Border Yeomanry website[15], the memories on the 51st Highland Division website (especially Captain Taylor[16] and Corporal Jack Kidd[17]), the WW2 Talk forum[18], the Vickers machine gun blog[19], Annabel Venning's article[20] for the Mail Online about how families spent Christmas 1939, John Clinch's website[21] on those from 51st Highland Division who attempted to escape, and Neil Tweedie's article[22] for The Telegraph on the day that war was declared.

The Mass-Observation project which ran from 1937 to the early 1950's is an excellent source of information about everyday life in the period. One of the most extensive diaries contributed to the project was that of Nella Last. Her diaries have been edited into a series of books by Profile and they were very useful in adding some realism to the Monkwearmouth sections of this novel.

An Angel at My Table: The Complete Autobiography and *Faces in the Water* by Janet Frame were very useful to understand the life of a patient in a psychiatric ward as was *The Bell Jar* by Sylvia Plath and *One Flew Over the Cuckoo's Nest* by Ken Kesey, both of which gave interesting perspectives on electroconvulsive shock therapy. *Wisdom, Madness & Folly: The Making of a Psychiatrist* also gave an objective view of the psychiatric wards of the peri-

12.   http://www.bbc.co.uk/history/ww2peopleswar/stories/21/a4646621.shtml

13.   http://www.bbc.co.uk/history/ww2peopleswar/stories/80/a9023780.shtml

14.   http://www.bbc.co.uk/history/ww2peopleswar/stories/68/a4019168.shtml

15.   http://www.1stlothiansandborderyeomanry.co.uk/campaign_in_france.html

16.   http://51hd.co.uk/accounts/1_gordons_deploy_to_the_saar#ixzz4qruMrh24

17.   http://51hd.co.uk/pow/jacks_road#ixzz4pOK0wB1c

18.   http://ww2talk.com/index.php?threads/fighting-withdrawal-to-st-valery-en-caux.25560/page-3

19.   https://vickersmg.blog/

20.   https://www.dailymail.co.uk/news/article-1239303/Christmas-edge-abyss-How-wartime-families-festive-holiday-special.html

21.   http://home.clara.net/clinchy/neeb1.htm

22.   https://www.telegraph.co.uk/history/world-war-two/6128589/Second-World-War-The-day-the-balloon-went-up.html

od. Annalee Newitz's article[23] in Wired magazine helped me to understand the history of the lobotomy, as did Hugh Levison's article[24] for the BBC. The Encyclopedia of New Zealand has a photo of a seclusion room[25], which gave me an idea of what a similar room in Broadgate Hospital might have looked like in the 1940s.

The Shipyard Girls by Nancy Revell is also set in Monkwearmouth and helped me get a feel for the period and *Call the Midwife: Shadows of the Workhouse* by Jennifer Worth was inspired by the same workhouse that Jim and Beattie, my mother and uncle, found themselves in in 1941.

The reader may find some of the language gender biased or archaic. I am aware of this but have left the old phrases to remain consistent with the language and ideology of the period.

---

23.   https://www.wired.com/2011/03/lobotomy-history/

24.   https://www.bbc.co.uk/news/magazine-15629160

25.   https://teara.govt.nz/en/photograph/29407/asylums-seclusion-room-porirua

GET LIVING WITH SACI

Building a relationship with my readers is the best thing about writing. I occasionally send newsletters with details on new releases, special offers and other bits of news.

And if you sign up to the mailing list, you can download my first novel LIVING WITH SACI **for free**, just by signing up at https://bookhip.com/KVKVDA

ABOUT THE AUTHOR

M J Dees is the author of *Living with Saci*, *The Astonishing Anniversaries of James and David, Part One* and *When The Well Runs Dry*. He makes his online home at www.mjdees.com[1]. You can connect with M J on Twitter at @mjdeeswriter[2], on Facebook at www.facebook.com/mjdeeswriter[3] and you should send him an email at mj@mjdees.com if the mood strikes you.

---

1. http://www.mjdees.com/

2. https://twitter.com/mjdeeswriter

3. http://www.facebook.com/mjdeeswriter

ALSO BY M J DEES
Living with Saci[1]

Living with Saci is set in the sprawling metropolis of São Paulo, Brazil. It tells the story of Teresa da Silva, an overweight, depressed, drink dependent, and her struggles in the city. Estranged from her daughter, who lives with the ex-husband in England, life seems to constantly deal Teresa a bad hand. She begins to wonder whether the mischievous character from Brazilian folklore, Saci, might have something to do with it. Events seem to be taking a turn for the positive when she meets Felipe, who asks her to marry him. But when he disappears, Teresa finds that she is the object of suspicion.

1. https://bookhip.com/KVKVDA

The Astonishing Anniversaries of James and David, Part One[1]

How do you know if you have achieved success? No matter how successful he becomes, James doesn't feel happy. Meanwhile, his twin brother, David, seems content regardless of the dreadful, life-threatening events, which afflict him year after year. *The Astonishing Anniversaries of James and David* is as much a nostalgic romp through 70s, 80s and 90s England as it is a shocking and occasionally tragic comedy.

---

1. https://dl.bookfunnel.com/4s5q5rf2un

When The Well Runs Dry[1]

In a country divided by civil war, one city stands above the chaos. Since the system collapsed, citizens are struggling to survive. Marauders are destroying what little is left. However, not everyone is quite ready to surrender. The Alder and her loyal supporters find themselves caught in a life or death struggle to save, not only themselves but also those around them. The future of the nation is at stake. *When The Well Runs Dry* is the first book in M J Dees' dystopian series set in a future where resources have all but run out. Read this book while there is still a future in which to read it. .

---

1. https://dl.bookfunnel.com/ssu0ck4ozi

DEDICATION

To my maternal grandparents Fred and Leah Wooll without whom this book would obviously not be possible.

Also to the British and International Red Cross and Red Crescent organisations and mental health charities all over the world for the amazing and valuable work they do.

ACKNOWLEDGEMENTS

In addition to the thanks which I have already expressed in the endnotes, I am indebted to the following for extra special help: My own mother, Beatrice Leah Dees for providing much of the background information need to begin the story. Major Chester Potts for filling many of the blanks. Bill Reynolds for giving me additional perspectives on his grandfather, Leah's dad James, and some family recollections of Leah. Catherine Rogers for reading the book which included not only her grandparents but also her father. Jackie Wyant for giving great feedback and for designing another great cover. Genevieve Montcombroux , Fallacious Rose, Jane Ballard, Jane Ingram, Peggy Coppolo, and the rest of the Beta readers whom I can't thank personally because their invaluable comments and suggestions were anonymous.

I would also like to thank the Self-Publishing Community for all their support in helping me to get this book published and my Advance Reading Team for their help with last-minute feedback and, of course, those all-important reviews.

---

1. http://www.saltandunicorns.com